By Eldon Murphy

(Writing as Dean Murray)

Reflections	Dark Reflections	The Awakening
Broken	*Bound*	*Reborn*
Torn	*Hunted*	*Immortal*
Splintered	*Ambushed*	*Endless*
Intrusion	*Shattered*	
Numb	*Burned*	
Trapped		**A Broken World**
Forsaken		*The Society*
Riven		*The Destroyer*
Driven		*The Warlord*
Lost		*The Founder*
Marked		*The Desolation*
Left		

Reflections
(Dean Writing as Eldon)

The Greater Darkness

A Darkness Mirrored

The Compelled Chronicles

Stone Heart

The Guadel Chronicles

Frozen Prospects

Thawed Fortunes

I'rone

Brittle Bonds

Shattered Ties

A Darkness Mirrored

Eldon Murphy

A Darkness Mirrored is a work of fiction. Names, characters, places and incidents are the products of the author's imagination or are used fictitiously. Any resemblance to actual events, locales, or persons, living or dead, is entirely coincidental.

Published by Fir'shan Publishing

ISBN 978-1-9393632-1-3

www.FirshanPublishing.com

First Edition

For my girls

May your dreams be worthy and may you obtain them all

After a suitable struggle

Most kids never know real fear. Sure, they may be scared of the dark or think that there are monsters under their beds, but they always know that they have one or more parents less than a dozen feet away who will protect them from anything they can imagine happening.

Even as a child I knew what real fear was. I knew what it meant to be sure that you weren't going to survive to see another sunrise.

My father—not my biological father, who knows what happened to him—didn't tuck me in at night or tell me how much he loved me, but I always knew that he would do his level best to kill anyone who threatened me. For most little girls that wouldn't have been enough, but it was for me. That and he gave me a sister, an older sister who I knew would sacrifice almost anything to save me.

Of course I didn't understand all of that until I was much older. As a child I just knew that I felt safe when Geoffrey, my father, was around. The nights when he stayed in our house with me were the only ones where I didn't wake up screaming in the middle of the night.

It wasn't until later, after I found his journals, that I really learned how I came to live with him and understood why it was that he made me feel safe. I didn't need to fear the other monsters because I had my own personal monster a terrible, wonderful monster that I still don't understand completely, not even after he made the ultimate sacrifice to keep me safe.

Geoffrey Journal Entry 1

December

One of the great tragedies of human existence is that most of them, most people, never live long enough to realize it when they are paid a visit by one of those unique, life-changing opportunities that come around only a handful of times in the span of any one human lifetime.

Of all the gifts inherent to my condition, time is without a doubt the single most valuable. No amount of speed or strength can ever surpass the power of a keen mind. There will always be a surplus of thugs lining up for the scraps that fall from the table of the man of intellect and time is one of the most powerful tools when it comes to sharpening one's mind.

Today was one of those rare opportunities, a development that offers the possibility of fundamentally shifting my fortunes to the better in a lasting way. The interesting thing about opportunity is that you can't plan for a specific development, because you'll never know quite what form it will take. You *can* however plan for the inevitability of the opportunity.

If you keep your eyes open, eventually opportunities will arrive and the more you can do beforehand to prepare yourself for their inevitable arrival, the more benefit you can parley out of them.

So much of it simply comes down to time. Time and a willingness to accept the unavoidable level of risk that comes with any attempt to better your station.

I was playing dutiful errand boy for Imastious again tonight. He wanted a message delivered to the local tribe of the Latin Kings to make sure that they knew they were trying to muscle their way onto the wrong block.

The actual hit was simple. Three gangbangers with cheap pistols and no training are no match for a trained operative. I dipped the hand of one of the fallen in a pool of his own blood so that Imastious' calling card was evident at the scene of the crime, and then disappeared into the night with the four kilos of cocaine that the three of them had been about to cut with baking powder.

Imastious still thinks that he's got me on a tight financial leash, but it's finds like this over the last two decades that have allowed me to build up the resources I'll need to eventually free myself from him. As long as I continue to promptly spend everything Imastious gives me in suitably flashy ways, he'll never wise up to the fact that he's lost one more hold over me.

I've infiltrated the White Tears deeply enough that I can use them to move any drugs I come across. That means that I shouldn't have any problems liquidating this batch of drugs and using the cash to quietly invest in a promising biotech company I've had my eye on for several months. I've already made a significant purchase there, but liquidity concerns have kept me from investing as heavily as I'd like.

I was more than two miles away from the hit, walking in slow circles in an effort to confirm that I hadn't been followed, when I heard her. She was gagged and tied, partially trapped underneath an abandoned couch in an alley that was filled with rotting garbage.

Even in New York, people still take pity on children, and this one couldn't have been more than three or four. Once I got far enough into the alley I was able to see her without needing to actually get within more than a dozen feet or so of her.

I don't have nearly as many enemies as Imastious, and there shouldn't have been any possible way for an enemy to know in advance that I would be coming by this particular alley, but I've been doing Imastious' dirty work for long enough that I've largely inherited Imastious' enemies and some of them are incredibly powerful.

I knew that the safest route would be to simply walk away and leave the girl there to die, but the biggest inconvenience of my condition is keeping myself properly fed. New York has long had a significant population of homeless derelicts, but while few people notice them while they are alive, once they start turning up dead in greater than normal numbers the police invariably get involved.

This girl obviously had been left outside on purpose. A kidnapper would have just killed her rather than risking that someone would find her before she died from exposure. Only parents could have left her here like this. They'd desperately tried to create a situation where her death might look like an accident.

They might even have reported her as kidnapped, but they would have been sure to leave her far away from her home so as to ensure that she wouldn't be found. As long as I was careful to dispose of the body no one would be asking any questions.

I sent tendrils of thought out in every direction questing for other minds, but the area was unusually devoid of other people. Once I was confident that the girl didn't represent some kind of trap, I let some of my mental probes touch her. The reaction from her mind when I touched it sent me stumbling back into the side of the building behind me.

Other vampires, pyromancers or telekinetics, are sometimes able to detect when someone tries to insert a tendril into their minds. Other mentalists, unless they are so young as to not have developed their abilities at all, invariably know as soon as another mentalist tries to influence their thoughts, but this time was the first instance where I'd encountered such awareness from a human.

She didn't just know that I was inside of her mind, she grabbed ahold of my probes and used them to push an intense burst of fear inside my mind. I broke off the contact instantly, half expecting her to follow me back and attempt some kind of mental attack, but she remained trapped, both physically under the sofa and mentally inside of her own mind.

I watched for several seconds as tears continued to trickle down her tiny cheeks and muffled sobs shook her fragile body. The possibilities were almost limitless. She could serve as the perfect trap. It would no doubt be a project requiring years of effort, but given the strength she'd already displayed, it was possible that I could use her to break free of Imastious in one fell stroke.

There was nothing threatening about her exterior, but if I played my cards right, that unassuming form could hide a warren of blind alleys and dead ends. Imastious would touch her mind carelessly and find himself pulled in deeply enough that it would take all of his concentration and strength to keep from having the pathway back to his body severed. He would finally be completely at my mercy.

It was the lowest-risk path, but there was another route that promised even greater rewards if it worked correctly. I could keep her alive until she was old enough to turn, and then if she survived the change I could train her up as my disciple. If she was this strong as a mere human, then she'd be an exceptionally strong mentalist once she was a vampire.

In many ways I realized I was in the same situation that Imastious had found himself in many years ago. It wasn't necessarily something designed to be reassuring, but if I were able to avoid making the kinds of mistakes with her that Imastious had made with me, then she could help me kill Imastious. Even more importantly, she might also provide me with a strong enough power base to avoid being sucked into the clutches of one of the other vampire elders after Imastious was dead.

The risks of the course I was considering were terrifyingly real, and I've found that immortality has the effect of making one even less willing to risk death, but in the end there was only one valid decision. It might be another two or three decades before I come across another opportunity like this girl. I'd be willing to wait if I thought that the intervening time would decrease my risk in undertaking the endeavor, but ultimately it wouldn't. I already have enough wealth that even doubling or tripling my assets wouldn't add appreciably to my security, and I knew that my mentalist abilities would grow only slowly over the next century.

In the end, I realized that there wasn't anything to stop me from terminating her a year from now or three years from now or even two decades from now if the risk became unacceptable. I moved the couch off of her, untied her, and then helped her to her feet. Her name is Lucy, she confirmed that she is indeed three years old and she agreed to come home with me where it was warm.

It wasn't until we got back out onto the main road and into better light that I realized why Lucy looked so familiar to me. It was obvious that she wasn't going to be able to keep up with me, I was reaching down to pick her up when it hit me. The tear-streaked face looking up at me was almost a perfect match for Beth.

Slender face, soft brown hair, and brown eyes that seemed wiser than anyone her age could possibly be. I tried to deny the likeness, but it was unquestionably real.

In hindsight, I believe that I handled things well despite my shock. It is only reasonable to expect that over hundreds or even thousands of years that I'll continue to run into people who bear a strong resemblance to someone from earlier in my life. As I think back over the last decade or so, I can remember no fewer than three other instances where I saw someone who looked like a younger version of some past acquaintance. This is just the first time that someone has reminded me of the older sister who took on the bulk of the work involved in raising me. Right up until Imastious killed her.

Geoffrey Journal Entry 2

January
Lucy's Age: 3

The operation against the Latin Kings was an even bigger success than I expected it to be. Not only did the tribe I hit pull back away from Imastious' pets, the Red Hand Consortium, they also pulled back slightly with regards to their ongoing harassment of the White Tears. I'd tipped my contacts in the White Tears off to the fact that the Latin Kings had experienced a reversal in fortunes recently and the White Tears had taken advantage of the commotion my operation caused to kill two of the tribe's lieutenants. There was some kind of collateral damage, I think one of the lieutenants had a family, but for the next couple of months I'll get a cut of the drugs moved in the territory that the White Tears just took over, which should amount to a tidy sum.

Given that I currently have no choice but to do all of the things that Imastious is unwilling to do himself, it's always nice when I can cash in on the work and get something out of it for myself.

In other news, I fully expected that Lucy would represent a significant change to my lifestyle, but I'm still surprised on a regular basis by just how much time and attention she requires. The first couple of weeks were nearly enough to cause me to rethink the child's usefulness. There was an alarming amount of tears and very regular temper tantrums, but I managed to procure a new apartment for the child and engage the services of a nanny, one Mrs. Clarissa Agosti, and since then things have settled down somewhat, albeit not completely.

A single woman in her fifties, Mrs. Agosti came highly recommended and seems to be making some headway with Lucy. It seemed as though Lucy was initially unnerved by Mrs. Agosti's shockingly white hair, but it appears as though she's gotten past that and is about as comfortable with her new primary caregiver as could be expected.

From a pure time-management perspective, it would be tempting to simply leave Lucy with Mrs. Agosti on a full-time basis, but I know that would be a mistake. The few hours of reading which I've been able to squeeze in around caring for the child has indicated that children bond best when they are younger. If I'm to expect

Lucy to bond with me to the degree that I need her to, then I'll need to spend at least as much time with her as a father would.

I'm finding that feigning interest in Lucy is also much more difficult than I expected it to be. The things about which the child cares are ridiculous. For instance, last week she became quite overwrought because I couldn't tell her how many days it would be until her birthday. She seems convinced that her birthday is in January, so I held up a calendar of the month and told her to pick a day. From henceforth we will be celebrating her birthday on the twenty-fifth of January.

While this calmed Lucy down slightly, there has still been a distressing amount of tears even since then. I've told Mrs. Agosti that Lucy's parents were killed in a car accident, and that the child was trapped inside the car for an extended period of time before being rescued. The cover story of me being Lucy's uncle should go a long way towards heading off any questions that would otherwise arise about how Lucy came to be in my care.

Unfortunately setting up the new apartment, providing food and clothing for Lucy, and hiring Mrs. Agosti has cut much more deeply into my liquid capital than I expected it to. The payoff from the cocaine I lifted from the Latin Kings ended up being redirected to caring for Lucy rather than being invested as I'd originally planned.

Predictably the company in question has done very well over the last three weeks which means that I've forgone more than a hundred thousand dollars in profits by not following my original plan. It's not an insubstantial amount of money, but I continue to find that I'm unable to free up the time required to go out and recoup the shortfall via other means.

Geoffrey Journal Entry 3

February
Lucy's Age: 3

The Red Hand Consortium just had one of their brothels firebombed. Apparently the Latin Kings tribe that I trimmed back at the end of last year went up to their regional council for help. Imastious is extremely vexed by the development, but I'm actually looking forward to whatever punitive expedition he's going to send me out on next. Anything that escalates tension between the Latin Kings and the Red Hand Consortium is going to generally increase the influence and power of the White Tears, which should eventually pay dividends to me.

After some thought, I've decided that Lucy was two going on three rather than three going on four as she initially tried to tell me. It's a matter of little if any importance, but it seems that the more such things are settled the less distraught Lucy is on an ongoing basis.

I don't interact with the rest of society very much, but Mrs. Agosti was adamant that Lucy needed a birthday party last month, even if it was nothing more than a cake and some presents with just the three of us.

After three consecutive days of subtle but constant nagging I realized that I either needed to acquiesce and pick up a cake and presents or I'd be forced to avoid Lucy's apartment for a couple of weeks after her birthday.

Interestingly enough, it turned out that Mrs. Agosti was more excited about Lucy's birthday party than Lucy herself. The child showed no interest in her presents or the cake, instead huddling in the corner of the living room and refusing to be coaxed into unwrapping or eating anything.

After passing half an hour in such a supremely futile activity, I stood to leave, but Lucy broke into inconsolable tears. I expected Mrs. Agosti to handle the outbreak, but the woman quite literally threw her hands up in despair. Instead I found myself with a sobbing three-year-old in my arms and no real idea of what to do with her.

Mrs. Agosti made rocking motions at me, so I paced around the living room, dodging toys and the glass coffee table, until I realized that I had a better option within my power for calming Lucy down. I cautiously sent a few wisps of thought into Lucy's mind and started siphoning some of the fear away. It was the work of only a few minutes to calm Lucy down to the point where I could follow Mrs. Agosti into Lucy's room and put her in her bed.

I'm noting the experience here because it has turned out to be significant in several ways. Firstly, Lucy demonstrated none of the advanced mentalist tendencies that originally intrigued me. Another individual might have been tempted to dismiss the events of that first night as nothing more than imagination, but I am convinced that the girl has some latent predisposition that can be harnessed with time and training once she's been changed.

Secondly, this wasn't the first time that the girl launched into a fit that Mrs. Agosti couldn't calm. As luck would have it, I've been present at the apartment each time and been able to help the child pull herself together, but it seems as though the repeated exposure to my mentalist abilities are causing some kind of transformation in the child's psyche. It doesn't appear that the fear inside of Lucy has lessened in any degree, but it required less effort to calm her down during each subsequent fit.

I can hardly go to Imastious with questions about raising a child with the kinds of abilities that Lucy has displayed, even assuming that her case and my case were parallel. I'm therefore left operating on little more than guesswork.

I've never come across any other instances where repeated tampering on the part of a mentalist caused a human to become less resistant to mental probes, but I've already established that Lucy isn't like other children.

I've therefore decided that it would be best if I were to avoid further mind-to-mind contact with her. Given the amount of resources, not the least of which is my own time and energy, I'll be investing in Lucy over the next two decades, I'm unwilling to do anything that could result in her abilities or mental defenses being compromised.

Geoffrey Journal Entry 4

April
Lucy's Age: 3

The White Tears have begun overreaching themselves. Imastious' response to the firebombing was typically overdone, but I was only able to take partial advantage of it because I wasn't involved in all aspects of the operation.

Imastious has always been careful to keep the different parts of his organization tightly compartmentalized up until now, which is only common sense, but this time he brought in another operative to assassinate two people. The first was the girlfriend of one of the local Latin King leaders while the second was the mother of another leader. While that was going on, I was dispatched to intercept a drug shipment.

Frankly I would have rather traded assignments for a number of reasons. Wet work against unarmed targets is a lot less risky. Not only that, if his other operative had been the one responsible for the drug shipment then they would have been forced to leave more tracks. Even if everything goes well on a shipment interception, the drugs still have to be handed off somewhere, presumably to one of Imastious' Red Hand Consortium contacts, which generally means that someone has seen you and can be pressured into revealing at least some information about you.

Not only that, if someone else had intercepted the drug shipment then I could have arranged for the White Tears to get their hands on it a few days later. As it was, it would have been too suspicious if the drugs had subsequently gone missing after I got ahold of them for Imastious.

I've started a file on Imastious' new pet assassin, but I doubt I'll make much progress tracking him down, at least not unless Imastious continues to use us on related operations. If I do figure out who Imastious was using I'll, of course, do my best to kill them. As long as I'm tied to Imastious, I may as well be getting as much action from him as possible. The more ops I run, the more opportunities there are for me to profit from the bits and pieces that he doesn't know about.

No, that was all just a slight inconvenience. The real problem was that my contacts in the

White Tears weren't able to keep the grunts in the organization under control. As soon as word of the Latin King's most recent round of losses made it out onto the street, the White Tears staged three separate hits on Latin King territory.

Conflict between the Kings and the Tears is only valuable to me inasmuch as I can find a way to profit from it. Conflict between the Tears and the Red Hand Consortium is slightly better as it at least hurts Imastious even if it doesn't directly help me.

Frankly this one left me perplexed for a day or so until I realized that the best option was to just spread the conflict out more broadly.

I staged two different hits on the White Tears over the next week. The first was a seizure of two hundred thousand dollars of cash from a bodega that the Tears had been using to launder some of their drug proceeds. I cut down all six grunts working the operation and made it look like Red Hand Consortium work.

Then I broke into the apartment of one of the rabble-rousers inside of the White Tears and left Latin King graffiti on his wall as a rather pointed message that he wasn't safe, not even at home. That might have been enough to refocus the membership of the White Tears away from the Latin Kings and onto the Red Hand Consortium, but I also paid a visit to two of my most highly-placed contacts in the White Tears and suggested that they go to the Kings with an offer of truce so that both gangs could go after the Red Hand Consortium.

Neither man was very receptive to the idea until I pushed hard with my abilities, but I walked out of both meetings confident that the command that I'd implanted in each of their minds would stick.

I didn't have the kind of intel on the Kings that I had on the White Tears, but when all was said and done, I didn't need much information to carry out the last piece of my plan. I waited until well after midnight and then cut down three of the Latin Kings on the southwest corner of their territory.

Everyone knows that the Red Hand uses big knives, so I probably could have gotten away without seeding the scene with bloody hands, but subtlety is generally lost on the average gang member, so I went ahead and painted the right hand of each of the dead men with their own blood.

It's probably premature to be celebrating the op as being totally successful, but I think it will probably accomplish what I set out for it to do.

Lucy is unfortunately continuing to take up large amounts of my time. Mrs. Agosti has assured me repeatedly that it is common for children who have been traumatized to go through a period of increased neediness though, so I will continue to soldier on, as it were.

A DARKNESS MIRRORED

The instances of inconsolable tears have started to decrease slightly, but Lucy continues to calm down only for me, which has necessitated that I spend more time at Lucy and Mrs. Agosti's apartment even when I'm not actively playing with Lucy. I have tried to come up with another way forward that still allows me to avoid making all of the mistakes that Imastious made with me, but so far have yet to arrive at a workable plan.

Mrs. Agosti was nearly to the point of quitting and I fear that Lucy will become even more intractable if she were to lose another caregiver so soon after arriving here, so I have reluctantly started spending most days there in the second apartment.

So far Mrs. Agosti continues to believe my cover story that I'm a highly-paid bodyguard, which helps explain the weapons and the fact that I'm gone so frequently in the evening and spend the daylight hours sleeping.

I've continued to refrain from accessing Lucy's mind directly, but have been under no such compunction with Mrs. Agosti. I've spent nearly a dozen hours to date reinforcing her tendency towards being patient and longsuffering, which should help assure that she remains in my employ despite the difficulties that I anticipate will continue into the foreseeable future.

I've likewise made sure to curb any native curiosity and her natural inclination to gossip. I should begrudge this time away from my work in the same fashion as I resent the time that Lucy takes up, but I find instead that I'm quite intrigued to see the long-term effects of my work on Mrs. Agosti.

Previous to this, the workings I created on humans were principally short-term in nature and correspondingly crude. This will be the first time that I've had cause to shape a person's mind on an ongoing basis, combined with an excuse to remain in proximity to them for long enough to see the results of my work.

More and more I suspect that my work with Mrs. Agosti will prove to increase my effectiveness, if not my raw power, and will therefore be a profitable investment. Given the narrow line I walk in my efforts to eventually kill Imastious and set myself up as a major power inside of this city, I can't afford to let arrogance cause me to miss the small, but very real, opportunities that exist for increasing my power.

I had intended on summarizing my recent financial activities as there are several lessons there that I think are valuable enough to record for later review, but Mrs. Agosti has convinced me to take Lucy out to Central Park today.

Geoffrey Journal Entry 5

May
Lucy's Age: 3

Now that a month has passed, I feel safe in saying that my efforts to turn the Latin Kings away from the White Tears were successful. There has been some low-level violence along the border that the two gangs share, but nothing like what I'm sure we would have seen without my successful attempt to frame the Red Hand Consortium for the hits on both of the other gangs' holdings.

If all that had come of my frantic work last month was for the Latin Kings not to send in half a dozen real heavies from their regional group to roll through the White Tears, I would have been satisfied, but things are even better than that.

The White Tears and the Latin Kings have pushed the Red Hand out of an entire block, and the fighting was exceptionally bloody. My initial estimates put the Red Hand Consortium as having lost more than forty members just in the last week alone. Losses on the part of the White Tears and the Kings are roughly in line with that, but given that the losses are split between the two gangs, they are in much better shape than Imastious' pets.

Needless to say, the news has gone a long way towards easing my concerns about the White Tears suddenly folding. I got a text about the first of the successful attacks while I was at the park with Lucy and the knowledge that things were improving there allowed me to pass the interminable wait with much more equanimity than I otherwise would have been able to.

Lucy of course had no idea that I'd just pulled off a behind-the-scenes power play that would have done Machiavelli proud, but that too will come eventually. For now it's all I can do to tease a few words out of her from time to time in an effort to try and sidestep the tantrums and tears that are still a regular occurrence.

If the losses sustained by the Red Hand were the high point of the trip for me, the yellow flowers we saw at the park were the high point for Lucy. She still said very little, but every time I looked down at my phone I would invariably look up to find that she'd wandered back over to one of the two gardens that were filled with the same dull yellow flower.

I initially just thought that Lucy was fascinated with flowers in general, but after the sixth time of following her back to the same part of the park I finally realized that she didn't care about any of the other flowers, just this one particular type.

Before the trip, Mrs. Agosti went on and on about Lucy needing a chance to go outside and run around. It turned out that Lucy was absolutely uninterested in doing anything of the sort. I took her to play on the swings, but she just stood next to me and watched the other children.

The large grassy area a few hundred yards from the playground was equally fruitless. I'd finally agreed to Mrs. Agosti's proposed excursion because I'd been hoping that once she was outside Lucy would entertain herself to some extent. It seemed like a chance to multitask on my phone while still putting in my required weekly allotment of time to bond with the child.

I was sadly mistaken as it was all I could do to even pry one hand free from Lucy's chubby fingers so that I could use my phone while we walked around the park. I'm starting to wonder if Lucy is too damaged to serve my purposes down the road.

Unfortunately, I'm currently at a loss with regards to the problem she represents. I've never had occasion to use my mentalist powers to try to actively heal a damaged mind, but in theory that should be possible. Unfortunately that is precluded since I've already established that further manipulation of her thoughts could ruin whatever predisposition towards mentalist abilities she's already shown.

A psychiatrist is likewise out of the question as I can't risk her relating the full story of how she came to live with me.

That reminds me, I need to start collecting the proper fake documents for her. The sooner I start that process the more bulletproof her backstory will be. As long as I'm out shopping, maybe I should see about getting a potted version of that stupid yellow flower from the park.

If it calms her down even just once a week when she'd otherwise cling to me sobbing in despair, then it would be well worth the effort of procuring one.

Geoffrey Journal Entry 6

November
Lucy's Age: 3

Lucy has become extra morose as the holidays have gotten closer and closer. She still speaks very little, so I can only assume that she's linked this time of year to her abandonment by her parents. I've had to speak to Mrs. Agosti several times about not decorating the apartment, but each time I return after an extended absence I find that she's hung up a decoration of one kind or another.

At various times she's hung up strings of popcorn running from the crown molding on one side of the room to the other, poinsettias next to the leather sofa, chains of paper rings around the coffee table, even plain glass balls that had been decorated in a dozen ingenious ways. I quite honestly had forgotten there were so many different kinds of Christmas decorations.

After the last couple of times, I confronted her, speaking quite sternly about the matter, but she just looked repentant and pointed out that she hadn't hung up any particular kind of decoration that I had expressly forbidden. I tried backing the prohibition up with a shaping, but it didn't seem to make any difference.

She continues not to put up anything I've expressly told her not to display, but is still finding new types of decorations which to her mind are still acceptable. I could force the issue if I was so inclined, but that seems to be a losing proposition.

Using non-mentalist means is likely to just make her extremely unhappy and risk driving her away while exercising my powers could very well strip her of some of the initiative that makes her a valuable employee.

I suspect that I'll continue to refine my ability to work the kind of subtle shapings required to avoid ruining a human after just one or two services, but for now I've definitely come up against boundaries beyond which I'm not going to be able to influence Mrs. Agosti. In the future, I'm going to experiment more with just implanting a desirable belief inside her mind.

I'll probably still run into problems with the way she sometimes interprets a given group of beliefs, but it should be better than what I've done in the past. Inserting workings into a person that are solely focused on creating a specific action hasn't proven as reliable as I would like, and it's much more crude and limited in scope.

For now I suppose that Lucy will just have to toughen up. If she's to be any use to me, then she'll experience much worse than this before all is said and done. Even so, I've taken to spending even more time at the house than I was before. I'm able to manage most of the aboveboard business transactions remotely with my laptop, and that is where I'm spending the bulk of my time lately.

I continue to successfully identify market opportunities that provide a reasonable rate of return on my capital. Given that I'm maintaining my expenditures at a level well below my earnings, over a long enough period of time I will be able to achieve any level of wealth imaginable. Realistically, I'll probably eventually reach a point where I no longer have sufficient time to manage all of my working capital, but I'm unlikely to arrive there anytime soon.

While the return on the legitimate forms of commerce helps put me at ease regarding the future, I'm still seeking faster growth, to which end I've continued to use the White Tears to move various illegal commodities as I come across them while working for Imastious.

Things have slowed considerably since the Red Hand Consortium was knocked back on its heels, which has meant that Imastious hasn't used me as frequently as normal. I've considered creating some opportunities by stirring trouble back up between the Latin Kings and the Red Hand, but have schooled myself to patience.

I can't expect to be able to carry on that kind of shell game indefinitely and it's better to accept a lower rate of return in exchange for avoiding creating a confrontation with Imastious that I can't yet win.

Because of my lower mission load, I haven't been leaving the second apartment as often during the early evening, which has resulted in Lucy coming into my room more frequently than she has in the past.

She then waits until I'm absorbed in some bit of analysis or another before climbing up onto my lap. I sternly told her that she wasn't to touch the keys on my laptop, and after that one attempt she has never tried to push any of the letters.

I've got a desk that the computer actually sits on, but it's still almost impossible to do any typing with a three-year-old on your lap. As inconvenient as her newfound habit is, it's one of the first real signs that she's starting to bond with me, so I've decided to let her continue with this new nightly ritual. I've been able to rearrange my workflow slightly such that I'm mostly doing research in the evenings now so that Lucy isn't interrupting as much as she otherwise might be.

A DARKNESS MIRRORED

My efforts to convince Mrs. Agosti to turn the thermostat up to a more reasonable range in the evenings have so far failed to meet with any success, but I find that once Lucy is on my lap, sometimes with her arms around my neck, sometimes just with her back to me as she watches my screen, that I'm no longer cold. Her tiny little body puts out an astonishing amount of heat.

I need to remember to make some notes regarding some new recruits to the White Tears that I could possibly groom to take over the gang once I've spent some time applying some of the loyalty conditioning techniques I've been developing on Mrs. Agosti. It will have to wait until tomorrow though as Imastious has ordered me to rendezvous with him down in the financial district. Hopefully whatever job he's going to throw at me is less boring than the last few have been.

Geoffrey Journal Entry 7

December
Lucy's Age: 3

Imastious has just given me the best Christmas present I could have hoped for, and the most satisfying part of it is the fact that he doesn't even realize what a boon he's just provided to me. He came prepared for a serious confrontation of wills, so I was forced to play along, but when he told me that he'd recently turned another vampire and that he wanted me to be the one to train her, all I could think was that this was the perfect dry run for what I'm going to be doing with Lucy a couple of decades from now.

The girl is a scared eighteen-year-old whom Imastious kidnapped from her house a couple of days ago. Her real name is April, but I've decided that she needs to be brought down another few steps before she's going to be ready to start learning instead of just whining about the terrible things that Imastious has done to her.

I'll be calling her Venice from here on out; and once she starts to respond to that name, I'll begin feeding her something more than starvation rations. From there we'll move onto simple unarmed combat and see where her talents lie.

She's incredibly beautiful with a slender build and platinum-blond hair, so I rather expect that she'll do well when it comes to any missions requiring seduction. Imastious has historically been pretty heavy-handed on the operational side though, so unless he's about to turn over a new leaf, she's going to need to at least be able to defend herself against a run-of-the-mill normal human.

As much as I'd like for things to be otherwise, Imastious is planning on keeping tabs on her training, so I've been ordered to continue to use the containment facility that he has set up for her.

Not only would it be easier on me if I could relocate her somewhere closer, but I think it would probably be easier on her as well. Imastious has had a taste for blondes for as long as I can remember, and I suspect that her current quarters were at least partially chosen so that she's close enough at hand to wherever Imastious is living that he can stop in whenever he feels like it.

Which just goes to show that convenience is not always the best answer. If Imastious took a more hands-off approach it would make my job of using him as a common enemy to unite us much harder.

No, the current setup is ultimately much better. With any luck I'll be able to turn Venice into an ally. She's unlikely to have any real power for decades still, but assuming that I'm ultimately able to train her up to a reasonable degree of proficiency with a sword then she'll still be useful when I'm finally ready to try and kill Imastious.

Speaking of which, I need to make sure that I begin her mental conditioning sooner rather than later as well. I'll need to be very careful not to do anything that Imastious can detect, but there are a number of ways that I can go about weakening the suggestions he implants in her mind. Even better would be if I can manage to reinforce others slightly such that the overall working has different consequences than he intends for it to. Ultimately I'll need to simply limit the amount of conditioning he's able to implant while I get her to the point of being able to defend her own mind against casual intrusions.

The best option would be if I could convince her to let down her defenses for me at a later point so that I can implant some loyalty conditioning of my own, but that may be unachievable.

A DARKNESS MIRRORED

Lucy has begun talking a little more lately. She still seems to view Christmas as something to be scared of, but I've promised her that I won't be sending her away for Christmas.

It was a small thing to promise, which seemed to make a big difference in Lucy's disposition, and if circumstances were to change in an unforeseen manner, there is nothing she could do to ensure that I live up to my word. Children are much more blindly trusting than I'd realized, but I'll have to take care not to break trust with her as it would doubtlessly have a negative impact on our future relationship.

I've recently had to chastise Mrs. Agosti regarding the amount of television that she is allowing Lucy to watch. I clearly remember when the devices were invented and despite having been exposed to them for years, my opinion of them remains unchanged. They are nothing more than a distraction which serves no good purpose and there is little if anything useful that they do which cannot be better performed by way of the written word.

What little news is shown on the various networks is barely more than superficial talking points which are manipulated by various power blocs. Rather than being constrained by being spoon-fed information at a rate that the lowest common denominator can understand, I've long advocated reading from various sources as being a superior method of informing oneself.

Understanding current events is a necessary investment of time, but there is no reason to turn it into a kind of entertainment that occupies hours and hours.

Unfortunately, Mrs. Agosti has quite a different view, and my attempts to reprogram her away from the activity have proven unsuccessful so far. It is interesting to see how her psyche is reacting to my efforts though. I've rarely seen such a strong reaction out of anyone before when it came to trying to change their behavior.

I have decided, at least temporarily, to cease fighting this particular battle with Mrs. Agosti, but it has raised a very valid concern of what I would do if she and I were ever to come to a point where our differences became irreconcilable.

She has no close friends or family who could be used as leverage, and threatening her personally is likely going to just result in her telling Lucy about my behavior. I've already established from prior incursions into her mind that money will not be a very good motivator for her, which leaves me with little in the way of options where she is concerned other than the voice of reason, which I've also established is not always successful.

I've decided that it would be prudent to start investigating some kind of backup option. I'm not taking this course lightly because of the sheer amount of time which will be required to begin inserting the proper constructs in the mind of whoever ends up being my backup option.

It appears that I have found yet another way in which I drastically underestimated the level of inconvenience that Lucy would bring into my life. There are a large number of problems in life which I've found can be sidestepped simply by picking up and leaving. This is, unfortunately, much less of an option now that I'm responsible for Lucy.

In many ways this presents a novel, if fairly irrelevant, tactical problem which I've yet to fully solve. For now, I've decided that I'll need to spend slightly more time with Lucy in order to provide her with an alternate activity.

Mrs. Agosti tends to watch most of her television in the evening, so I've begun reading bedtime stories to Lucy before putting her to bed each night. I initially tried just ordering an assortment of options from an online retailer, but this proved less than acceptable for Lucy for some reason or another.

She displayed absolutely no interest in any of the books I'd selected, but Mrs. Agosti recommended I take Lucy to the public library for story hour. I'm finding that her suggestions are nearly always very reasonable, so much so that I can rarely disagree with them, but I'm increasingly finding that I'm taking over duties with regards to Lucy's care that I never intended to assume.

I will have to give the matter additional thought, but for now the important factor is that while story hour wasn't in and of itself a rousing success, it did lead to a triumph. Lucy didn't want to sit down and listen with the other kids, but she was absolutely fascinated by the stacks.

She wandered along the narrow corridors between the bookshelves with a subdued expression of delight on her face that was her equivalent to screaming for joy. We ended up going home with more than a dozen books, and Lucy apparently does like listening to stories, she just doesn't like being around large groups of other children.

The beginnings of a plan are starting to coalesce in the back of my mind. It's not far enough along yet for me to know exactly the opportunity that is approaching me, but I've been down this road before and I recognize the feeling. Hopefully this particular plan will come together quickly. Taking care of Lucy, and Venice, albeit in very different ways, is incredibly inconvenient, but I suspect that it is the boredom that will do me in first unless Imastious either assigns me a suitable mission or I come up with something myself.

Geoffrey Journal Entry 8

February
Lucy's Age: 4

I have to admit to being rather more impressed with Venice than I thought I was going to be when we first met. She's still a complete mess, but she's showing much more in the way of willpower than I expected her to.

I don't know how Imastious always seems to pick incredibly, one could say almost psychotically, determined disciples, but he apparently has some kind of hidden talent there. It's a reminder to me that I need to be careful not to underestimate him.

Imastious isn't particularly subtle, but he is good at breaking people and usually he manages to keep them broken once he's achieved his aim. Honestly I'm not sure how I managed to maintain so much independence. All I can assume is that Imastious' methods work better on adults than on children.

Venice continues to whine about the hand that life has dealt her, and she still refuses to answer to the name I've given her, instead insisting that I call her April. While her strength of will should eventually help make her a better operative, right now it's a barrier that needs to be destroyed so that I can get on with the process of rebuilding her into something more useful to me.

Her sense of modesty continues to be one of the most effective tools I have with which to break her. Despite the terrible things that Imastious has already done to her, she continues to be the most unnerved by the fact that her clothes are little more than rags. She's little more than a scarecrow now, but if anything, that seems to have increased Imastious' desire for her.

I'd hoped that the starvation and Imastious' efforts would be sufficient to break her without the requirement of more direct action on my part, but so far she's withstood all of the more passive tortures I've inflicted on her.

I'd happily continue to wait her out, but Imastious has started expressing his displeasure with how long my methods are taking, and while I'm more than prepared to suffer through whatever punishment he might decide to concoct for me, I can't afford to have him take over her training.

A DARKNESS MIRRORED

Last night I tied her to her bedframe and ran a low-amp, high-voltage current through her, slowly increasing it over the course of the session. I think that this is the start of the breakthrough with Venice that I've been looking for. In hindsight it is apparent that she'd accustomed herself to the level of discomfort that was being inflicted on her. She didn't enjoy the torture, but she'd realized that she could survive it and therefore it had ceased to have as much of a motivational impact on her.

I believe that the secret to breaking Venice will be the perpetual promise of worse things waiting in the wings. I've also realized that I've been stretching myself too thin and focusing on the wrong things over the last several months.

Lucy is important to my long-term plans, but it's not as though she'll turn against me two decades from now because I shave a couple of hours per week out of the time I'm currently spending with her. I should have been spending more time with Venice than I have been. Her unusually strong will makes it harder than normal to get a real picture of what is going on inside of her mind, but that is a poor excuse.

If I'd spent more time exploring her thoughts rather than just the minimum amount of effort required to counteract the constructs that Imastious has been placing there, I probably would have hit upon the proper course of action weeks ago. It is a worthwhile reminder that not all of the tasks that may need done are truly equal in importance or results for a given amount of effort.

There is however one area in which I think I've been especially wise when it comes to investing time and energy into an undertaking. The plan that I could feel starting to come together a couple of months ago has been carried out and it worked flawlessly.

Because of all of the operations that I've run for Imastious, I've gotten to know some of the Red Hand Consortium leadership and there was one individual who stood out to me last year on the couple of occasions that I interacted with him.

As nearly as I was able to tell, Antoine was recruited several years ago and went to college on a basketball scholarship in an attempt to leave the gang life behind. An unexpected injury sidelined him partway through his first year, which wouldn't have necessarily been the end of his attempt to get out, but his mother suffered a stroke shortly after he was injured.

Based on everything I'd observed, Antoine considered his life to be a failure, but the more I learned of him the more impressed I became. He'd returned home and once again became active in his gang because that offered the best prospect of paying for his mother's medical bills, but he'd managed to avoid the more violent aspects of activity in the Red Hand Consortium.

A DARKNESS MIRRORED

Antoine was smart and he'd put his brief time in college to good use. He wouldn't be giving any Harvard MBA's a run for their money in the near term, but he wasn't up against Harvard MBA's. Antoine streamlined the gang's drug operations and then moved on to establishing a protection racket inside their territory.

It was Antoine's intelligence that originally caught my attention, but it was the fact that he'd returned home to care for his mother that had given me the handle on him that I'd been looking for.

A little additional research revealed that Antoine had a wife and a six-year-old daughter and he'd relied on anonymity as their main shield against the hazards that were part and parcel of his gang activity.

Once I knew where Antoine lived, it was a simple matter to kidnap his daughter, whom his wife had left at a daycare center. Possession of the child gave me all of the leverage that I needed in order to get her mother to meet me at the station under 125th Street.

Antoine hadn't ever been loyal to his gang. If I'd had any doubt it would have been put to rest by the speed with which he gave up locations, shipment schedules and account numbers. Antoine's loyalty was first and foremost to his family, which is ultimately what killed him.

Any rational person would have known that I wasn't going to let his wife and daughter go free.

The sensible thing would have been to cut his losses, but he walked right into my trap and he came unarmed and alone, just like I told him to.

I'd spent a week before the Antoine operation developing a new contact with the Bloods, which proved to be unusually wise in hindsight. I'd suspected that the information I'd get from Antoine would be more than I could successfully capitalize on my own, but I'd underestimated just how much Antoine knew.

Under other circumstances I might have been inclined to let Antoine go. There is something to be said for the idea of keeping the dumbest breeding stock in circulation. The stupider the average human is, the easier it is for vampires to continue to go unnoticed in the shadows.

Antoine's lack of survival instincts certainly put him towards the bottom of the barrel despite the intelligence he displayed in most other aspects of his life, but he'd recognized me, which meant that I couldn't let him live. Besides, he was the major force behind Imastious' favorite money machine. With him gone I knew that Imastious would have a much harder time recovering from the losses that were about to sweep through his organization.

I cut all three of their throats and then disposed of their bodies in suitably violent ways. Antoine was stuffed into the trunk of his own car, his wife was hanged from the ceiling of their apartment, and I left their daughter in a nearby park.

A DARKNESS MIRRORED

Even while I was doing it I knew that it was probably overkill, but it was a key part of my effort to link the killing to the Bloods. As soon as the bodies were taken care of, I texted my contact in the Bloods with most of the information I'd extracted out of Antoine and then went out to make off with three of the juicier targets. I ended up several million dollars richer, the Bloods now owe me a major favor, and Imastious has lost an incredible amount of money and influence which will ultimately lead to a loss of manpower.

Lucy's presence is, in a way, responsible for all of this. Before she came into my life and reminded me of a sister long since forgotten, I wouldn't have thought to attack in this manner. An intellectual understanding by itself doesn't carry sufficient power to really take advantage of those kinds of familial bonds. All in all, it's been a very profitable few weeks.

Things have continued on much the same as before with Lucy. This year her birthday was a very subdued affair, which seemed to suit her just fine. Although the last year since I found her at times felt as though it was moving with glacial slowness, looking back at it now it's hard to believe so much time has passed already. I very much hope the next eighteen years go by equally quickly.

Geoffrey Journal Entry 9

May
Lucy's Age: 4

It has finally started to happen. Venice doesn't realize it yet, but she's started breaking. She's still being difficult in many ways, but I can tell that she's just going through the motions now.

Imastious continues to paint himself as the villain of the piece by the simple fact that he can't seem to control his baser instincts. I, on the other hand, have started providing Venice with tiny luxuries whenever I'm able to do so without arousing Imastious' suspicion. It's still very slow going, but it's only a matter of time now.

Given her increased reasonability over the last few days I've decided to begin teaching her the beginnings of unarmed self-defense. It's possibly a little earlier than normal for me to begin doing something like that, but it will give her a defense against Imastious, which will go a long way towards binding her more tightly to me.

This will also mean that I'll need to start her on the meditation and visualization exercises required for her to be able to keep Imastious out of her mind. In a perfect world I'd be able to rely on the fact that her defenses would be successful, but at this point it would be foolhardy to do so. That means that I'm going to have to be very careful to cloak my instruction in such a way that Imastious won't have proof that I set out to have her injure him.

I've already increased her rations slightly, not enough for her to start putting weight back on, but enough that she's coming back from the edge of starvation. She's going to need to rebuild muscle mass if she's going to have any chance of landing a blow hard enough to give Imastious any kind of pause.

Her being in better shape physically will go a long ways towards increasing her mental defenses as well. Speaking of which, she's only taking in the minimum amount of blood that she needs to survive. Considering that it's all been bagged blood so far that doesn't bode very well for her long-term survival.

Given the sheer number of vampires in New York it is difficult, if not impossible, to guarantee a consistent supply of bagged blood.

The hospitals and the Red Cross have even been known to use armed guards in some instances.

A very powerful mentalist can usually still manipulate his way into the supply rooms, but I'm not to that point yet. Doing a working on someone with whom you don't have regular contact, who's already suspicious, and who is healthy or otherwise not run down by starvation or torture is very difficult.

Imastious seems to be able to manage it on occasion, but I suspect that most of his successes are because he ingratiates himself with his targets beforehand in some form or fashion. It's just another way to get around the obstacle of a healthy mind. I tend to, instead, generally choose targets whose self-interest would already lead them to do whatever I want them to do in the first place. That way all I need to do is give them a slight nudge rather than rewire something critical.

All of which is a rather long, complicated way of saying that it's generally just cheaper and less effort to kidnap a living person rather than trying to get your hands on bags either by force or subterfuge.

Someone like Venice won't have any problems getting men off on their own once she's back to her normal weight. Any number of hot-blooded males would be eager to take her back to their place where her superior strength will make them easy victims. That of course is predicated upon her getting over her squeamishness first though.

As I've considered the problem I've realized that this is the perfect way to hide much of what I'm doing to prepare her to injure or even kill Imastious. I'll tell him that I've decided it's time to break her of her blood aversion. Blood-starving a vampire is always hard on their system, which would explain giving her higher-calorie rations, and I can tell him that I started running her through some basic defensive techniques as an illustration of what she'll need to know later on once I start introducing larger victims into her cage.

Of course the first human I feed her will likely have to be small so that she doesn't overdo it because of the hunger, but given how quickly she's going to move from kids up to adults it's a reasonable precaution to start right now.

As far as the mediation and visualization exercises go, I can bill them as something designed to help her focus on something other than the act of actually feeding. Again it's a stretch as a better solution would be for her to just grow to love feeding, but it's workable.

Geoffrey Journal Entry 10

July
Lucy's Age: 4

Venice has finally done it. She showed a remarkable amount of willpower, but even she couldn't withstand the constant hunger for blood. Based on how quickly she moved into the hallucination stage she wasn't getting quite enough blood in her diet before, but in many ways I would have rather that she had lapsed into incoherence even sooner than she did.

The rate of progression through the various stages of blood starvation are so different from one vampire to another that I was forced to wait just outside of her cage for the entire time. That meant that I came prepared for a long vigil.

I selected my captive the day before, once again from a daycare center. As always, victim selection is the hardest part of the entire process.

A DARKNESS MIRRORED

This center had a higher than normal percentage of little girls in it. I watched them all file out with various adults over a period of four days and three potential targets jumped out in short order.

Most of the children were picked up by the same adult on all four days. A few of the children were picked up by two different adults, but these three, a boy and two girls, were picked up by a different adult on each of the days that I watched the facility.

After the fourth day I followed Cynthia, one of the daycare workers, home and then later that night I followed her to a dance club. Given that she was primarily at the club to find companionship for the night, it was incredibly easy to slip a few tendrils inside of her mind and convince her to leave with me.

We had dinner at a high-class establishment. I paid with cash to make sure that there wasn't any paper trail, and then subtly pumped her for information over oysters and lobsters. It was almost too easy. She really cared for the kids she worked with, so when I expressed an interest about her day job it took only the slightest of mental nudges for her to open right up.

The three I was interested in appeared on the surface much the same where my purposes were concerned. All three had busy, single mothers who used an ever-shifting group of friends, family and occasionally boyfriends to pick up their children from the daycare.

I tried to get Cynthia to tell me more about the kids in question, but my tendrils started to pick up the beginnings of suspicion inside her mind, so I smoothly turned the conversation another direction. As we headed back to her apartment after dinner I debated my options.

There weren't any substantial differences between the three children in anything I'd heard or seen so far, but some gut-level instinct was steering me away from the two little girls. It's a small thing, but after having seen so many operations go bad, I've learned to listen to my instincts.

By the time we made it to her place I was confident that I had the best target picked out, so I put her under with chloroform, and then once the chloroform started to wear off I injected her with my favorite tranquilizer. In addition to keeping her out of circulation for twenty-four hours, it had the very desirable side effect of memory loss.

When I finally left her apartment I was wrung out and shaking, but I was confident that my efforts, along with some significant help from the drug, had been sufficient to erase any memory she had of the evening we'd spent together.

I picked the kid up the next afternoon. A combination of my most winning smile and a trace of mental compulsion convinced one of the daycare employees to release the child into my care. It was almost too easy by the time I got to that step. The poor woman was obviously exhausted from a long day of making do without Cynthia and the last thing she would have wanted was to be responsible for the boy any longer than she had to be.

Venice's eyes got exceptionally wide when I walked into her apartment with the boy, drugged and cradled in my arms as though he'd fallen asleep. She begged me not to make her kill him, but I kept pointing out to her that she wouldn't be able to subsist on blood bags forever. She might make it a few weeks or even months, but eventually she'd end up without a supply. *I* knew it was only a matter of time until she fed and killed, it was just a matter of showing her that fact.

Like anything else, there are benefits and disadvantages to being one of my kind. The benefits are clear and unarguable. Strength and speed, rapid healing and a complete, or at least near-complete, halt to the aging process.

The disadvantages are less clear, but are especially difficult for new vampires to deal with. Feeding and leaving one's victim alive is a recipe for being killed, either by the humans when they realize what you are, or by the various vampire elders who have a vested interest in keeping our existence a secret. An extremely powerful mentalist would be able to leave the humans they fed on without any memory of the event, but for new vampires there isn't any such possibility. What's more, without the control developed over the course of decades or even centuries of feeding, it is very rare for a vampire to be able to feed without losing control and sucking their victim dry.

I remember having some of the same concerns as Venice when I was first turned, but I've since come to realize the irrationality of it all. For the most part we vampires feed on the castoffs of society—people who have fallen through the cracks, people who some parts of society still claim to care about, but whose lives ultimately have less value than five liters of bagged blood.

A society that would put armed guards in place to stop the theft of blood from a hospital but not provide the same security to its homeless doesn't truly value all life equally and I knew that Venice would eventually come to see the truth of my words.

Even knowing that didn't stop her tears from being vaguely discomforting. I've been feeding on, and in most cases killing, humans for decades now, and while it's been a long time since I've looked back with doubt on my decision to live rather than just killing myself, I was still somewhat uneasy as a result of listening to Venice's arguments for such an extended period of time.

It was a decided relief when Venice finally got to the point where I could tell that the hunger had taken over. I put the boy in there with her, waited while she drained him, and then left to dispose of the body.

Lucy usually runs to me and wraps her arms around my legs when I come back after an extended absence, but for some reason she barely even acknowledged my presence tonight. Her indifference bothered me more than it should have. One off evening doesn't mean that she's stopped bonding with me, though. It's probably nothing more than the fact that Mrs. Agosti had purchased a number of new picture books for her earlier that day.

It's actually quite astonishing the way that Lucy devours new books. She spends much more time 'reading' than I would have expected for someone so young. I suspect that some of that is just a natural tendency to ape the adults in her life, specifically me, who spends most of my time reading off of a computer screen.

In fairness though, I do have to give some of the credit to Mrs. Agosti. The woman seems to have absolutely no inclination to read herself, but she has made a real effort to foster a love of reading in Lucy. It was Mrs. Agosti who purchased a kit of plastic letters and first started teaching Lucy the alphabet. At this rate Lucy will be reading well ahead of schedule and months before any of the other children her age.

Geoffrey Journal Entry 11

September
Lucy's Age: 4

I've been much too busy to realize it before now, but looking back I must admit that it has been a particularly difficult few months. I badly underestimated Venice, or maybe I should say that I overestimated her instinct for self-preservation.

After making her first feeding kill, she tried to kill herself. Fortunately, while I hadn't anticipated needing to perform an active suicide watch, I had taken the basic precaution of making sure that there wasn't anything in her cage with which she could carry out a successful attempt. She lost a fair amount of blood, but nothing that her system wasn't able to bounce back from in slightly less than forty-eight hours.

Imastious was the one to find her, and after texting me to demand that I go take care of her, he then dropped off of the face of the earth for three days. Predictably when he did show back up to Venice's apartment, it was to beat her within an inch of her life.

By and large Imastious is a calculating, emotionless creature, but he seems to become less logical when women are involved and when things aren't going his way. I've seen the tendency in him previous to this, but Venice seems to have gotten under his skin more than I realized.

There really isn't much more that Imastious could do to make Venice hate him at this point. Beating her accomplished little other than forcing me to spend two more days making sure that she recovered from her latest round of injuries.

To say that I resented him creating yet more work for me would be an understatement; however, even very ill winds do blow some good. I used the fact that Venice's injuries had decimated her natural mental defenses to my benefit and spent the otherwise idle time laying extremely fine, extremely subtle constructs in different areas of her mind.

I simply couldn't spend additional extended blocks of time on suicide watch, so I capitalized on her animosity for Imastious and her natural attraction to me. She doesn't like me, which is hardly surprising. Although in my own way I'm just as much of a captive as she is, she's yet to realize that and I haven't wanted to emphasize that fact because she needs to view me as a player in this game rather than just another of the pieces.

Her feelings are too strong for me to just nullify them and replace them with something more positive, even assuming I'd been willing to risk Imastious finding out just how powerful my abilities have become.

Instead I focused in on the physical attraction she's feeling, strengthening it and extending it into other areas. If things work as I think they will then she'll experience even greater levels of physical desire for me, but more importantly she'll start finding non-physical attributes about me to admire.

It may be something as simple as appreciating punctuality or something else equally irrelevant, but as I gradually build on that I should end up extending the framework to the point where she no longer hates me. I doubt that I'll have access to her mind for long enough to bring that about solely by way of mentalist constructs, but if I can build it up sufficiently, then my actions, especially viewed against the needless sadism of Imastious and others of our kind, should help accomplish my desired goal.

These are all steps that Imastious should easily be able to take, but either he's so enamored of blunt force that he doesn't think in these kinds of terms anymore, or he's just become far too irrational where Venice is concerned.

Ultimately it doesn't really matter what the reason is as long as he continues to behave in the same fashion as he has so far. Venice has mostly recovered now, but I've left her on better quality rations despite that fact, and her training continues apace. While she was too weak to feed on a human I continued to provide her with blood bags, but now that she's nearly back to full strength it is time to arrange for another live feeding.

Geoffrey Journal Entry 12

November
Lucy's Age: 4

Tonight I celebrated. Most of the time when I need to feed I simply take from among the homeless and the junkies, but occasionally, in special instances, I treat myself to something extra.

Venice has shown another burst of remarkable progress. Her mental shields are stronger and stronger each day and she's showing a real flair for unarmed combat. We haven't progressed to anything too complicated yet, but she seems to have an instinctive sense of which openings are just feints and which ones are opportunities that need to be pursued with everything she has.

The physical activity, along with increasingly infrequent mental constructs, has served to distract her from the last of her suicidal tendencies. After nearly beating her to death last time, Imastious then proceeded to make himself scarce for nearly two months, which meant that he didn't have a good feel for where Venice was at mentally, or physically, when he finally did come back.

Obviously I wasn't there when it happened, and Venice wasn't in much of a position to relate events to me when I dropped back in for a visit, but from the visual evidence as well as the bits and pieces that she was able to relate to me, it appears that Imastious tried to take advantage of her again and she connected with an elbow strike to his throat.

That's not actually something I'd taught her, but it demonstrates a certain level of raw aggression that I can't help but be proud of. Unfortunately rather than following up with a killing blow she proceeded to kick him in the ribs. Once the initial advantage of having surprised him so completely had passed, Venice was no match for Imastious and he ended up throwing her into the bars of her cage with enough force to kill a normal human.

Despite the advantages the change brings our kind it was nearly enough to kill Venice as well.

It's entirely possible despite my best efforts that I've left too much of a trail inside of Venice's mind, that or Imastious ultimately may not even care whether he has any proof.

Under either of those scenarios I'm going to end up paying for my audacity in pain when Imastious decides to torture me, but hopefully I've succeeded in binding Venice to me more tightly as a result of all of this.

All in all the occasion felt worthy of a celebration, so I went to one of the more popular nightclubs in the city and picked up a delicious young woman who was barely into her twenties.

Things with Venice are long past the point where I'm using the imminent threat of nudity as a punishment, but since she's started returning to a healthier weight I've started to find her more and more attractive. Her reward, although I can't term it as such because of the high probability that Imastious will eventually break into her mind again, was a new set of clothes to replace the rags that she was captured in.

My pretext for providing the clothes was that she needed something presentable for when Imastious ordered us to move onto training the interpersonal skills like seduction. Predictably she threw them against the walls of the cage and yelled profanities at me, but when I returned the next day she was wearing them and not only did she seem happier, she was really quite fetching in them.

Her reward was clothing and mine was a meal that tested the bounds of my decision never to be like Imastious and let the desires of the flesh get in the way of the goals that I've set for myself.

Geoffrey Journal Entry 13

February
Lucy's Age: 5

I saw this coming, but unfortunately there was little I could do about it. Imastious took several runs at Venice before managing to bypass her defenses. Venice didn't know exactly what was going on, but there was plenty of evidence that he'd visited her, and she was worse for the wear after each time he went to her apartment.

As always, the anticipation was almost worse than the actual torture. In the weeks leading up to Imastious breaking Venice I considered running more than once, but I abandoned the idea each time for the same reasons that I've always abandoned it in the past.

I'm fairly certain that I've rooted out all of the hooks that Imastious placed in my mind when I was a child, but I can't be positive, in fact I may never know for sure. That means that there is always the possibility of some kind of involuntary reaction that will be triggered by any attempt to run. Imastious views controllable pawns as the best route to further power and therefore has specialized in inserting hidden constructs inside of his subordinates' minds.

It is entirely possible that the first time I stepped on a bus, a train or an airplane my heart would cease to function, but that's not the sole reason that I'm reluctant to leave the city. The truth of the matter is that leaving the city would mean leaving the beginnings of a power base that I've spent many years crafting. That power is the only thing that has the possibility of really freeing me.

If I were to relocate somewhere else, even assuming that I could keep from starting some programmed behavior that would allow Imastious to find me, it would still only be a matter of time before I was pulled into the web of some other vampire elder.

The only thing that can protect one of my kind is to be at the top of the food chain. Vampires don't just prey on humans, they prey on weaker vampires as well and I'd be just as dead killed in some low-level power struggle in Atlanta as I would be if Imastious killed me here in New York.

Given that it was only a matter of time before Imastious came for me, I returned to spending most of my time in my apartment, rather than in the second apartment with Lucy and Mrs. Agosti. It was the most prudent course if I were to avoid accidentally leading Imastious back there, and with any luck the easier it was to find me, the better mood Imastious would be in when he started in on me.

Spending so much time by myself was oddly different than I remembered it being. It wasn't exactly that I missed Lucy or her minder, but it was as though there was something missing from my environment that I'd become accustomed to having around.

The furnishings were the same hand-stitched leather and dark wood that I picked out years ago, but somehow I took less comfort in the black granite surfaces than I had previously. I've always prized my peace and quiet, but my apartment felt too quiet now.

Things have been strained between Lucy and I for the last several months, for no reason that I've been able to detect, but as I sat in the comfortably furnished set of rooms that had been home to me a short time ago, I realized that for better or worse I'd started thinking of Lucy's apartment as home instead.

It smacks of the beginnings of weakness, which wasn't a fact designed to reassure me as I waited for Imastious, but I've always believed that self-delusion is the first step on the pathway to failure.

I was actually thinking of Lucy when Imastious opened the door to my apartment and walked in. I'd left it unlocked because I didn't want to deal with the hassle of replacing the door. As always, Imastious cloaked his torture in platitudes that vaguely echo whatever religion he grew up in, but for someone who's known him as long as I have, it was obvious that he'd succeeded in ransacking Venice's mind and he was here because of what he'd seen there.

My sword was within easy reach, and for the briefest of seconds I considered grabbing it and trying to kill Imastious, but I knew the effort would be futile. Imastious is still, and may always be, a stronger mentalist than I am, and he's started to develop the beginnings of a telekinetic gift as well over the last few decades.

I'm a much better swordsman than I used to be; but even if I got lucky and somehow killed him, it wouldn't change the fundamental problem that I didn't have enough power yet to be anything other than someone else's pawn.

The actual torture was almost a ritual between Imastious and me. We'd been in the exact same situation so many times before that we almost didn't need to talk. He shackled me to my bedframe and then used the same set of batteries and wires on me that I used on Venice such a short time ago.

A large pot from the kitchen served to collect the blood from the shallow wounds that he used to bleed me out, wounds that took a process that otherwise would have required days down into something that was only a few hours.

Once I was weakened by blood loss and torture, then the true battle of wills began. For all of his power and ruthlessness, Imastious was used to dealing with young vampires, and I'd developed several tricks over the years that went a long ways towards addressing the imbalance he'd created by bleeding me out.

The first was the old analogue clock on the wall. I'd figured out a long time ago that Imastious tracked how long it took to break me. It was an effective, if blunt, measure of my strength. It was very easy to lose track of time while being tortured, but with the clock just barely in visual range, I was able to make sure that I let my defenses start to crumble at the right time. Too soon and Imastious would know that I was trying to play him, too late and I'd be tipping my hand and letting him know that I was actually much stronger than he realized.

Years ago, before I'd realized the reason behind much of what Imastious does, I'd given him a very good view of my baseline power. Since then I'd been successful in maintaining the illusion that my powers were growing much more slowly than they actually were.

Given the glacial slowness with which vampire powers increased, the difference between my actual level of power and the level of power that Imastious thought I possessed was very, very slight, but it was a real advantage, and one that should continue to grow by the tiniest of bits each year.

The clock let me start displaying the signs of imminent physical failure before my body would have started showing them on its own. Again, the margin of difference was very small, generally less than half an hour, but it represented another tiny reservoir of strength that Imastious didn't know about.

The most potent tool at my disposal is a level of control over my memories that has only a little to do with my mentalist abilities. I spent nearly a decade shortly after I was turned looking for a way to increase my mentalist powers to the point where I could beat Imastious at his own game.

I studied with several master yogis and half a dozen different martial arts masters before I finally gave up and acknowledged the fact that nothing I did was going to cause my powers to grow any faster than they were already growing. While I didn't buy into all of the mystical nonsense that my teachers had tried to instill in me, I did find that semi-regular meditation helped keep my mind clear and focused on my goals. I thought that rather tiny tool was all I had to show from so many years of effort until I unlocked the ability to destroy my own memories.

When I first started using my powers, I got little more than vague impressions regarding my own mind, but somehow the meditation allowed me to visualize my mental landscape with much more vividness than I ever would have believed possible.

From bits and pieces that Imastious has let drop over the years, I think that his perceptions are stronger than mine were when I was first turned, but that they are less developed than mine are now. As I spent more and more time meditating and exploring the incredibly detailed world inside of my mind, I brushed up against one of my memories with more force than I meant to. To my surprise I found that the memory shifted position slightly. It was as though it unanchored and then re-anchored again in a new spot in the pool of my mind.

The memory lost a certain vibrancy, but it was all still there. I knew at the time that I'd just discovered something significant, but it took me several months to come up with a way to capitalize on it.

By shifting a group of memories over to one edge of my mind, I was then able to create the illusion that my mind ended before it got to those memories. To follow a visual analogy, if my memories all float in an irregularly-shaped pond of water, I simply move one section of the banks inward such that it conceals part of the water.

I stumbled onto an equally useful ability, that of erasing specific memories at will, by accident. I was moving a memory regarding where I'd secreted a stash of valuables and I used too much force in the process.

Between one instant and the next I ceased to have any knowledge of where the jewels were located. I knew they were out there, I knew that I'd stolen them and then hidden them, but the memory of actually hiding them was gone.

Those three skills, the ability to move memories, destroy memories, and secrete a cache of memories off on the very edge of my mind, are the foundation I use to keep Imastious from knowing just how actively I'm working against him.

The fact that the most important memories, the ones that I'm saving by hiding them from Imastious, lose some of their solidity is an unfortunate byproduct, but the real complication is that I'm only able to store so much in the way of information inside the blind that I create on the edge of my mind. That means that I have to be very selective regarding what I keep versus what I choose to simply destroy.

Given that I'd known this was coming, I'd already mostly sanitized my mind, which means that I was left only with the choice of what to destroy this time around. Interactions with Mrs. Agosti were an easy decision. My daily journal entries mean that I've got a summarized list of my key interactions with her. It will likely mean that things will be a bit awkward between us for the next few months, but that is a price that I'm willing to pay.

A DARKNESS MIRRORED

I'm always very careful to keep my business holdings relatively concentrated as a way of decreasing the amount of information that will need to be stored there, but that has always been the largest block of information requiring hiding. Memories of my key contacts inside the White Tears and other places generally round out the rest of the available space.

My memories of time spent with Lucy were what gave me such a pause this time as I went about the task of preparing for Imastious' visit. It is ultimately hard to say whether Lucy or my business activities will prove to be most valuable, but the business information consists of relatively dry facts combined with the lessons I've learned over many decades of negotiation and analysis.

The memories of Lucy, however, are of a nature that won't store well on paper and ultimately I decided that it was more important to keep as much of my time with Lucy as possible, even with the insubstantiality that will result from the move, than it would be to eke out a few extra percentage points where my return on capital is concerned.

Venice was much less of a quandary. Most of my interactions with her are sanctioned by way of Imastious having ordered me to see to her transformation from a helpless co-ed to a useful tool. I did however decide to keep those bits of memories that related to the interactions with Venice that Imastious wouldn't have approved of.

The logic is simple once you realize that the situation with Venice is much like the situation with Lucy—she's just a weaker tool which should pay off after correspondingly less investment.

I made careful records of all of the business information that I was destroying, and then removed the memories in question. I remember the act of making the list, through an emotionless veil, but will still need to study the entries in detail before I can hope to make substantial use out of it.

Things went much as I expected them to as far as the actual invasion of my mind by Imastious. He drove me right up to the edge of my physical limits and then entered my mind, ransacking nearly every bit of it. Although I don't believe that he processes everything that he touches, in the past he's always been able to understand enough of what he sees to be able to track down and examine anything traitorous in very fine detail indeed.

The small margin of strength that I bought myself through all of my efforts at concealing my true strength was sufficient once again. I managed to maintain the hiding place around my block of ghostly memories long enough to satisfy Imastious that I hadn't actively been trying to get Venice to kill him.

Once Imastious was gone, I pulled myself over to the fridge and consumed all of the small supply of bagged blood that I keep for exactly these kinds of emergencies, and then I began the task of reviewing the journal entries that have been marked as containing something I lost.

I'll need to go see to Venice soon, but that will have to wait until tomorrow when I've regained enough strength to walk.

All in all, I would have to say that the encounter was a success. I've continued to hide the extent of my strength from Imastious, but I have to wonder why I chose to put myself in such a situation.

It had been a long time since I'd been faced with one of Imastious' torture sessions, so maybe I'd just forgotten the sheer disorientation resulting from destroying so many memories. I've lost the emotional overtones for much of what was moved, so possibly there were non-rational reasons for what I did, that or maybe I believed there was a greater chance that Venice could actually kill Imastious.

There is a chance that I will find something in my journals that will shed more light on my decision, but I don't believe the likelihood of that is very great. To use the old expression, I've made my bed and now must lie in it. The things that I lost over the last few days will not be coming back to me, and while I need to learn from the experience to the extent that I made a mistake, I know from times before that a certain amount of self-doubt is natural when one loses so much information so quickly.

Geoffrey Journal Entry 14

April
Lucy's Age: 5

I've lost so much of my frame of reference when it comes to Lucy that it's hard to tell for sure, but I think that things are worse than they were before. Apparently I'd become accustomed to the frustration of dealing with Lucy. I can't think of any other reason that I wouldn't have made note of the fact in my journals.

Lucy has stopped speaking to me. I don't recall us ever carrying on long, involved conversations before this, but in the past it wasn't uncommon for her to run to the door when I came home. Now she just hides in her room whenever we aren't sitting down to eat.

Despite repeated promptings from Mrs. Agosti, Lucy still refuses to tell me about her day, and when Mrs. Agosti pressed her about the cause of her actions, she said that I was different.

It is incredible to think that a child would pick up on the fact that I've lost information, that my memories of her are a pale shadow of what they once were. Mrs. Agosti certainly hasn't, but that is the only explanation that I've been able to come up with for this change.

I keep meaning to spend some time with Mrs. Agosti and ask her for ideas on how to draw Lucy back out, but have been consistently sidetracked by my efforts with Venice. It's almost as if there is indeed some kind of cosmic balance there. Things with Venice are considerably better, to a degree that it almost seems to offset the problems with Lucy.

I made it to Venice's apartment less than forty-eight hours after Imastious tortured me, and while I did my best to not exhibit any sign of what had happened, Venice is more perceptive than I gave her credit for. She correctly deduced that Imastious was the one who'd tortured me, and while it's not as though I've been forgiven for everything that has passed between us, it does seem to have created a bond there.

I have to admit that our new connection has caught me off guard. It is…nice…to have someone around with whom I can discuss things. I'm not so foolish as to think that I can confide in Venice, but I have an astonishing number of things in common with her. It's more than just the fact that we are both little more than slaves to Imastious, or the fact that we're both vampires and therefore have an almost unlimited potential stretching out for centuries ahead of us.

It has a surprising amount to do with the fact that recent discussions with Venice are causing me to remember some of my own early concerns with what I would become once I accepted the changes that came along with being a vampire.

I will have to guard against becoming too familiar with Venice. She's a vampire. It means that she's no longer one of those weak humans, but it also means that I can't ever really trust her. It's a sad state of affairs, but it is simply the way of the world. In order for someone to become strong enough to be appealing they have to leave behind the weaknesses that would allow me to trust them.

Geoffrey Journal Entry 15

August
Lucy's Age: 5

Two developments have come to pass which I did not anticipate in the slightest. Lucy has warmed back up to me, but the cause was odd to say the least. Last Tuesday I spent the night out doing surveillance on a target for Imastious. The target was active until midmorning on Wed, so I ended up sleeping later than normal which meant that I was running late for my weekly trip to the library with Lucy.

I'd been spending most of my time at my apartment, so the trip over to Lucy and Mrs. Agosti's apartment ate up additional time as well. By the time we made it to the library, we had less than an hour before closing time.

It was already dark when we left the library and headed back to Lucy's home. It has been so long since someone attempted to mug me that for a second I couldn't believe it was happening. Apparently having a child with me makes me look like an easier target.

My personal training sessions since Imastious tortured me have been largely focused on aikido, so when the mugger came at me with a knife I simply used a knee-drop throw to put him into the building that until a second previously had been at my back.

Lucy has been so fragile lately that I expected her to break into tears due to the sheer violence of my response, but she simply looked at the unconscious mugger for several seconds before asking if I could teach her how to do that.

To be honest, I'd been reconsidering the advisability of my past decision to try and turn Lucy into a weapon. When looking at the chain of events with the cool dispassion granted to me by having so much of the emotional overtones ripped away from my memories, it had become very hard to justify continuing to spend both time and money keeping her alive and trying to bond with her.

I'm beginning to change my appraisal of the situation. I've found a very exclusive health club that is only a short walk from her apartment and booked an exercise room for Lucy and me four times a week. The training is progressing well. Lucy is younger and smaller than Venice, but there is a ferocity to her that tells me she will eventually be quite dangerous, for a human, if she continues her training.

Lucy continues to ask for additional training times, which is inconvenient considering how much distance there is between her apartment and my apartment, so I've once again started spending more time there than at my own apartment.

I started today's entry by stating that there were two unexpected developments. The second development was that Venice tried to run away. When I say it was unexpected I don't mean that I didn't anticipate that she would run away, I mean that I'd expected it to happen sooner than it did. We'd unlocked her cage and moved her to a new apartment weeks ago, so when she didn't make a break for it, I'd assumed that she'd made her peace with her situation.

Apparently she is both smarter and stupider than I thought she was.

The conditioning worked just as expected. Imastious isn't strong enough to make her love him, or even like him, but he's created a subconscious tendency to trust authority figures, and then topped it off with an incredible level of paranoia that kicked in once she tried to leave. She was gone for less than thirty-six hours before Imastious went and collected her. She wasn't in any condition to be able to tell me where she'd gone, but given how quickly he found her, she must have gone directly where he programmed her to go.

Imastious sent me a text ordering me to go take care of her shortly after he got her back to her apartment, which was inconvenient on several levels. Firstly, it meant that I missed one of my training sessions with Lucy. Secondly, based on the fact that Imastious had surely tortured Venice, it meant that I needed to bring her a blood source.

It would have been easiest to simply pick up one of the homeless outside of her building, there's a reason we picked such a terrible neighborhood to base her out of, but instead I detoured all of the way back to my apartment to grab one of the blood bags that I'd managed to stockpile since the last time that Imastious had bled me out.

By all rational measures I should make her drink from the vein. She's continued to resist that aspect of her new nature and the sooner I can break her of her squeamishness the better off she'll be. I justified the decision by telling myself that it would further bond her to me and undercut Imastious' loyalty conditioning, but I can't escape the feeling that it was simply a rationalization.

Geoffrey Journal Entry 16

November
Lucy's Age: 5

Venice has started training with a sword. On the one hand, I'm undeniably pleased with the fact that I've been able to bring her so far in such a short time. She doesn't like killing to feed, but she's come to accept that she doesn't have any other option.

Her defenses are completely secure which means that she's safe inside her own mind, even from Imastious or me, as long as she doesn't do anything to trigger one of Imastious' fits of rage. It means that she's come up in the world by an incredible amount, which has made things between us even more companionable.

On the other hand, arming her has made her even more dangerous than she was before. As long as she continues to view me as a nominal ally against Imastious, or at least the lesser of two evils, then I should be safe. If, however, she decides that she wants to kill me, then it's going to be harder than normal to stop her from succeeding.

Imastious controls the time and place whenever he and I meet, which means that I'm always at some disadvantage. It's much more difficult to maintain that level of control when you're actively training someone, and it's impossible to do it without generating a lot of ill will.

Once again, I'm walking a very fine line. Venice has been nothing but pleasant lately, but after she tried to escape last time, I promised myself that I wouldn't underestimate her ability to dissemble.

With regards to Lucy and Mrs. Agosti, things remain much the same. Mrs. Agosti continues to be remarkably stubborn in many respects while Lucy continues to soak up information at a phenomenal pace. She doesn't always remember the name of a given technique, but it's obvious to me that she's been practicing at home because she almost always responds to each attack with the right counter.

It's like she's absorbing every bit of knowledge she's exposed to and not just when it comes to her self-defense training. Mrs. Agosti has continued to work with her and she's starting to read, and not just the very simple words I would have expected from someone her age. I apparently haven't displayed enough amazement at the accomplishment because Mrs. Agosti was quite put out with me for several days at my response to being informed of Lucy's accomplishment. I suspect that is mostly because Mrs. Agosti views it as Mrs. Agosti's accomplishment more so than Lucy's accomplishment.

If Lucy continues to do well with the softer, more defensive techniques then I'll expand into teaching her hard, striking techniques from other disciplines and see how she does there. At this point, I'm feeling like past me was fully vindicated in his decision where Lucy was concerned.

Even if she were to prove no more skilled as a mentalist than any other newly-turned vampire, the simple fact that she's going to have nearly two decades of training behind her by then will make her much more dangerous than her age would otherwise indicate.

One way or another I'm going to end up with my weapon.

Geoffrey Journal Entry 17

March
Lucy's Age: 6

Once again, much has happened. Starting with the trivial, Mrs. Agosti made quite the fuss last fall about the fact that Lucy needed to enroll in kindergarten. Back then I told her that I wanted to wait, to give Lucy the benefit of one more year at home before sending her off into an unfamiliar environment.

At the time I assumed that Mrs. Agosti was just looking to reduce her workload by several hours each day, but I'm starting to think that she's genuinely concerned about Lucy's lack of social interaction. Lucy has had another birthday and Mrs. Agosti has begun talking about kindergarten again. Each time the issue is brought up I counter with the fact that Lucy gets quite a lot of interaction with Mrs. Agosti and me, but in typical fashion Mrs. Agosti has refused to let the matter drop.

I've tried creating some additional constructs inside of Mrs. Agosti's mind, but so far it hasn't alleviated her infernal stubbornness. I've offered to bring in a maid service to lighten Mrs. Agosti's load, but that hasn't swayed her. All I can assume is that there is something other than the reduced amount of work represented by kindergarten that is serving as Mrs. Agosti's motivation.

I have no good reason, nothing concrete tells me that it would be a bad idea to let Lucy go to a public or even a private school, but so far my instincts have been correct with regards to Lucy and something is telling me that it would be better to keep her sequestered away from the rest of the world. Only here in the apartment am I able to control, to a large degree, the influences to which she is exposed.

Based on the same gut feelings that caused me to bring Lucy home in the first place, I've decided that her education will be carried out by a series of private tutors. To say that Mrs. Agosti is unhappy would be a severe understatement, but ultimately Mrs. Agosti continues to believe that I am Lucy's legal guardian, which means that there isn't anything she can do to contest my decision now that I've made it.

The other major development, this one much less trivial, is that Venice tried to kill Imastious again last week. Predictably, she failed despite the fact that she was armed and he wasn't. On the one hand, I initially figured that this was a good sign inasmuch as it indicated that she'd decided that Imastious really was the one responsible for everything that has happened to her. Given the amount of interaction the two of us have, it would have been much easier for Venice to have tried to kill me. The fact that she didn't probably means that she considers me at least a nominal ally.

The bad thing is that Imastious very nearly killed her. This wasn't a normal beating designed merely to break down her mental defenses, this was a rage-fueled punishment aimed at ensuring that Venice never repeats her assassination attempt.

It was only chance that I arrived at Venice's apartment less than an hour after Imastious left, but it is the only thing that saved her from bleeding to death.

Even having arrived so soon after the beating, I still wasn't sure I would be able to keep her alive. Imastious had bled her out as well as breaking several ribs and both arms and leaving her with a severe concussion.

As nearly as I've been able to piece together, it appears that Imastious took Venice's sword away from her, probably using his telekinetic abilities, and then sliced her open along the left side of her chest, collapsing a lung and narrowly missing her heart. The rest of the injuries, broken bones and more superficial cuts, were simply to drive the point home that she'd made a very big mistake.

Venice was already hallucinating by the time I arrived, which meant that I didn't have much time. I got most of the bleeding stopped and then was faced with a more difficult decision. Venice had no bagged blood because she doesn't have the ability to obtain any on her own yet, and I've purposefully not been providing her with any because I wanted to force her to continue to drink from the vein.

It seemed like a good idea at the time, but I should have told her to bag blood from one or more of her victims for a time like this when she needed blood in a hurry.

I debated for several seconds and then decided that I wouldn't be able to go out, find someone who wouldn't be missed and make it back before she deteriorated too far to be saved. If I wanted to keep her alive then I only had one course open to me.

I rolled up my sleeve, opened one of the smaller veins on my arm, and then put it in her mouth. There is always a degree of risk anytime a vampire feeds from anyone. An older vampire is likely to have more control over their hunger, but they are correspondingly stronger so if they do lose control then you're in for a much bigger fight when you try and get them to disengage.

Venice was injured, which worked in my favor because I knew she was almost guaranteed to lose control. Even as I was doing it, I knew that my actions weren't rational, that this wasn't like me, but I did it regardless and just took the only action I could think of at the time to increase my chances of survival.

Her mental shields were in ruins, so it was a small matter to insert my probes inside her mind and connect with her. I expected that; what I didn't expect was the way that she welcomed me inside. Even more surprising was the fact that as she fed, as she got some of her strength back, she still didn't push me out.

Venice has been invaded so many times by Imastious that I'm sure she knows when someone is inside her mind, but even so she left her defenses down, let me continue to see what she was thinking as she sucked greedily on my arm.

The sense of connection between us was...profound. I wish I had a better way to describe it, but I don't, and the fact that it is almost certainly manufactured doesn't change how real the experience *felt*.

The constructs I put in her mind months ago as a way of strengthening her natural physical attraction for me and expanding it to include an appreciation of some of my other attributes have grown beyond my wildest dreams. Venice is in love with me, and while I didn't ransack her thoughts the way that I could have, it was obvious to me that it's a surprisingly mature, pragmatic kind of feeling on her part. She understands, at least a little bit, what a relationship between us would mean, but apparently her feelings have grown to the point where she wanted to share them.

I started to get lightheaded after only a couple of minutes, but when I tried to pull away from Venice, rather than fighting me, she let me go, albeit with a visible shudder.

If I'd had any doubts about the strength of her feelings toward me that experience would have washed the doubt away. All of my original thoughts about what the attack meant were suddenly revealed as being so completely off base that I was almost ashamed to have thought them.

Venice didn't attack Imastious because she hates him, or at least not just because she hates him. She attacked him because she was trying to get both of us out of his clutches. I suspect she didn't involve me simply because she wanted to shelter me from Imastious' wrath if she failed.

I bandaged my arm, double-checked Venice to confirm that the bleeding was under control, and then stumbled back towards my apartment to get the bags of blood that I'd cached there. It wasn't until I made it back to my apartment that I realized my mistake.

Imastious was waiting inside of my apartment and I realized in a sudden rush that I had an incredible amount of information inside of my mind that hadn't been moved off to the safe corner where I could hide it from Imastious.

My mind whirled, frantically looking for a solution as Imastious stood and approached me. I figured that I could probably destroy large chunks of the most important information during the early stages of the torture, but it would still be a risk.

Maintaining the carefully controlled charade during the actual torture was going to be next to impossible if I was busy trying to catch up on the housecleaning inside my mind. I would be risking Imastious realizing that I'd been concealing the true extent of my physical endurance as well as my real level of power. That, or he might even realize that I was busy doing something inside my own mind and decide to launch his attack earlier than normal.

Given that I was already weak from donating blood to Venice, it wouldn't take long for him to break me if he had a reason to bring all of his superior power to bear.

All of the progress I'd made over the last several decades was at stake, along with my very life and a future that was literally incalculable when it came to what might be accomplished in the long years ahead of me.

The longest two minutes of my existence slowly stretched out as Imastious looked at me with cold eyes that I knew almost better than my own and then began speaking. When Imastious finally left a couple of hours later I hadn't been tortured, but Imastious had told me in no uncertain terms that he knew of Venice's feelings for me, that he didn't think I'd had anything to do with putting her up to her attempt to try and kill him, but that if he ever came across any information that said otherwise that he'd simply kill me and start over with a new disciple.

As soon as he was gone I tossed back a bag of blood to try and get my shakes under control, and then took my last two bags over to Venice.

There is no denying that I dodged a bullet, but it leaves me with a number of questions that will need to be answered. What do I do about Venice? It seems obvious that I should capitalize on her feelings, on the weakness that they represent, but once again my gut is telling me otherwise and I can only think of one reason it would be doing so.

Eventually Venice will break through the conditioning, eventually she'll come to see me with an unbiased eye, and if I've been using her between now and then, she'll turn on me so fast that I'll never even realize what hit me. She failed against Imastious because she was still young and inexperienced. If she decides to kill me, then I'll stand almost no chance of surviving.

The second question seems like it should be a non-issue, but it is likewise causing me to second-guess myself. I've become lazy and overconfident in my own way. I've gone for so many years able to predict when Imastious would choose to try and break into my mind that I've forgotten the terror of those first few decades.

The logical answer is to spend a short time each day moving any incriminating memories off to the blind at the edge of my psyche. With the business side of things, that is of lesser concern. Among all of the changes I made in preparation for my last session with Imastious was to create a central repository on an encrypted drive on my laptop where all of my relevant business information is stored. Account numbers, passwords, holdings, it's all there.

It's Lucy who is holding me back from doing what I know I need to do. With our frequent training sessions we've become quite close and I'm reluctant to do anything that will reproduce the emotional distance from the last time I was forced to move memories around. It's a small thing, but I'm starting to realize that it's the small things that matter in a relationship, at least over the long term.

I risk losing Lucy and the investment that I've made into her either way I proceed—it's just a question of which risk seems to be the lesser evil.

Geoffrey Journal Entry 18

June
Lucy's Age: 6

I ultimately decided to take a mixed approach, although I'm not sure that any of it matters at this point. I've left my memories of time spent with Lucy alone, but I've ruthlessly destroyed or moved all memories of traveling back and forth to her apartment.

It means that Imastious can find out about her, but given the size of the city he shouldn't ever be able to find her. It seemed the best route, but recent developments have once again caught me off guard.

The other night I was picking up some of Lucy's books off of the floor and a picture slipped out of one. It was an old-style five-by-seven print, the kind of thing that I remember coming and then going once digital really took hold.

The picture was of a park that looked very familiar, but that wasn't what drove me into a fit of rage, at least not initially. There were dozens of pictures secreted inside of Lucy's books, and based on the differing outfits I had to conclude that they were taken over a prolonged period of time. There were other kids in the pictures, not just random kids playing in the background either. Someone had posed Lucy and the other kids so that they could take pictures together.

It went against every order I'd ever given Mrs. Agosti. I wanted Lucy kept safe, wanted her isolated from disruptive influences, from the kinds of attachments that could lead Imastious to her.

Already angry, I opened my mouth to call for Mrs. Agosti and ask her why she had disobeyed my orders and established a playgroup for Lucy, and then I saw it. The last picture was of Mrs. Agosti and Lucy and it was the same park as all of the others, only now I recognized it. I recognized it because Lucy was leaning against the exact same piece of playground equipment where I'd left Antoine's child after killing her.

My heart stuttered as I realized why I'd had such a hard time placing the park. I'd meant to destroy all memories of the incident. I had in fact destroyed everything obvious in an attempt to make sure that Imastious never learned about my having caused most of the reverses suffered by the Red Hand Consortium lately, but somehow among all of the other killings over the years I'd missed expunging this particular murder.

I connected it to the events from my journal almost out of instinct. There wasn't any way for me to be positive that I was remembering the time I'd killed Antoine's daughter, but I'd killed so few children during my life that I was fairly sure that I'd connected this particular death back to the proper incident.

The resemblance was uncanny and my heart raced as I realized that Lucy was now the same age as Antoine's daughter had been. I don't know that I've ever been full of so much rage. I've been angry before, but there was something different about this feeling. I was simultaneously in complete control of the situation and utterly powerless.

I could punish Mrs. Agosti in any fashion I chose, anything from firing her to killing her instantly, but I couldn't force Lucy to do anything, not really. The two of them had conspired together against me, had conspired to keep Lucy's friends a secret, and this was just a foretaste of things to come.

It took every ounce of control that I've been able to develop since I was turned, but I stopped myself from rampaging through the house. I carefully put the pictures back in Lucy's books and then I went into my room and began activating the contingency plans that I'd put into place back when Mrs. Agosti first started displaying the stubborn streak that has been an almost constant thorn in my side these last several years.

Renworst has little in the way of personality left after all of the constructs I've placed inside his mind over the last few years, but he's utterly loyal to me which is a difficult quality to find, even in a human. My fine control over my powers has continued to grow, but I probably couldn't have carried off such a successful conditioning campaign if not for the fact that Renworst desperately wanted somewhere to belong, someone to trust, a higher cause than merely his own miserable existence.

He'd been patiently waiting in a property I'd purchased in Yonkers for a time when I'd need him, and I could practically hear the eagerness dripping from his voice when I told him to get the car and meet me in front of Lucy's apartment.

I knew it would take a while for Renworst to make the drive down, even well after midnight, so I used the time to the best advantage possible. I packed a few things from my room. I didn't need much really—my laptop, a change of clothes and my journals. Then I drugged Mrs. Agosti, tied her up, and gagged her, all without making any real noise. Lucy didn't even wake up until I picked her up from her bed and moved her into my room so that I could pack some of her possessions, and even then she went right back to sleep once I set her down on my bed.

A DARKNESS MIRRORED

Once Renworst arrived I took Lucy out to the car while he retrieved the suitcases from inside the apartment. The drive up to the house went smoothly and was finished well before I needed to go to bed, so I've taken this opportunity to update my various journals.

I'll spend tomorrow with Lucy to help her adjust to her new surroundings and then I'll head back into the city and deal with Mrs. Agosti.

Geoffrey Journal Entry 19

June
Lucy's Age: 6

I didn't expect the transition to be easy for Lucy, but I didn't expect it to hit her as hard as it has.

I considered lying to Lucy when she woke up in the new house and asked what had happened to Mrs. Agosti, but I suspected that would just come back to haunt me later on, so I told her the truth. I told her that their efforts to keep the playgroup at the park a secret hadn't been successful and that there were consequences to breaking the rules. For her the consequences were living in a different house without Mrs. Agosti.

The result was crying, but not a temper tantrum. Lucy's cries were the cries of someone who'd lost the person who meant the most to them.

A DARKNESS MIRRORED

I've been alive for a very long time, and I've spent enough time inside of other people's heads to have been exposed to nearly every emotion imaginable. I never suspected before now just how much paler those emotions are when experienced secondhand.

Lucy is devastated and I can't do anything to help her. Actually that's not true. I could reunite her with Mrs. Agosti, but I can't do that and keep her safe in the process. I think out of everything that has happened that I'm the most surprised over how badly I wish I could do something to make Lucy happy again.

If I were a lesser man I might have found myself wavering in my resolve to protect Lucy, but I stayed firm. I have altered my plans slightly, though. Rather than dealing with Mrs. Agosti in a more permanent fashion, I've moved her to a safe house which has adequate soundproofing and a cage that resembles the one that Imastious was using to keep Venice captive until a few months ago. Killing Mrs. Agosti would be simpler in almost every way, but I'm strangely unwilling to do so. If I'm going to continue to tell Lucy the truth then at some point I'm going to be faced with a direct question as to whether or not I killed the woman who has been her mother for the last three years.

I knew that they'd bonded, but I apparently underestimated the strength of that bond. If I were to kill Mrs. Agosti and Lucy were then to find out,

I'm convinced that she would never forgive me, which means I'll have to try and wipe Mrs. Agosti's memory and then send her on her way.

To be honest, I'm not entirely sure that what I'm trying to do is possible. It is one thing to destroy my own memories when I want them gone, or to destroy the span of just a couple of hours. It's quite another matter altogether to destroy the long-term memories of someone else, someone who desperately wants to hang onto those memories.

The process has already taken much longer than I'd expected it to, but to be completely honest I'm not entirely unhappy at the prospect of having to spend more time down here in the city. The looks that Lucy has been giving me lately make me remarkably uncomfortable. Not only that, being on the island means that I have more time to spend with Venice, who has finally recovered from the damage Imastious inflicted on her after her failed murder attempt.

Venice is still young enough that she doesn't heal much faster than a normal human, but that too will change given enough time.

Between running the occasional hit for Imastious, getting Venice started training again, and spending more hours than I'd like mucking about inside of Mrs. Agosti's mind, I'm the busiest I've been in a long time. I would have expected that to be enough for me, but I very much miss teaching new techniques to Lucy.

A DARKNESS MIRRORED

I suppose I thought that our bond was strong enough to compensate for the loss of Mrs. Agosti, but reality has been far different than I expected.

Lucy Journal Entry 1

July
Lucy's Age: 6

Dad always writes in his diary when something is bothering him. I asked Renworst for a diary of my own and he gave me one. I don't write very good yet, but I don't have anyone now. Maybe writing will help me like it helps Dad.

I'm sad all of the time now. I went outside to the park with Mrs. Agosti and I made friends even though my dad told me not to. Dad got really mad and then took me away from home. It's just me and Renworst and he doesn't play with me. I miss Mrs. Agosti a lot, and I miss Dad, but mostly I miss Mrs. Agosti because she didn't choose to leave me but Dad did.

Geoffrey Journal Entry 20

August
Lucy's Age: 6

I've taken no joy in torturing Mrs. Agosti, but the last few months have been an interesting learning experience. She's started to develop shields around her mind. It's like nothing I've ever seen before, but it appears to be some kind of reflexive effort to protect herself and preserve the memories of Lucy that I've been working so hard to try and destroy.

The memories become much more blurry for her each time I attempt to remove them, but for a while there it was as though something was creating a new set of memories, pseudo-memories if you will, faster than I could destroy them.

I was pretty sure that the protective mechanism and the memory creation mechanism were two separate things, but I was nearly to the point of giving up on my plan to try and keep Mrs. Agosti alive by the time I finally figured out what was going on.

Mrs. Agosti seems to have followed my example. She's been writing everything she could remember of her life with Lucy in a journal and then re-reading it over and over again for months. All I can assume is that she grabbed it from her room when I moved her to the safe house.

In hindsight, possibly I should have just kept her sedated and moved her at night with the car, but moving an unconscious body is generally more difficult than having someone walk around under their own power. I knew that I'd properly incentivized her to keep her mouth shut and not try to escape, so I'd chosen the easier route. It's a moot point now though as I've taken away her journal and resumed eliminating her memories.

Things seem to be progressing better now. The mental defenses that were giving me so much difficulty are still present, but now when I destroy a memory it doesn't spontaneously regenerate somewhere else over the next couple of days.

I suspect that I've still got several weeks of work ahead of me, but at least there is now an end in sight. I look forward to finishing this particular project, and not just because of the time that it will free up. My distaste for what I'm doing grows day by day. I've even caught myself occasionally making up excuses to delay our sessions, reasons not to visit the cold, sterile apartment where I've imprisoned her.

Things with Venice have proceeded apace. Imastious has started throwing missions at her. Apparently he's decided that her being trained enough to try and kill him means that she's trained enough to kill other people as well.

Venice has shown the expected qualms when it comes to the amount of killing involved in working for Imastious, but I've been able to, by and large, get her past all of that over the last few weeks.

Lucy Journal Entry 2

October
Lucy's Age: 6

I kept thinking that Mrs. Agosti would find me, or at least that Dad would come back so that it wasn't just me and Renworst at the house, but it's been forever now and it's still just me and Renworst here.

Renworst was talking to Dad on the phone the other day so I asked if I could talk to Dad, but when I told him how lonely I am he didn't promise to come visit us.

I have tutors now. I guess that means that I'm less lonely, but they don't care about me, not really, not like Mrs. Agosti cared about me. At least I think she cared about me. It's hard to know for sure anymore.

Geoffrey Journal Entry 21

November
Lucy's Age: 6

Mrs. Agosti has been taken care of. Her memories from the last three or so years have all been purged. The memories that had Lucy in them were the hardest to destroy, but once they were gone Mrs. Agosti seemed to lose some of her fight.

Once that happened, things moved along at a reasonable clip. I can't be absolutely sure that I got everything, but I do know that I got everything featuring Lucy and then everything featuring our apartment and everything that included me.

I used a rather broad brush, figuratively speaking, so my efforts should have tended to destroy most of the memories even tangentially associated with those three things, which meant that I felt safe releasing Mrs. Agosti.

I sedated her for a couple of days while I did one last check of her mind to make sure I got everything related to the last few months of captivity as well, and then dropped her off in front of the Presbyterian University Hospital.

With all of the rummaging around inside of her head that I'd done, I was able to get all of her banking information and it turned out that she had saved the bulk of what I'd paid her over the last three years, so I made sure to sew her account information into one corner of her shirt along with her ID's.

I hired a very high-end private investigator to keep an eye on her for the next few months and then expected that I'd be able to forget about her. Instead I found my thoughts returning to her several times over the subsequent few days.

I don't regret what I did, not exactly. Mrs. Agosti knew that she was going against my orders, but time is the only resource humans really have. That's true of vampires as well, but we have a potentially unlimited store of it while humans do not. My wiping away more than three years of Mrs. Agosti's life represented a very real loss for her.

I debated for nearly two days before I finally gave into the nagging voice inside of my head and arranged for several hundred thousand dollars in cash to be deposited into Mrs. Agosti's bank account. Ultimately, that amount of money means very little given the size of my current holdings, and if giving it to her will allow me to return my focus back to other more pressing issues, then I'll make it back several times over in short order.

Lucy has asked to talk to me twice recently. The first time was simply to tell me that she's very lonely. I wouldn't have thought that someone so young would be able to inject so much guilt into a simple statement.

I refuse to take the blame for all of this. I'm merely trying to keep her safe from all of the people out there who would hurt her without a second thought, and if she'd simply followed my wishes then the three of us would still be living in the apartment together.

We're past the point where Lucy's education should have started, so I've gone ahead and finalized the arrangements for her tutors to begin daily sessions with her. Not surprisingly, it's taken an incredible amount of work to provide even the most rudimentary security where the tutors are concerned. I've engaged additional private investigators to monitor each of the tutors, but that is more a matter of making sure my due diligence is taken care of. The real guarantees will be implemented over the next few months as I continue the weekly conditioning sessions that I've already implemented. I've rented out apartments adjacent to each of the tutors and thereby have been able to position myself physically close enough to them to work on them while they sleep.

Once Lucy has learned what she can from each of them, I'll sanitize their minds much like I did with Mrs. Agosti. I'm not looking forward to the ongoing level of work involved in replacing an entire set of tutors every couple of years, but although I don't feel like it right now, I know that Lucy is worth the investment. Hopefully the tutors will help somewhat with her loneliness.

The second call was just to ask me if I would be going home for Thanksgiving. I'm beginning to wonder if the bond between Lucy and I is even weaker than I thought. She hasn't asked about resuming our training sessions and her inquiry about Thanksgiving was said with such casual indifference that I'm not convinced that she really wants me there.

It's probably for the best. Maybe I should let some time pass, let things calm down a little before trying to reestablish my bond with Lucy. It seemed to work reasonably well that way the first time around with Mrs. Agosti, I just need to make sure that Renworst continues to be obedient so that we avoid another round of upsets.

I suspect that Venice will need even more time in the near term, so possibly it's smartest to concentrate my efforts on the investment that has the quickest payback.

Geoffrey Journal Entry 22

January
Lucy's Age: 7

Lucy is officially one year older. I considered making a pilgrimage up to Yonkers for the occasion, but instead opted to simply send a present and a note expressing my excitement on her behalf.

Renworst was only marginally helpful when it came to picking out a present. From all indications he is very diligent when it comes to making sure that Lucy is fed, clothed and makes it to bed on time, but he doesn't seem to have any real sense of Lucy's interests.

After realizing that this is likely the main contributor to Lucy's ongoing unhappiness, I've ordered Renworst to spend more time with Lucy, to interact with her, to go have fun. I must admit to a certain degree of frustration.

With Mrs. Agosti my problems all revolved around the fact that she wanted to do too much with Lucy and she wasn't loyal enough to me personally. Now I've gone to the other end of the extreme with Renworst who is fully loyal to me, but who doesn't actually care about Lucy at all.

In some ways that is good as it should mean that Lucy will readily bond with me again once I have a bit more time and can continue spending time with her, but I do spare the idle moment or two each day wondering about the long-term impacts the situation will have on Lucy's psyche. Unfortunately I can see no other way to move forward. Renworst is no Mrs. Agosti, but he will have to do for now.

I had hoped to be done with Mrs. Agosti entirely. In a world that was in any way sensible I would be. Unfortunately I ended up with a few spare minutes on my hands last week and I picked up the journal that I'd seized from Mrs. Agosti and started to peruse it.

There is an amazing amount of overly sentimental garbage all throughout her entries, but if I'd needed another bit of evidence as to the fact that she loved Lucy then the journal would have proved it. I honestly can't say what compelled me to read through four years of entries, but I found myself starting from the beginning of the journal with entries that predated our association and then reading on through to the last few entries that she wrote while locked inside a cage in my safe house.

Maybe it was the same curiosity that causes a voyeur to watch someone night after night, vicariously living the life of whomever it is that he's spying on. I'd been inside of Mrs. Agosti's mind, so one could be excused for thinking that there wouldn't be anything in the journal that could surprise me, but reading someone's mind is never that simple.

I can access facts and feelings, discrete packets of information, but it is incredibly difficult to form a coherent narrative from something like that. This, however, was a perfect picture of Mrs. Agosti's life and for the two days that it took me to read through it I felt an almost godlike omniscience.

I got to see Lucy, and even to a limited extent myself, through another set of eyes. There wasn't anything earthshattering there. No, instead I was struck by the black depression that had been consuming Mrs. Agosti in the weeks just before I offered her a job.

In my conditioning sessions I'd always focused on the present, or at least recent events, and I'd always been most concerned with Mrs. Agosti's underlying character rather than the emotions that might come and go over time.

I'd correctly understood that she was at her core a simple, happy woman, but I'd never understood just how bitterly she'd regretted never being able to have a child of her own. The journal alludes to at least one failed marriage early on, but is silent about the incident after she became Lucy's nanny.

The middle of the journal was full of the minutiae of childcare interspersed with milestones in Lucy's life, most of which I hadn't been around for, and then the end became once again interesting. Mrs. Agosti hadn't expected to live, not after I took Lucy away from her and locked her up. She'd expected, even wanted, me to kill her.

She'd gladly spent years tending to Lucy, loving Lucy, only to have the object of her feelings ripped away from her and the loss had been made all the more acute by the way that her memories of the time were becoming unreliable.

As I closed her journal and sat back to think about what I'd read, some of the reports from the investigator following Mrs. Agosti took on a new light. She didn't know what she'd lost, but the more I thought about it, the more confident I became that she was in many ways right back where she'd been four years ago. Only now she no doubt had a persistent feeling that the world was somehow wrong, that something more important than she could describe was missing.

I once again find myself in a quandary. Lucy loves Mrs. Agosti, much, much more than she loves me. Would my alleviating Mrs. Agosti's suffering be a marker that I could call in at some future date if Lucy were ever to become unwilling to do something I needed done? Is there even any way to call in such a marker without risking a reunion between Lucy and Mrs. Agosti?

Geoffrey Journal Entry 23

June
Lucy's Age: 7

I confess that I'm not sure whether or not I've made a mistake with Venice. While I've been peripherally involved with the training of two young vampires in the past, this is the first time that I've more or less had a free hand when it comes to nearly every aspect of the training.

Imastious has continued to turn up the pressure on the two of us over the last several months to the point where I hardly even have time to keep on top of my business holdings. There have been instances in the past where I've been forced to run missions on back-to-back days before, but never for such a long period of time.

I suspected something out of the ordinary was happening, but I didn't realize the root cause until Imastious ordered Venice and me to capture another vampire. Given the fact that our target, a male named Horace, is a known flunky for a vampire elder named Perdition, it was a safe bet that Imastious was gearing up for a covert war with Perdition.

Horace was easy to find and once I'd located him it was only a slightly more difficult task to capture him. Venice happily participated in the capture. She waded into the fight without any hesitation despite the fact that Horace easily outmatched her. Venice trusted that I would stop him from overpowering her, just as the plan said.

It made for a quick, painless fight, which made me uneasy. Vampires rarely work together because there is too much chance that your 'partner' will seize upon any given fight as a chance to turn on you. There have been attempts in the past, some of which I remember, where multiple vampires banded together in an effort to bring down a more powerful adversary, but they'd met with only limited success. Younger vampires are more trustworthy but even when working together in a group of two or three they usually still aren't strong enough to bring down a vampire who is several hundred or more years old.

That means that the group needs one or more older vampires, which introduces a whole new level of risk. Older vampires invariably have an extensive list of grievances and they play a very long game. The last time that a group tried to take down a seven-hundred-year-old vampire, it turned out that the group's target had been working with the second most powerful member of the group all along. The two of them easily killed everyone else in the group and the rumors that the city was heading into a new age where younger vampires would finally be able to throw off the chains of the vampire elders stopped overnight.

If Venice and I could continue to work together, to trust each other, then we'd wield power far and away greater than our mere numbers and age would otherwise indicate, but that is the problem. I can't trust her, not really, not as long as she is bound to me by nothing more than a construct-created infatuation.

I've known for months now that I need to change our relationship to one of mutual self-interest, but I haven't been able to make it happen. She's still too naive and I continue to make the wrong decisions around her.

Events immediately after we captured Horace were a perfect example of everything I'm doing wrong. We took him back to Imastious' safe house, the one where Venice spent so many months, and strapped him to the bedframe, at which point Venice started protesting.

It's standard procedure really. Imastious would never risk his own mind inside of an unknown vampire, one who could turn out to be much stronger than anyone realizes. It's rare, but occasionally one or another of the older mentalist vampire elders, one of the ones whom nobody has seen face to face in centuries, masquerades as a low-level grunt in someone else's organization and then proceeds to manufacture an incident that causes their real target, a younger mentalist, to capture them and try to question them.

The last time that happened wasn't pretty. The older vampire hollowed out the mind of the younger mentalist and used him as a puppet to destroy the younger vampire's entire organization. I didn't particularly like the fact that I was the sacrificial lamb designed to trigger any mental traps, but the way that Venice reacted was almost worse than that.

First she protested because she didn't want to be party to torture, and then when I explained the situation more fully she didn't want to proceed because she didn't want me to endanger myself.

I tried everything I could think of. I explained that Horace had doubtlessly tortured dozens of other people. When that didn't work, I pointed out that Imastious would torture and eventually kill her if she didn't proceed, but even that had less impact than I'd been expecting for it to have.

I'd been handling things more or less correctly up to that point, but then I made another big mistake. I grabbed her arm, pulled her into the other room and told her that if she didn't go through with the torture that I'd be forced to do it myself which would greatly increase my risk when it came time for me to jump inside of Horace's mind.

It wasn't the rational appeal to her own selfishness that I should have used, that would have worked with any other vampire who'd been alive for more than four or five months, but it worked. She squared her shoulders and then went back out into the main room and started torturing Horace.

The rest of the evening went fine. We bled him to the point where he fainted and then we bound his wounds back up and I sent tendrils inside of his mind while Venice stood at the ready, prepared to cut off his head if I started evidencing any of the signs of the kind of prolonged fight that would be required for even an extremely powerful elder vampire to take over my mind.

Our mission was a success. We got the information we needed, the location of some obscure contact that Perdition was using to move military-grade weapons, as well as everything else I could find inside his mind about Perdition's operations. But even that was wrong.

Before Venice's arrival I never would have trusted another vampire to stand with a bare blade less than three feet from me while I delved so deeply into someone else's mind that I completely lost track of my surroundings. It wasn't right, it wasn't natural, but it was the only way that I could get Venice to work with me.

More and more I'm convinced that I need to break her of her infatuation even if it means alienating her for a period of time. I have to strip her of some of her illusions if I'm ever going to be able to make this partnership work.

She's got so many things ahead of her that she's not going to want to do. Torture and murder are useful tools in most instances, but eventually Imastious is going to put her in a position where she has to use something other than brute force and I can't see any way in which simple love for me can cause her to seduce some target so that Imastious can fatten his financial holdings by a few million dollars.

She needs to do it for the same reason that I do it. Because it's the best way for her to get ahead and end her servitude to that monster. I can't work with her if she's going to continue to be some kind of knight-errant fairy godmother idealist.

It seems as though everywhere I look lately that I'm dealing with one frustration or another. Renworst has taken my order to 'have fun' with Lucy to heart, but while I reiterated the prohibition against establishing a routine involving friends who could be used to track Lucy down, I neglected to establish boundaries with regards to what is appropriate fun for a child.

Renworst took Lucy to some kind of slasher movie and then was stupid enough to complain to me when she woke up in the middle of the night screaming. Every time I turn around I'm forced to deal with incompetents.

It took nearly all of the willpower I had to stop myself from going up to Yonkers and cutting Renworst's throat. I've gone to incredible lengths to try and avoid exposing Lucy to the worst parts of my life. Given the fact that her biological parents left her to freeze to death in some filthy New York alley, she's bound to have some very severe residual traumas, and unlike Imastious, I've always believed that a sound tool is better than a flawed tool that I can 'control' completely.

Lucy needs to be sheltered from the worst parts of life. I didn't think I'd have to spell that out quite so bluntly to Renworst, but apparently he's not capable of thinking for himself at all.

Lucy Journal Entry 3

March
Lucy's Age: 9

I'm so hungry right now it hurts. Last week I snuck a letter into the mailbox with Mrs. Agosti's name on it. I knew that it probably wouldn't ever make it to her, but I had to try something. The mailman sent it back because there wasn't a valid address on it.

I guess I knew that it wouldn't work, but I kept hoping that someone at the post office would find a way to track her down and deliver it to her. I wish she would come take me away, but if she doesn't know where I am then there isn't any way for her to come get me.

Usually I'm the one to get the mail. It's one of the few times I get to leave the house since Renworst even has our food delivered right to our door. Yesterday I lost track of time though and Renworst went and got the mail instead.

He was mad, really, really mad, and I think a little scared when he found the letter. Not of me, but of my father. I could tell that he wanted to hit me, but I remember the one and only time that Renworst hit me. He was in a cast for what seemed like forever. Dad broke his arm and then made sure that I knew he'd done it so that I understood that Renworst wasn't to hit me anymore.

Instead of hitting me, Renworst locked me up in my room without anything to eat. I fell asleep crying last night and I've cried a lot today, but Renworst has refused to come unlock my door. I'm starting to get tired again. I hope that he lets me out soon to eat or I'm not sure that I'll be able to sleep tonight.

For a few minutes I thought maybe that Renworst would have to let me out when my tutors came by, but then I remembered that today is Saturday. They won't be by until Monday, so there isn't anything to stop him from being as mean as he wants to be.

I had the nightmare again last night. Everything is on fire and then someone steps toward me and he's got something sharp in his hand.

The nightmares are always the worst when Renworst locks me up or punishes me somehow. They'll probably be really bad tonight.

Lucy Journal Entry 4

July
Lucy's Age: 11

It looks like my dad was up from the city sometime within the last couple of days. He didn't bother stopping by to visit me though, or if he did he must have come while I was asleep. It's not like it's a surprise. He hasn't made it to any of my last few birthdays, why would he stop by for a lesser reason?

Apparently Dad saw me at some point though because he's decided that I'm fat. Renworst kept muttering something I couldn't understand while he was setting up the treadmill in the other room, but really there's no other explanation.

Renworst has been saying for months that I should spend less time reading my books and more time moving around, but it's not like that's even an option for me. How am I supposed to get any exercise if I'm barely allowed out of the house?

Dad seems to have come up with a solution to the problem though. Instead of letting me outside like sensible people, he is going to basically stick me in a little metal ball and make me run like some kind of trained gerbil.

I was ready to yell and scream, not that it would have made the slightest bit of difference, but then I saw the huge, huge TV that some random guy was helping Renworst haul into what is apparently going to be the exercise room.

It took them more than an hour to get it mounted on the wall opposite the treadmill, but I was completely stoked the entire time. I'm never allowed to watch television. There's exactly one other TV in the entire house. It's in Renworst's room and I'm not allowed to watch it. I'd sneak in and watch it anyways, but he's never gone. Ever.

If walking on a stupid treadmill meant I could watch unlimited amounts of TV then I'd happily walk until my legs fell off.

Unfortunately it turned out that the television wasn't going to be hooked up to cable or anything. Instead it and the treadmill both hook up directly to some kind of computer in a box about the size of my fists.

I don't get to watch any shows, and I don't get to go outside, but this is pretty much the next best thing because the whole point of the television is to simulate hiking outside. There are like forty different hikes that I can choose from and then the treadmill changes how steep it is during various parts of the hike so that it matches up with what I'm seeing on the screen and what I'd be experiencing if I were walking it in real life.

I can even plan out the route I want to take and decide where I want to stop and look around. I usually stop a lot, but I've started hiking some of the easier ones without a break. I still hate Renworst and my dad, but things just got a little better.

Lucy Journal Entry 5

September
Lucy's Age: 13

No big surprise here, but my life still mostly sucks. The nightmares pretty much stopped after we got the treadmill, but that's really the only thing that has improved in years.

Most kids are starting a new year of school this time of year, but not me. If I'm lucky maybe I'll get a new tutor to replace Jack. Dad hires the best tutors around, but 'the best' doesn't mean that they have any more of a personality than Renworst does.

Also, you can be pretty smart when it comes to knowing facts and figures but still be a complete idiot in every other way.

Jack has been busy congratulating himself on how well I'm doing in Geography, but if he had any brains at all he'd realize that I've sped up my progress there just so that I can get rid of him faster. Once I've demonstrated mastery of a particular subject Dad always lets me move on to something else, and since Jack doesn't have any other areas of expertise he'll be out the door as soon as I pass my Geography finals.

Samantha, on the other hand, I've stretched out now for almost two years. It helps that she's smart and that she knows lots of things in four different subjects, but if I'd hated her like I hate Jack I could have gotten rid of her months ago.

I'm just glad that Dad ended up hiring Samantha. I shudder to think about just how much more life would have sucked without her. Can you imagine being a teenage girl surrounded by nothing but old men? Yeah, it would have sucked.

Samantha still has her own life and stuff, and I only see her three times a week, but she's still a breath of fresh air every time I see her. Samantha is the first of my tutors to try and get me to engage in something other than their subjects.

The treadmill in our exercise room is starting to look pretty worn out, but I still run fifteen or so miles per week. When Samantha found out about my runs she tried to get me to join the junior high cross-country club. I knew even before I asked Renworst that it wasn't going to happen, but it was a nice gesture on her part.

Samantha has been bugging me to try and reconnect to my dad. I keep telling her that he's not worth the effort, but she still seems to think it's important. The tough thing is that I can't even really remember any time when the two of us were actually tight.

The closest time was back when he used to teach me aikido, and even then he always seemed a little distant. It was a long time ago, but I can still remember the day that he came home and everything was different somehow, he was different somehow.

It's like my entire life has been one big series of disappointments. First my dad cares, and then he doesn't, and then he does again but he takes me away from Mrs. Agosti and sticks me with Renworst, of all people.

I guess that the truth is that I'd like to be closer to my dad, but I'm just not sure how to go about it, or even if it's really worth the effort.

Geoffrey Journal Entry 24

October
Lucy's Age: 13

When looked at from a big-picture perspective, I feel fully vindicated in my decision to have spent the bulk of my time and energy developing Venice. Things have progressed in ways that I didn't originally anticipate, but she's become an incredible asset.

I still occasionally have to help her with regards to maintaining the proper mindset. There's a tendency there for her to be softer than she should be, but she continues to make good strides.

I've tried very hard to keep knowledge of just how good our working relationship is from Imastious, but I'm not sure we've succeeded, which is unfortunate although not entirely bad. Imastious is unlikely to mess with what I'm sure has become his star team of mission-runners, and if he does, Venice will now have additional incentive to protect me.

I have to admit that I would have more of a difficult time now cutting her loose if the situation demanded it than I would have had just a few years ago, but ultimately I would do what was necessary to survive.

I've discussed these kinds of issues obliquely with Venice but she seems unconcerned with the fundamental imbalance in our relationship. While I never felt honor-bound to warn her off, it is nice to know that my efforts to do so have failed to cause her to reassess her position. Ultimately my efforts at being honest with her should decrease, however slightly, the odds that she'll turn on me at a later date.

Despite my overall satisfaction with how things have gone with Venice, I can't escape a nagging worry over the situation with Lucy. She called me a short time ago and asked if it would be possible for us to resume the kind of martial arts training she'd enjoyed so much when she was younger.

A part of me wanted to say yes, but after some thought I told her no. I didn't explain any of my reasoning to her, but it would have put her at too much risk. Venice would have quickly noticed if I'd started disappearing for large blocks of time. She's also jealous and resourceful enough to eventually track me back to Lucy if our training sessions had gone on for more than a few weeks.

I almost reconsidered my decision not to explain my reasoning to her before I got off the call, but she's only thirteen, she's not ready to be exposed to my world yet.

This does highlight the fact that I'm going to need to find a way to put some distance, emotional and physical both, between Venice and I. Doing so without ruining things between us will be difficult, but I'm starting to think that it might have been a mistake to leave Lucy unattended for so long.

In the meantime, I've decided that it would be best to make a trip up to Yonkers and scout out an appropriate dojo for Lucy. I'm not going to be able to oversee her training personally, but I can still give her the opportunity to resume preparing for the life ahead of her.

In many ways I'm pleased, both with her desire to resume training and her desire to spend some time with me. This is the first time since we installed the virtual hiking appliance at the house that Lucy has shown any signs of life.

Lucy Journal Entry 6

July
Lucy's Age: 14

I think I went too far this time. I blew out Renworst's elbow last night and shattered one of his knees. I think that Renworst would have killed me if he wasn't so loyal to Geoffrey. He could have probably succeeded too. I've been training again for nearly a year, but Renworst has something like eighty pounds on me and he fights dirty.

I hate the idea of being beholden to Geoffrey for yet another thing, but there it is. Geoffrey put me in this situation and now I owe him for saving me from Renworst, who he saddled me with in the first place.

First Geoffrey told me that he wouldn't start training me again, and then he showed up a few days later with a uniform and tells me that my training for the next year has been paid for at the dojo three blocks from our house.

He didn't act glad to see me or embarrassed that he's pretty much ignored me for half of my life. He just calmly turned my life upside down once again. After handing me the uniform he told me not to get too close to any of the other students, and then left.

The sensei at my new dojo turned out to be okay. It's a really big operation, for the most part the newer students don't get any real time with the head sensei, they just take classes from the other first and second-degree black belts.

Apparently Geoffrey worked out some kind of deal with the sensei though because after my first month I started getting private one-hour lessons each week.

Things went pretty okay for the first few months. Renworst would take me into class whenever I asked and then wait until I was done so he could take me back home. It was still pretty much like being in prison, but it was a ton better than what I'd been living with before. It even seemed like it was good for Renworst to get out of the house occasionally too. He was less grouchy after I started going to my dojo.

At first I just randomly went to whichever of the beginner lessons I felt like attending, but that didn't last long. For one thing some of the junior instructors were idiots, for another, after a month or so I found an instructor that I liked.

No, I mean really liked, and not just his teaching style.

Parker wasn't like the other guys in the dojo. He was one of the best karatekas in the dojo, but he didn't take himself as seriously as the rest of the instructors took themselves. When I started he'd just turned seventeen, so he didn't have any interest in me, but I worked really hard to change that.

At first it was difficult. My body still sort of remembered the techniques that Geoffrey had been teaching me when I was just a kid and this stuff was completely different. I had to break myself of the habit of redirecting energy and controlling my opponent's balance and get used to punching and kicking, but after a little while I realized just how much fun it was. Even better, it was something that I could practice without a partner, so I practiced a lot at home.

Renworst grumbled when I asked for him to mount a heavy bag in the exercise room, but I kept asking and finally he ordered one off the internet. At first I could hardly move it, but I got better over time. I still can't move it as much as if I were a guy and weighed more, but there's something incredibly satisfying about kicking something nearly as heavy as you are and seeing it swing back from the force of your blow.

With regards to Parker, once I finally started to catch his eye I tried to mix things up, sometimes missing training altogether or sometimes going to a session taught by another instructor, but it wasn't to confuse him, it was to keep Renworst from realizing what was going on.

It helped when I got onto the competitive kata team. Parker was on it too, which meant that I was occasionally able to use the team as an excuse to spend time with Parker outside of the regular practices.

It was kind of tough to keep Parker interested because we could only steal away to talk or hold hands when Renworst wasn't looking. It was like two opposed forces. Parker, who needed more attention, and Renworst, who would ruin everything if we were too obvious about what was going on.

It was like the first taste of love and freedom all rolled up in one. I should have known that it couldn't last forever. Renworst figured out something was up last week. It took him several days to put all of the pieces together, but once he had the full story he completely freaked. He threatened to call Geoffrey. He said he was going to pick up and move us just like Geoffrey had done the last time I tried to make a friend.

The next thing I knew we were both yelling and then Renworst went too far. He told me that he was going to catch Parker in a dark alley somewhere and take a baseball bat to him.

I went to storm out of the house and Renworst grabbed my arm. I was so angry that I just kind of let my training take over. I extended his arm and then did a palm strike to his elbow. He screamed, but before he could do anything else I hit him with a side-thrust kick to the knee, destroying the joint and dropping him to the ground.

I almost just left him there sobbing in pain, but he pleaded with me not to leave. He said that Geoffrey would kill him if I left. There wasn't any reason to believe him, not really, but it made me stop anyways.

I hate Renworst. We're mostly civil to each other, but if you would have asked me before that, I would have told you that I would have celebrated if something were to happen to him. I guess maybe I care about him more than I realized.

As much as I hate him he's still the only family I've had since Dad, since Geoffrey, took me away from Mrs. Agosti. Maybe Renworst only does what he does because he's scared of Geoffrey, but that's better than nothing. I still remember what it was like to be freezing to death underneath a pile of garbage. If it's a choice between prison and dying then I'll pick prison every time.

Geoffrey is supposed to be up here sometime in the next hour or so. I guess we'll see how bad things are then. After everything that has happened in the last twenty-four hours, it wouldn't surprise me if the nightmares started back up.

Geoffrey Journal Entry 25

August
Lucy's Age: 14

My last trip up to Yonkers made it painfully obvious that something had to be done about Renworst and Lucy. It was starting to look like the two of them would kill each other if I left them up there by themselves for much longer.

I did a surface probe of Renworst's mind and it appears that some of the loyalty conditioning has started to wear off. Interestingly enough it's being slowly replaced by paternal feelings for Lucy. Renworst will never be another Mrs. Agosti, but with enough time around Lucy he could eventually turn into a caring individual.

As it is right now, he's been experiencing a constant state of low-level inner conflict between his diminishing loyalty to me and his nascent loyalty to Lucy. I believe that is why he overreacted the way he did at the prospect of Lucy dating this boy from her dojo.

Given the way things currently stand, I can see no alternative but to move the two of them back down to the city where I can keep a closer eye on them. It is going to cause a number of problems with Venice, but I can't see a way to sidestep that, not if I'm going to preserve the investment that I've made in Lucy so far.

I've already made the necessary arrangements, now it's just a matter of time before Lucy and Renworst will be moving into their new apartment here on the island. Only time will tell what kind of impact them being here will ultimately have on my life.

Geoffrey Journal Entry 26

September
Lucy's Age: 14

I feel like I've been caught out again, It's not that I'm not making an active effort to keep my memories sanitized, it's just that there is so much information that needs to be stored safely if I'm going to keep it, and even more in the way of memories that I'm reluctant to shift into the secure part of my mind because I don't want to lose the emotions that go along with them.

Based on my journals I've felt this way in the past, but the concerns always disappear once I've completed the process of relocating or destroying all of the relevant information that I'm so reluctant to see disappear.

I have to wonder though what I'm truly giving up. Did I really feel as bad at the prospect of losing a part of myself then as I do now? In many ways I feel like I'm losing more this time.

Unfortunately I don't have a choice, not if I'm going to survive what I suspect is coming.

Imastious hasn't contacted me for months, which usually means that he's processing the results of an operation. Even for Imastious, draining someone dry of information can take a lot of time, so I didn't think anything of it, just like I didn't worry when my contacts inside the White Tears told me that their accountant had disappeared back in June.

I figured that was just the natural outcome of putting someone intelligent in charge of all of the money for a criminal enterprise. It doesn't take a rocket scientist to figure out that taking a chunk of cash and running is the smart way to ensure that you live long enough to enjoy the fruits of your labors.

I didn't realize just how much in the way of potential problems were about to come crashing down on me until Imastious showed up in Venice's apartment with orders to conduct a series of hits on the White Tears that ended with a snatch and grab of all of the White Tears' leadership.

A neophyte might have dismissed it as nothing to worry about, but I knew better. I'd gone to great efforts to try and confuse the issue by using the Bloods and the Latin Kings as foils for most of my personal operations against the Red Hand Consortium, but it's obvious to me that Imastious got ahold of someone inside the

Bloods or the Latin Kings who knew that they weren't responsible for one or more of my hits.

That in turn led him to make a grab for the White Tears' accountant who would have had a clear knowledge of the money trail for the gang and the fact that they had several unexplained windfalls that had come at the expense of the Red Hand.

I've been very careful not to leave any direct evidence linking me to the White Tears, but there is enough indirect evidence there to cause Imastious to come looking for me and all it would take is a single foray into my mind for him to correlate all of the seemingly unconnected facts with what he'll have already learned from his various other sources.

I've never tried to sanitize all of my memories regarding the White Tears because to do so would have resulted in great difficulties the next time I needed to work with them, but it appears that I have no other choice.

I'm going to have to wipe my memory of all interactions with them, and arrange for several of their key people to die, preferably in ways that make it look like they succumbed to natural causes, all while helping Venice plan and carry out the hits for Imastious.

It's going to be a wearing few days just trying to take care of that, but I've also been forced to reconsider my strategy where Lucy is concerned. Previously I was satisfied with simply protecting

Lucy's location and the extent of her probable power, but I've realized that underestimates the sheer scope of Imastious' power. Once he knows that she's out there and just how big of a potential asset she could become, he'll expend every effort conceivable trying to track her down.

I need to shift everything about Lucy into the safe part of my mind and I'll just have to deal with the inevitable increase in friction between the two of us that will result.

I've also been forced to reconsider things with Venice. The prospect of having Imastious inside of my mind has finally stripped me of some of my illusions where Venice is concerned. I've been telling myself that Imastious ultimately couldn't use Venice's feelings against her because I represent too great of an asset to him. Anything he could possibly get from her simply wouldn't justify further straining the already poor working relationship he and I have.

That is still true, but I've realized that if Imastious looks into Venice's mind and sees the depth of her feelings for me that he'll immediately look into my mind as well to verify the extent of my feelings, if any, for her. In the past I've told myself that Venice's best protection was the fact that I don't love her in return.

I'm no longer able to fool myself into thinking that Imastious will find nothing but indifference with regards to Venice inside of my mind. A few years ago I would have said that a pairing between two vampires would have been impossible, but Venice has found a way to make it possible.

The depth of her feelings, the fact that she trusts me unreservedly has allowed me to begin to feel something for her that, while only a pale shadow of what she feels for me, would still be more than enough for Imastious to seize upon it to advance his agenda at her expense.

I'm going to have to sanitize the vast bulk of my memories where Venice is concerned. The early memories can stay as well as some of the more recent memories where we are doing something mundane, something distasteful, but all of the memories of us together enjoying each other's company will have to either be destroyed or moved to safety.

Around everything else I'm also going to have to think of something to tell Venice which will explain my sudden distance, but which won't tip Imastious off as to what I've done to shield certain memories from him.

I'm faced with too many memories to save everything I'd like to where both Venice and Lucy are concerned. I'd say that I'm being forced to choose between my future success and love, but that would be hubris.

What I feel for Venice isn't love, not really—not yet, and nothing I can do at this point could save my feelings for her. I have no choice other than surviving or not surviving. My feelings for Venice will all be gone before the week is out.

Lucy Journal Entry 7

October
Lucy's Age: 14

Geoffrey—I refuse to refer to him as my dad—came up and drove us down from Yonkers himself. It was weirder than I expected because he actually tried to make small talk with us.

Of course Renworst just sat there in a semi-worshipful silence the entire time. About all he could manage were basic yes and no responses to Geoffrey's questions.

I'm not sure what made me respond to Geoffrey. It would have been a lot easier to just give him the silent treatment. I guess I was curious. I mean what kind of guy takes a child in and then pretty much ignores her for ten years?

I thought maybe if I could understand him better it would make it so that I didn't care so much that he'd neglected me for so long. I mean if he turned out to be some kind of raging psychopath or something then I could just chalk it up as a win that I hadn't had more interaction with him.

I've created a lot of different reasons over the years for why it's just been Renworst and me for so many years, but none of them fit. Billionaire workaholic was my favorite for a long time, but what kind of billionaire throws muggers into walls hard enough to put them in the hospital? For a while I thought he was some kind of CIA operative or something, but if he is then he's got to be dirty somehow. I've seen the amount of money that Renworst pays out in rent every month and I'm pretty sure that you can't afford that on any kind of government salary.

I tried to just put all of that out of my head and listen this time around and I was surprised at what I heard. I think in his own way he is as trapped as I am. He gets to move around the city at will, but there was something there that made it feel like he wishes that he could travel to other countries.

I figured that I didn't have anything to lose, so I asked if we would be able to resume training together now that I was back in the city. He paused, not just a short pause, a long, noticeable pause while he thought it through, but in the end he just shrugged. He said that he'd like that, but that he wasn't sure that it would be possible, at least not for a while.

I went to bed that night thinking that maybe life in the city wouldn't be too bad, but then Geoffrey showed back up a few days later to talk to Renworst and it was like he was a whole different person. He barely even spoke to me, and when I tried to talk to him about some of the stuff that we'd touched on during the drive down he answered curtly, like I was getting in the way of the real reason for his visit.

Maybe Geoffrey really is a psycho after all. Hopefully the fact that we're in the city won't mean that we see him any more often than we did before.

Geoffrey Journal Entry 27

November
Lucy's Age: 14

It appears that I've weathered the storm, as it were, but there were some interesting developments along the way.

I realized that I didn't need to destroy or move my memories of Venice into a safe spot, either one. Instead I simply moved each memory slightly which served to strip away all of the emotion associated with them, thereby making them safe and providing Imastious with exactly what he would expect to see. Plenty of time spent together, attraction and even love on her part, and an almost complete lack of emotion on my part.

Cleaning up the loose ends among the leadership of the White Tears likewise went acceptably well. Not only was I able to kill all three of my direct contacts in the gang, I was also able to arrange the deaths in such a way as to help avoid any suspicion that there was any kind of overall guiding force behind them.

I used one of their wives to stage a murder-suicide in one instance and simulated a mugging gone bad for my second contact, but it was the third hit that was the easiest to pull off. My third contact has a brother with a much younger, very attractive wife. It took less than six hours of observation to establish that my contact was indeed sleeping with his brother's wife. I simply arranged for the brother to find out and let him kill my contact for me.

In reflection, the whole process was much easier than I seem to remember thinking it would be back before I started sanitizing my memories.

Imastious did in fact show up a few days ago to scan my mind. I'm nearly recovered from the effects of the torture, and as far as I've been able to tell he wasn't able to find anything which would link me to his unknown opponent.

Venice was likewise tortured and scanned, but is taking much longer to recover from the effects of her session with Imastious. It appears that Imastious is more worried about the potential threat we represent than he is about maintaining our effectiveness as a team. He apparently told Venice what he found in my mind and even despite my warnings beforehand, she's having a hard time with things.

A DARKNESS MIRRORED

I've taken the prudent course and moved out of her apartment while she processes everything and decides where she wants to go from here. It's inconvenient from the standpoint of our working relationship, but I believe that it has some offsetting benefits which I'm planning on taking advantage of. The main one of course is the fact that increased distance between Venice and I will mean that I'm able to spend additional time with Lucy and Renworst.

I think that the biggest plus to come out of this whole round of adjustments is that I'm feeling remarkably clearheaded. Looking back at some of my recent actions has caused me to realize that I've been making suboptimal decisions in a number of areas.

Becoming involved with Venice was certainly an enjoyable experience, but in hindsight I didn't need to become as attached to her as I seem to have gotten. In fact, I'm becoming quite certain that my feelings for Venice caused me to neglect Lucy and Renworst to a much greater degree than I should have.

I'm going to spend much more time trying to repair my relationship with Lucy now than if I'd simply made sure to be at least a small part of her life on an ongoing basis. I believe the root of that problem however wasn't Venice, or at least not just Venice. Ultimately I think that I allowed anger at Mrs. Agosti to persuade me to leave Lucy upstate much longer than I ever should have.

I've always viewed sanitizing my mind as something to be avoided as much as possible, but I think that it is time for me to consider a program of regular emotional purges as a way of optimizing my decision-making process.

Honestly, I'm surprised that I haven't decided to do so sooner. My feud with Imastious has an undeniable set of core reasons which are entirely valid. He is enslaving me and I live under a near-constant risk of death that has only little to do with my own actions. That being said, the way that I've chosen to proceed with my shadow war against him has had a very strong emotional basis which hasn't advanced my cause in the slightest.

I've undertaken numerous operations against Imastious which had only slight economic benefit to me and which had correspondingly slight negative impacts on Imastious. Looking at those activities, I'm hard-pressed to justify them under the cold mechanics of risk versus reward.

My financial situation is such that these types of vendetta actions don't add appreciably to my war chest, and I've therefore decided that I will no longer be pursuing any activities against Imastious that don't provide either a very large benefit to me or create a very large detriment to him. I'll need to spend some time deciding where the exact threshold should be, but certainly in the tens of millions of dollars at least.

I think that I may be the first vampire to have hit upon the ability to move my memories around and thereby strip them of emotion. Certainly one would expect that most of the low-level grudge fights going on between the various vampire elders would cease if they had the ability to look at things rationally.

Lucy Journal Entry 8

August
Lucy's Age: 15

It's been months, and I still don't really know what to think about all of this. After pretty much blowing me off when we first came down from Yonkers, Geoffrey then started showing up out of the blue to visit us.

Renworst was in heaven from day one, but I just kept waiting for the other shoe to drop. Geoffrey was really stiff and formal, especially for the first few months, but as time went on he seemed to loosen up.

He offered to begin my training again on his third visit which I accepted grudgingly. It was sort of childish, but I guess I wanted it to be on my schedule rather than his. He'd turned me down, twice now, and then seemed to think that he could just come around whenever and change his mind.

A DARKNESS MIRRORED

I would have just said no, but I really wanted to start back up studying some kind of martial art, and I figured that if I turned him down he probably wouldn't be very keen to pay for me to take lessons from someone else.

I said yes and then prepared to be disappointed when he stood me up. As it turned out, he didn't exactly stand me up, our sessions were just very fluid from a scheduling perspective. I'd get a text from him at random times of the day, usually early in the morning or late in the afternoon, asking if I wanted to meet up.

His cellphone number changed on a regular basis, so it was practically a full-time job just keeping up with his number, but if I said yes then he'd show up to collect me half an hour or so later. He seemed to have a membership to every gym in the area because we never went to the same place two times in a row.

At first I really resented the fact that I pretty much was just at his beck and call, but it didn't seem to bother him when I said no, so I started getting over my annoyance when I realized that he wasn't trying to be a controlling freak, he just had a really unpredictable schedule.

It took me a month to notice that we never went back home the same way that we came either. I would have figured it out sooner, but he was pretty sneaky about it. He'd wait until we were just about ready to leave the gym and then he'd mention a new café or a bookstore that he wanted to hit up on the way back home.

I was usually just so excited about the fact that he would be buying me something that I didn't clue in as fast as I normally would have. Once I did finally notice his paranoia, I tried to ask him about it, but Geoffrey just shook his head and told me that he had to be careful about stuff like that.

I would have kept asking, but the truth was that I didn't really mind. It wasn't like I had anywhere to be. Renworst still wasn't letting me out of the house other than to go buy food with him, so the trips to the gym were pretty much the high point of any given day. The fact that we just went home the long way meant that I got to see more of the city than I otherwise would have been able to.

Not only that, I didn't want to rock the boat when it came to our training sessions. Geoffrey was good, not just I've-been-doing-this-for-a-long-time good either. My old sensei had been hell on wheels on the tournament circuit six or seven years before he started teaching, but I was pretty sure that he wouldn't have lasted eight seconds against Geoffrey.

We'd moved on away from aikido or any kind of traditional karate by the time Geoffrey had been training me for a couple of months. The new stuff was like pure distilled violence and I loved it. It was all kill shots and elbows, destroyed joints and knees. I'd hurt Renworst pretty badly back in Yonkers, but even then I'd know that it had mostly just been because I'd caught him by surprise.

Aikido works against people who are bigger and stronger than you, karate does too, but you have to be so much better to compensate for their reach and strength that it's almost not even worth trying. This stuff was awesome though because it put me right up close to them, inside their reach where they would have a hard time hurting me as badly, and let me just wail on them.

If you had asked me a couple of months ago I would have said that I was happy. Renworst had mellowed out a little now that he wasn't just stuck with me for twenty-four hours a day, I got to go outside three or four times a week, and I had an almost unlimited supply of books.

I would have been lying though, because I was lying to myself right about then. I had a whole new batch of tutors, none of whom were any fun, and our new place, while pretty much obscenely large for the city, didn't have room for a treadmill.

I was so busy fooling myself for the first few months that I didn't even really notice how much of my old life was missing until I realized that I'd started watching the building across the street from us each night. I'd given a bunch of the families there nicknames and was making up stories about their lives to compensate for the fact that my life sucked in a major way.

Once I realized it was just another coping mechanism, I almost started just closing my blinds and going straight to bed, but then the 'Fightersons' got a new family member. I'd started calling them the Fightersons after I noticed just how angry they were at each other.

The dad wore a suit to work every day and worked late most nights, weekends too. The mom looked unhappy most of the time and went from unhappy to angry within about thirty seconds of the dad arriving home from work.

Just based off of their age difference I figured that the dad had been married before, but I wasn't sure until his son moved into the apartment. I could tell the kid was his instead of hers because the dad looked guilty a lot when he was around the boy and the mom was now angry basically all of the time instead of just when her husband was around.

I say kid, but he's not really a kid. I mean he's my age, or maybe a couple of years older, but what do you call someone our age? Anyways, I've been watching him for a few weeks and he seems really amazing. He's got all of these posters on his wall from the various DJ's and bands that he's gone to see live. I can tell that he actually went to see them live because he'll come back really late, there will be a yelling match with his parents, and then the next day he's got a new poster up in his room.

A few days ago he saw me watching him, but instead of getting mad at me he just smiled and waved. We've started writing messages to each other on loose leaf paper and then holding them up to the window.

That's how I found out that his name is Ryan, that he wants to mix music, and that he thinks I'm cute.

If Renworst finds out he's going to freak out. He's mellowed out a little bit over the last year or so, but he'd still freak out.

I'll just have to make sure that Renworst doesn't find out. I like Ryan and I'm not going to let Renworst or Geoffrey, either one, stop me from talking to him.

Geoffrey Journal Entry 28

December
Lucy's Age: 15

I just had a rather charged discussion with Venice. She's still not happy with the way things are between us right now. She's finally forgiven me for being so distant after my last run-in with Imastious, but I haven't been able to give her a good reason as to why we can't be together now like we were before.

I've told her that it's too dangerous for her, but she doesn't believe me. I suppose she has good reasons not to believe me though as it's only part of the truth. I am trying to protect her, but I'm also keeping her at arm's length because of Lucy. There wouldn't be any way to keep Venice ignorant of Lucy and Renworst if she and I were living together.

It's already somewhat difficult to keep her in the dark as it is. She knows entirely too much about my habits and activities already and I can't risk her finding out about the two of them. Venice's mental shields have continued to improve, but Imastious could still break her at any point assuming he's willing to invest the time and effort into doing so.

I've gone back through my journal entries from right before and right after the last time Imastious tortured me and I continue to be struck by the difference in tone between the two blocks of time. I've spent a significant amount of time contemplating the idea that I proposed of doing a regular cleanse of my mind to keep me from becoming too emotionally attached to any of the people around me. There are some definite things to be said about the option. It's been less than two years, and already I feel as though a significant percentage of my time is spent dealing with things related to maintaining a relationship with Venice or Lucy.

Just yesterday I spent an extra hour with Lucy shopping after our training session. What started out as an operational necessity to make sure that we weren't followed back to her apartment, has turned into a mini ritual.

And then, once we made it back to her apartment, I noticed just how old and tired Renworst is looking. At another point in my life I wouldn't have even given the fact a second thought other than maybe to make a mental note that I would need to replace him at some point in the next decade or so.

Instead of dismissing the information, I spent most of the rest of the day trying to come up with a workable solution to the problem. Renworst has plenty of vices and failings, but he's been a faithful servant for nearly a decade. More and more I feel like that kind of loyalty should be rewarded.

The obvious answer is to turn him. There is an element of risk to that, not everyone who is exposed survives the transformation process, but the risk is acceptable and the potential long-term benefit is sufficient that I'm nearly positive that Renworst would choose to be turned if educated and then given the option.

The only real difficulty is deciding when to attempt the turning. I know that Lucy and Renworst have had their share of friction over the years, but it wouldn't be fair to her to take away the man who's been more of a father to her than I've ever been. I won't risk turning him when he's still living with her, though, because new vampires are still too unpredictable. That means I can't turn him before I turn Lucy, but by the same measure I can't turn the two of them at the same time because bringing along two new vampires at the same time would be much too big of a time commitment. There would be no possible way for me to keep that a secret from Venice or Imastious either one.

A DARKNESS MIRRORED

I briefly considered having Venice take care of Renworst after I turned him, but Imastious would eventually know anything Venice knew and if Imastious found out that I was making new vampires he would kill me in a heartbeat.

The only solution seems to be to wait a few more years, turn Lucy, get her stabilized, and then turn Renworst and stabilize him as well. It's workable, but it sentences Renworst to a number of additional years of aging. Being turned tends to reverse some of the aging process, but I'm not sure how far it will go. I wouldn't want to doom Renworst to an eternity in a tired old body that wouldn't be suitable for the incessant combat that is vampire life.

It's a sticky problem which I'll no doubt spend many additional hours pondering, but I don't begrudge Renworst that time. I think that is the fundamental difference between who I am now versus who I was immediately after sanitizing my mind.

I know that there is an argument that I'm wasting time on things that are unnecessary. Renworst is probably never going to be anything other than a blunt instrument at best, but I want to spend that time regardless.

Not only that, I think that there is a perfectly valid counter-argument in that I've never managed to connect successfully with Lucy in the absence of emotion, and she still represents my best long-term chance of breaking free from Imastious.

She truly is amazing. I've begun teaching her kenjitsu and she's picking up techniques at an incredible pace. It's not just the physical aspect of things either, she continually displays the proper mindset for combat. It's still mostly a game to her, but I suspect that she will have no problem making the adjustment to life-and-death conflict when the time comes.

With everything going on, all the progress being made with both Lucy and Venice, I think that the thing I'm still happiest about is the fact that Lucy and Renworst are starting to get along better than they have been.

I've been dropping by a couple of times a week lately and working with Renworst after Lucy goes to sleep. I've learned a lot about implanting subtle constructs since my difficulties with Mrs. Agosti, and Renworst is taking to my latest round of suggestions very nicely.

The longer I work with Renworst the more I become sure that there was some kind of severe psychological trauma that had a central role in shaping his character. I could probe a little deeper into his memories to find out what it was, or even just ask him about it. His loyalty conditioning would make him tell me what happened, but that feels like a very poor trade in return for his loyalty.

A DARKNESS MIRRORED

Whatever the original cause of Renworst's mental scarring, I'm glad to be able to say that some of the worst effects of the trauma are slowly being reversed by the constructs that I've been implanting.

Lucy Journal Entry 9

February
Lucy's Age: 16

So Ryan and I have continued passing notes to each other by way of our windows. He's really funny and his dad sounds like a complete jerk, so we have a lot in common. Actually, I guess Geoffrey has been pretty good in the jerk department lately but if I just asked for permission to go out on a date with Ryan I'd definitely be told no.

Around Christmas Ryan started telling me that he wanted to meet face to face, and I had a hard time telling him no. His girlfriend had just broken up with him and he was getting a lot of pressure from his dad to pick a college, which was the last thing he wanted to do because it wouldn't help him with his goal of becoming a DJ.

A DARKNESS MIRRORED

I put him off for weeks and weeks, but finally I decided that I was going to give myself a birthday present even if Renworst and Geoffrey were going to forget about my birthday.

Coming up with a plan to get out of the apartment wasn't easy. We live on the fifth floor, but unlike Ryan's building, mine actually has a fire escape. My window, just like all of the windows in our apartment, is wired into the main security system, but I did a little reading and figured out that the contacts on the system are all magnetic.

The filter on our internet is super restrictive, but a couple of years ago I found an educational site that is whitelisted for some reason that has all kinds of stuff that Renworst probably wouldn't want me reading about.

Once I solved the problem of the alarm system then the only remaining hurdle was Renworst, who usually checks in on me a couple of times per hour during the day. The simplest solution seemed to be the best, so I just started adjusting my sleep schedule over the course of the few weeks leading up to my birthday. By the time my birthday actually arrived, I was habitually getting up at 4 a.m. and going to bed at 8 p.m.

Boredom has driven me to do some pretty crazy stuff over the years, so Renworst just rolled his eyes at me when I told him I was going to start watching tai chi instructional DVD's super early every morning. He adjusted his sleeping schedule slightly to increase our overlap, which meant that before long he was going to sleep by 9 p.m.

Ryan and I arranged our rendezvous through our normal channel of communication and then, almost before I knew it, the day for us to meet arrived. I made all of the usual preparations for bed and then closed my door and waited for Renworst to quiet down and go to bed himself.

I'd seen Ryan's family leave earlier that day, which meant that we were going to have his apartment to ourselves. I'd tried to convince him that we should go outside somewhere, but he'd correctly pointed out that it was too cold to spend much time outside unless we wanted to court a case of frostbite.

Once I was sure that Renworst was asleep, I snuck out my window and down the fire escape. Ryan buzzed me into the building and then met me at his door. I practically had stars in my eyes for the first hour we were together. It was everything I'd missed about being around Parker.

We just sat next to each other on the black sofa that his mom had purchased a few months before and talked. Ryan and I didn't have as much in common as I'd had with Parker, but he was funny, and he had all kinds of incredible stories. I made it until midnight before exhaustion started really setting in. I wanted to go back home, but Ryan waved off my announcement that it was time for me to go home and put a movie on instead.

I tried to stay awake for the movie, it was the kind of violent thing that neither Renworst nor Geoffrey ever would have let me watch, but by then I'd been up for twenty hours. I fell asleep before the first massacre really even got started.

I woke up halfway through the movie as Ryan was trying to put his hand down my pants. The reflexes that I'd spent the last few years training just kind of took over. I hit him with a palm strike to the base of the neck pretty much without even realizing what I'd done.

I did manage to pull most of the force behind the blow at the last second, but I wished that I hadn't a second later when he backhanded me off of the couch. I converted my fall into a roll and made it back to my feet about the same time that he came up off of the couch swearing and angry.

At the time I didn't realize that he was probably trying to rape me, but I didn't need to know the full measure of what he was planning because the way that he came at me told me that I needed to defend myself.

Apparently the techniques I'd learned when I was five were more reflexive than I'd realized because I took control of his arm and used his own momentum to put him headfirst into the wall. I expected that to deter him, but he came at me again so I put a knee into his groin and then used an elbow to break his nose.

That knocked him out, so I stumbled out of his apartment and back across the street. The experience rattled me so badly that I just went inside my building and up the elevator like I normally would have done.

I didn't realize my mistake until I was already inside of my apartment and Renworst came out of his room with a baseball bat in one hand. To say that I was in trouble would have been a complete understatement. I think that if Renworst had been able to get Ryan's name and address out of me that he probably would have gone over and beaten Ryan to death right then and there.

Renworst ended up calling Geoffrey, so now we're just waiting for Geoffrey to make it over here and decide what my punishment should be.

Geoffrey Journal Entry 29

March
Lucy's Age: 16

I'm not sure that Lucy or I, either one, have ever seen Renworst so mad before. In all fairness, I was pretty angry myself, but it was Renworst who required two conditioning sessions before he calmed down enough that I didn't have to worry about him hunting down Lucy's attacker.

By the time that I made it to their apartment and got both of them calmed down, Lucy was finally ready to talk. She still wasn't willing to tell either of us the name of the boy who'd tried to molest her, but she told me that she'd broken his nose, which was all that I needed to know.

I made Renworst promise not to do anything else to punish Lucy until I got back, and then I slipped out of the apartment and walked to the nearest hospital. I waylaid a nice female doctor who thought I was cute and convinced her that I needed access to the information on all young men who'd come into the hospital with broken noses during the last six hours.

The effort of overriding her normal suspicion left me shaking with exhaustion, but fifteen minutes after we sat down for coffee she invited me up to her office. Of the three patients who were a match for the criteria that I'd given her, only one lived close enough to Lucy's apartment to be the guy I was looking for.

After the manipulation I'd just exercised on the doctor, I was too tired to go do anything about the boy, so I just went back to Lucy and Renworst's place and fell asleep on their couch.

It wasn't until I woke up the next morning that I realized the impossibility of what I'd done. The level of power I'd displayed while influencing the thoughts of the doctor from the night before had been far beyond anything I'd ever managed previously, and I'd managed to do it with enough subtlety that I was reasonably confident that I hadn't done any permanent damage to her.

If I'd stopped to think about my plan, stopped to think about the impossibility of what I was trying to do I probably never would have attempted it, but I hadn't considered my course of action, I'd just gone and done it. The mere fact that I'd acted so impulsively was nearly as astonishing as the fact that I'd succeeded.

I've spent so many decades being deliberate that even when I'm impulsive my actions have been thought through more than most people's. Apparently emotion is even more of a double-edged sword than I'd realized. It is capable of driving me to feats beyond what I'd consider possible, but it is also capable of driving me to hasty, poorly-planned actions. That's incredibly dangerous for someone like me, someone who lives under constant threat of death.

It's not a thought designed to allow one to get much sleep, but it's not the only worrisome development as of late. Last week I realized that when I think about some of my memories featuring Venice they are no longer the emotionless things that they should be. Some of the emotions from before I moved the memories are reappearing.

While I'd like nothing more than to immerse myself in those memories of a slightly happier time and soak in the feelings associated with them, it means that the process of moving memories doesn't actually destroy the feelings associated with them, it just suppresses them in some way. It means that I know less about the process than I thought, which makes me wonder if the memories that I've destroyed are actually gone or if they are just buried somewhere, hidden from me, but still accessible to Imastious if he knows how to look for them?

Nearly as worrisome is just how hard this is going to make it to keep Venice at arm's length. I've already been struggling in that area as of late and this is going to make things even more difficult.

Lucy Journal Entry 10

April
Lucy's Age: 16

When I got back up the next morning after the Ryan incident I expected for Geoffrey to tear into me, but he didn't, not really. He just told me that we were going to have to make some adjustments.

I've read enough books over the years to know that a phrase like that usually means nothing but bad, but Geoffrey was actually pretty reasonable about things. He explained that the biggest part of why he's kept me secluded from the world is that he doesn't want people like Ryan to have access to me.

I'm not an idiot, so I didn't just swallow his line without thinking about it, but recent events have pointed out that there are more jerks out there than I had expected to run into. More importantly though is the fact that after Geoffrey told me that he didn't want me going out by myself, he said that he and Renworst would make an extra effort to accompany me on trips around the city for the next little while until he was able to finish teaching me all of the stuff that I needed to know to stay out of trouble on my own.

The first part sucks, not as bad as being confined to my room or anything, but it's still being locked up, just a different kind of prison. The second part is pretty cool though because it means that he's eventually going to give me some freedom.

The part that really blew my mind was when he calmly told me that he knew Ryan was the one who had tried to mess with me the night before. He even had Ryan's address and everything.

I was so busy being glad that Renworst wasn't around when he'd said Ryan's name that it took me a couple of minutes to realize that he was asking me what I wanted to have happen to Ryan. It was pretty weird, like maybe something you'd expect out of the Godfather or something. I'm pretty sure it was just a test though because I don't think that even Geoffrey would just calmly kill someone, even someone who was going to rape me.

I tried to dismiss his question, but Geoffrey was pretty relentless. I finally decided that I wanted Ryan to be put into the same kind of situation that he'd put me in. I didn't want him raped or anything, but I wanted him to be powerless and know that there wasn't anything he could do to defend himself because he was up against someone bigger and stronger than him.

That seemed to pretty much satisfy Geoffrey and that was that. Since then, Geoffrey and Renworst have both spent a lot more time taking me out to see different sights in the city. Geoffrey has also offered to take me running, which is good because lately it seems like Renworst is tired most of the time. He's lost a lot of weight too, which is odd because he hasn't been exercising.

All in all, life has been pretty good other than the fact that the nightmares have come back. They don't really scare me like they used to. Instead I wake up from them wishing that they'd continue for just a little longer so that I could get a better look at the man with the sword.

Lucy Journal Entry 11

September
Lucy's Age: 16

I feel like my whole world has gone spinning out of control. I should have known something was wrong when Renworst started spending so much time in bed. He's always been as strong as an ox. Maybe if I'd told Geoffrey that Renworst needed to go see a doctor sooner than I did, things wouldn't be so dire right now.

Renworst has cancer. There, I said it. Renworst has cancer, some kind of bone marrow cancer, and he's been going through chemotherapy for the last few weeks. Everything at the apartment is all turned upside down. We have a full-time nurse now, Janie, who watches Renworst pretty much around the clock to make sure that his vitals don't drop suddenly.

I've learned more medical terms over the last month than I ever even knew existed. I even know how to use about half of the medical equipment that has taken over Renworst's room and half of the living room, but I still feel so helpless.

Renworst was a complete jerk for most of the time we've been together, but he's actually been pretty nice over the last couple of years. Not only that, he's all I really have. Ever since Geoffrey took me away from Mrs. Agosti, Renworst has been the one constant in my life. Tutors came and went over the years, and Geoffrey wasn't much better, so it was always just Renworst and me against the world. In a lot of ways Renworst has been more of a father to me than Geoffrey ever has.

I have to keep reminding myself that the doctors are still optimistic. They say that there are still a number of different drugs and procedures that we can try, which means it's way too soon to give up hope. Renworst just looks so small and frail lying there in his bed hooked up to all of those monitors.

Geoffrey was around a little more than normal at first, but now he's around a lot less. He's cut out our training sessions, running, everything. He's off playing James Bond or business tycoon or something and is just leaving me here by myself to help Janie make sure that Renworst gets to the hospital three times a week so the doctors there can review his progress.

A DARKNESS MIRRORED

I kept saying that I wanted to get out more, but this wasn't what I wanted. I'd gladly spend the next six years locked away inside the apartment if it would mean that Renworst would be okay.

Geoffrey Journal Entry 30

October
Lucy's Age: 16

Renworst isn't going to make it. I've done the best I could to shield Lucy from the knowledge of how quickly Renworst's condition is deteriorating, but she has to suspect by now. There are too many visible signs for her to have remained completely in the dark all this time.

There was something in Renworst's doctor's manner when he reported in on Renworst's status a few weeks ago. I couldn't manage to pin him down over the phone, so I dropped in for an unannounced visit and pulled the truth from his mind over the course of an hour or so.

The entire medical team is just going through the motions now. They've never seen anyone come back from a case as bad as this. It's metastasized onto his spine. If they operate at this point it's going to leave him paralyzed from the neck down, and that still wouldn't guarantee that he'd survive more than a few weeks.

He and I are both worried about Lucy. She doesn't have the support network that a normal person falls back on when something like this happens. It's my fault, and I'm not sure how to help her through this. I'm not even sure if it should be me who tries to help her through it.

Despite the risk, I've made appointments for her to visit a psychiatrist, but she's refused to go each time, and Renworst said the last incident escalated into her throwing things and screaming at him and Janie.

I've been visiting Renworst at night when Lucy is asleep. It seems to be his most lucid block of time and it makes things easier on Lucy not to have to see me.

It's been getting harder and harder to get away so that I can keep up my normal schedule of visits. Venice is starting to ask questions that I can't answer, and I think she unintentionally let something slip to Imastious because he's started sending me on a whole host of trivial, time-consuming missions lately. They aren't dangerous in and of themselves, but it means that I have far less time and flexibility when it comes to trying to lose Venice.

The decision that I'd hoped to put off for several more years is now upon me, and I still don't know what to do. I've never heard of a

ELDON MURPHY

vampire developing cancer, so if I turn
Renworst, assuming he survives the process,
there is a good chance that his cancer will go
into permanent remission, but his odds of
surviving now, as weak as he's become, are very
low.

Not only that, there are a whole host of
complications to consider at this point. I don't
even begin to have the extra time required right
now to oversee Renworst's training post-
transformation, even assuming that I can ensure
that Imastious doesn't find out that I've begun
turning vampires of my own.

The fact that there are a dozen or so doctors
monitoring Renworst on a regular basis is
another wrinkle as it means that there will be
people asking questions if he disappears, but
that's not an insurmountable problem.

The biggest problem of course is Lucy. If I do
nothing, then Renworst will die. If I turn him,
then he may still die, but at that point I will be
the one who killed him. If I turn Renworst and
he survives then I'll have to keep him away from
Lucy, at least for the first few years, because I
don't want her exposed to the darker aspects of
my life, not yet. She's still too young for that.

It's been interesting to talk to Renworst about
all of this. He suspected some of the truth about
me, but there were other parts of my nature that
have come as a complete surprise to him. He's in
total agreement that protecting Lucy is the most

important part of this. We've agreed that no matter what else is decided, he's not to die there in the apartment with her. He doesn't want her last memory of him to be watching the life slowly leak out of his body.

Lucy Journal Entry 12

November
Lucy's Age: 16

Renworst took a huge turn for the worse last week. I could see it coming just by how non-responsive he was getting, but I kept telling myself that it was the new meds they had him on to help cope with the side effects of all of the chemo.

The monitors woke me up about midnight and I went into Renworst's room and found a complete madhouse. Janie was practically flying around the room as she checked readouts and prepped a cocktail of drugs to inject into his system.

She didn't have time to explain everything to Geoffrey and me, but I managed to piece together the fact that one of his vitals had just dropped into the danger zone. She figured that she could get him stabilized enough to transport to a hospital, and that once he was there that they could bring him back out of the immediate danger zone, but the implication was there for anyone who had spent as much time reading up on his condition as I had.

This was the beginning of the end. Now that he'd started venturing down into the danger zone his condition would just continue to deteriorate as time went on. They would inject him with stuff that would temporarily buoy him back up, but he would go back down after a little while and with each cycle he'd drop a little further. He was just circling the drain now and it was only a matter of time until he dropped so far that they couldn't bring him back.

I don't know what Geoffrey was doing at our apartment in the first place, but he apparently read between the lines of what Janie was saying as well as I did. He offered Janie ten thousand dollars to stay with me for the rest of the night, and then told me to stay put as he jumped into the ambulance with Renworst and the EMT's.

I spent the rest of the night pacing back and forth in the living room, waiting for Geoffrey to call and update me with how Renworst was doing, but he never called. It was the next evening before he finally stumbled into the apartment, obviously exhausted.

I tried to get him to tell me what had happened, but he just told me that Renworst was being taken care of according to Renworst's wishes. I threw a fit, complete with throwing things and swearing at Geoffrey, but that's all he would tell me, and then he said that we wouldn't be talking about Renworst anymore. That Renworst wanted me to remember him as he'd been before the sickness.

I managed to pull myself back together long enough to ask if I would at least get to go to Renworst's funeral and Geoffrey looked at me oddly before shaking his head. He told me that there would be no funeral and then walked out of the apartment.

This time I really threw a fit, right up to and including opening the apartment door to storm out after him, but there were two huge guys standing outside my door. They made it very clear that they were there for my 'safety,' which meant that I wouldn't be leaving the apartment.

Janie stayed with me for an extra day, and she did some calling around to her friends at the hospital, but nobody could tell her what had happened to Renworst. He'd checked in through the emergency room, the doctors had done their thing to get his vitals back up into more of a normal range, and then he'd disappeared a couple of hours later.

Janie said that her calls trying to hunt down Renworst were some of the oddest discussions she'd ever had with anyone because none of the people who'd been directly involved in treating

A DARKNESS MIRRORED

Renworst were the slightest bit curious what had happened to him. It was like it had all never even happened.

I hate Geoffrey. He's done it again. He's taken away the only person I had in the world who I knew loved me, and left me alone when I most needed someone to lean on. There isn't any coming back from this. I don't ever want to see Geoffrey again.

Geoffrey Journal Entry 31

November
Lucy's Age: 16

All of the arrangements have been made. By
the end I was practically seeing double, but they
are all made. Surprisingly, the bits at the hospital
were the hardest because I had to take care of
them personally.

I once again seem to have expanded the
fringes of what I'm able to accomplish with my
powers. Emotion really is a much stronger fuel
than I ever gave it credit for. Even so, only the
fact that I limited the number of people who had
contact with Renworst to a mere handful allowed
me to pull it off.

Most of them were so sleep-deprived and
exhausted that it was relatively simple to turn
their memories of Renworst foggy and then I just
created a very powerful construct inside of the

lead doctor's mind which caused him to discharge Renworst into my care as soon as Renworst had stabilized enough to be moved.

The rest was relatively easy despite my splitting headache. It's actually quite interesting the sheer number of laws that people will break in return for money. I've seen it again and again in the drug trade, but it still sometimes astonishes me what I can get away with through the application of relatively modest sums.

The fight with Lucy was difficult, not in the least because of how exhausted I was. I should have handled things differently. I could have just texted her that he was in surgery or some such and then come back and faced her when I was rested, but my only thought was that I needed to get back there and see to her arrangements there at the apartment before Janie needed to leave.

All through the fight I kept thinking that it was vital that Lucy not see Renworst. It is what he and I agreed to, but I fear that I've made a severe miscalculation there. I knew that his loss would strike her hard, but I didn't really understand on a gut level what the full results would be.

Lucy hates me. There's no doubt of that now. Based on her manner, her feelings have been quite varied towards me over the years. Rarely, she enjoys my company and looks forward to seeing me, more frequently she wishes that she didn't have to interact with me at all, but this is different.

She was so angry when we were talking that I could actually feel her rage flailing at me. I wasn't inside of her mind, but I didn't need to be this time around. The depth of her feelings had her nascent mentalist abilities going full force and there was an iron-hard core to her emotions that told me that there won't be any coming back from what I've done this time.

It would appear that my emotions did indeed get in the way this go-round. I've run back through the chain of events that led me to this moment and while I can see dozens of places where I could have done something different in hindsight, at the time I could only see one route forward that gave Renworst even a slim chance of survival.

Given how things ultimately turned out, it appears that I have traded away the largest strategic asset in my possession in a ridiculous attempt to repay the loyalty Renworst had shown me over the years.

I've secured a replacement guardian for Lucy. She's no Renworst or Mrs. Agosti, but she'll simply have to do for now. I'd be open to leaving her in place indefinitely if it seems that she and Lucy are getting along, but I very much doubt that will be the case.

She strikes me as a rather disagreeable sort, but I had to accept what I could find on relatively short notice. I should have begun looking for a replacement as soon as Renworst was diagnosed, but I simply couldn't bring myself to do so. It seemed somehow disloyal to his record of exemplary service to replace him much as one would a cog in a fine watch.

Ironically, my procrastination didn't make any difference to Renworst; it just meant that I accepted a poor candidate at the last second.

Lucy Journal Entry 13

December
Lucy's Age: 16

The nightmares are back. They started back up again with a vengeance the first time I tried to sleep after Renworst was gone. They're a lot worse than they were before too. There's a lot of blood in them now, and for all that I'm pretty sure that none of it is mine, I spend the whole nightmare scared that I'm going to die.

It means that I'm not getting much rest lately.

So in other news, it looks like Geoffrey did even worse than usual when it came to picking my latest babysitter. Mrs. Phelps is a terrible person. Honestly, I spent the first few days that she was living here wondering how she even ended up in this line of work.

She barely spoke three words to me during the first twenty-four hours, and after that when she did talk to me she mostly was just laying down the law. Sitting there and taking orders from a self-important granny who'd just spent her first three days of 'work' watching some trashy soap opera while she made a complete mess of the apartment was one of the hardest things I've ever done.

I could have broken her like a stick and then left the apartment to go find Renworst myself except for the fact that Geoffrey had left his overgrown gorillas outside our door. Apparently he wasn't any surer of my long-term ability to control myself around Mrs. Phelps than I was, so he gave her some muscle to make sure that I toe the line.

The other little benefit, from Mrs. Phelps' perspective at least, to having the two muscle-heads just outside our door was that she could go out shopping and just leave me back at the apartment because it wasn't like there was anywhere I could go.

Apparently Mrs. Phelps was used to working with younger kids though because she made a major mistake last week. She came back from shopping wearing a new pair of earrings that I'm pretty sure cost more than she makes in an entire year, even considering how much she probably gets paid to take care of the kind of self-absorbed, spoiled brats that she seems to prefer to tend.

It was one of those head-scratcher moments until I overheard her talking to Geoffrey yesterday. She told him that we'd had a rogue power spike fry a bunch of electrical equipment in the apartment and that the hospital was asking for damages on some of the equipment that had been hooked up to Renworst before he died.

It was a plausible kind of thing for her to be telling him except for the tiny fact that she'd had all of the equipment boxed up and sent back to the hospital within a few days of moving in. Everything came together for me a second later when she told Geoffrey that paying the reparations to the hospital had nearly depleted the store of cash that he'd provided her when she signed up for the job.

Renworst never really talked money with me, but I knew that Geoffrey left a large supply of cash in the safe inside Renworst's room. Apparently Mrs. Phelps hadn't been able to avoid the allure of all of that wealth and she'd splurged on a new set of earrings and then come up with a decent cover story to explain why she needed more cash.

I don't know what I'm going to do with this information, but it feels like a big deal. It feels like freedom.

Lucy Journal Entry 14

February
Lucy's Age: 17

So I figured out the best way to use what I found out about Mrs. Phelps. I'm blackmailing her into letting me do pretty much whatever I want. The expression on her face was priceless when I told her that I knew she'd been stealing from 'my dad,' and that either things were going to change or she was going to prison for a long, long time.

I probably shouldn't have felt so happy at how scared she got, but it serves her right. She's a terrible person. Hopefully something nasty will eventually happen to her, but for now I'm going to be able to come and go as I please.

I still have to make sure that I'm meeting with my tutors on a regular basis, but other than that the sky is the limit. I've rearranged all of my tutoring sessions so that they are in the morning, which means that I'm free to sneak out the window and down the fire escape each afternoon.

Mrs. Phelps will text me if Geoffrey happens to show up, but I'm not expecting that to happen given how scarce he's made himself lately. As long as I remember to go back up via the fire escape so that the two goons in front of our apartment door don't see me, I'm pretty much golden.

So far I've experienced more than two weeks of glorious freedom and it's everything I hoped it would be. I've found a wonderful little bookstore with a café that makes a really good espresso and where you get the wireless key for the day on your receipt.

That means I can spend a measly few dollars, sit down at my favorite tired, old wooden table and then read and play on my tablet to my heart's content. The wireless connection is unfiltered, so I can read current events or even watch internet television. Watching TV was an interesting novelty, but I'm realizing that the stories there, for the most part, aren't as good as my books.

That's okay though because there are a whole new set of books in the store that haven't been previously selected by Geoffrey or Renworst, and when I get tired of all of the new books I'll still be able to people-watch.

I still miss Renworst, but this is the best thing that could have happened short of him still being alive and here with me. I've decided that this is my birthday present to myself this year. Happy birthday to me.

Lucy Journal Entry 15

June
Lucy's Age: 17

The nightmares notwithstanding, things have been going so well that I should have known that something bad would happen. I've been going to the same café for months now with no problems despite Geoffrey's overactive paranoia. He really would freak out if he had any idea how much time I've spent outside of the apartment lately.

Anyways, everything was going fine until I decided to take a trip down to the Metropolitan Museum of Fine Art. It doesn't make any sense. There isn't any reason to think that somebody started following me there, but ever since then I get a really creepy vibe anytime I go to my normal café.

I think I caught a girl staring at me the last time I was there. I mostly noticed because she wasn't one of the regulars, but she just kind of hung out in the café rather than buying a book and leaving. She was about my age, maybe a couple of years older, with platinum-blond hair and one of those bodies that most girls would kill for.

Just looking at her I would have figured that I could break her in two with my bare hands, but something about her made me uneasy. I felt silly about it after I got home, but this time I used the kinds of tricks that I remember Geoffrey using to make sure we weren't followed home from the gym.

It was all pretty pointless because I didn't see her following me or anything, but at the time I was freaked out enough that all I was thinking about was making sure that she didn't know where I lived.

I haven't left the apartment in more than a week now and I'm going stir crazy. The smart thing would be to stay here for another couple of weeks until she loses interest and then just find a new bookstore, but that seems so incredibly paranoid that words can't even do it justice.

I'm not a little kid anymore and I'm not going to spend another day jumping at shadows. I'm going outside tomorrow and when I do I'm going to go to *my* bookstore and if she's there and looks at me sideways I'm going to put my fist into her pretty little face.

Geoffrey Journal Entry 32

June
Lucy's Age: 17

Something very odd is going on with Venice as of late. The last time I saw her she was giving off a curious combination of anger and smug self-satisfaction. The anger isn't necessarily unusual, not given the way that I've continued to try and keep her at arm's length, but the smugness isn't normal.

Under other circumstances I would currently be dedicating a significant amount of time and effort towards figuring out what has Venice acting the way she is right now, but I just can't tear away any more time to think about it than I have already.

Other projects, not the least of which is Imastious' ongoing low-level war with Reginald, another of the vampire elders, have kept me extremely busy. I'll simply have to hope that whatever it is that Venice is stewing over doesn't come back to bite me later on.

Present Time
Chapter 1

June
Lucy's Age: 17

I knew I was in trouble as soon as I arrived at the bookstore. The girl, the one with the platinum-blond hair, was waiting on my favorite couch, the green one that has the best view of the door. That's actually why I switched to it from the table that I'd used previously. I didn't like how exposed I felt sitting with my back to the door.

She looked up as I walked in, and gave me a smile that seemed to say that she thought I was too chicken to actually come inside and sit down. To be honest I was feeling pretty scared, but I wasn't about to let her get inside my head like that.

I went over and ordered an espresso and then sat down in my second favorite spot, the table that has a better view of the book shelves but not as good of a view of the door. I pulled my tablet out of my backpack and pretended nonchalance as I started reading *Atlas Shrugged*, which I'd finally decided to try and wade through. The truth was I felt like some kind of small animal being stalked by a lioness. My calm was an act and I was pretty sure that the blonde knew it.

I made myself wait for two hours though before I got up and walked out of the bookstore. It wasn't as long as I normally stayed, but it made the point, to myself if no one else, that I wasn't going to just let her run me out of my favorite hangout.

I'd been uneasy the entire time I'd been in the café, but I didn't realize just how much trouble I was in until I looked back a block later and saw her following me. A thousand ideas flashed through my head but none of them were particularly workable.

I suddenly realized that Geoffrey had always been more concerned with finding out whether or not someone was following him and less concerned with getting away from a tail. Despite my years of martial arts instruction I was very, very sure that I didn't want to tangle with the blonde who was walking just fast enough to keep me in sight without closing the distance any.

I turned left at the next corner, just so that I wasn't headed directly back home, and started looking for an escape route. There was too much foot traffic for someone my size to push their way through at anything faster than a walk, so I couldn't just turn another corner and then make a run for it. Besides, my endurance probably wasn't the best right now given how little running I'd done lately.

I was busy promising myself I'd get back into a regular routine of running if I made it home safely, and then I saw a subway entrance a block and a half over. It wasn't a great option, especially considering how little I'd ever ridden the subway, but at this time of day there would be plenty of other people around, and there was always a chance that I could jump on a train at the last second and lose her that way.

I made it down to the platform and then felt my anxiety ratchet up as she followed me down and then took up a position only twenty or so feet away from me. The train arrived and I boarded it and then jumped back off just before it started moving, but she smoothly exited at the same time I did and then I suddenly realized that I'd let her position herself between me and the stairs back out of the station.

I really started sweating then, but there were still a lot of people on the platform, at least for the next few seconds as they headed towards the stairs, so I walked towards her, planning on sliding past her and coming up with another plan for losing her.

I was still five feet away from her when she pulled a knife out of her jacket and stepped forward so that the weapon wouldn't be visible to any of the people still on the platform.

"How about if you just stay there for a couple of minutes so that we can talk?"

Everything I'd ever learned about facing off against an armed opponent stuttered through my mind, and it all came down to one thing. If I let her get me off by myself I was a dead girl. I had to act now, while there were still people around who could at least call 911 if nothing else.

Now that I was actually faced with a fight for my life, all of my muscles relaxed. I considered yelling for help, but I figured that would just ruin whatever element of surprise I might have. Instead I stepped forward and tried to immobilize her right hand as I lashed out with a kick to her knee.

She hadn't been expecting for me to fight back, that much was apparent by the way that her initial response was marginally slower than her follow-up techniques. She let me grab ahold of her knife hand, but she got her knee up high enough and angled enough that my kick was deflected harmlessly into the dirty, white tiled wall.

I landed an elbow to the side of her head with enough force that she should have dropped like a rock, but she shrugged the blow off and hit me with a left cross that felt like being hit by a twenty-pound bar of iron.

As I dropped to the ground and unconsciousness claimed me I realized that I'd forgotten to yell once the fight had started.

Chapter 2

June
Lucy's Age: 17

I didn't expect to wake back up, but since I did I wasn't particularly surprised to find myself tied up face-down on the floor in what appeared to be a very seedy hotel.

"Excellent, love. I was starting to wonder just how long you were going to be out. Now that you're awake we can get started. Not much use in torturing someone who's passed out."

I managed to roll over onto my back so that I could get a good look at my captor, not that I expected it to do me any good. She'd shed the light jacket she'd been wearing, so she was just sitting on the edge of the bed in jeans and a tank top while she played with the knife that she'd pulled on me earlier.

I'd been hoping that she'd at least be bruised or something from the elbow that I'd landed, but nothing marred the side of her face. It was like the fight had never even happened for her, but the pounding inside my skull was plenty of evidence that I'd been hit just as hard as I remembered.

I tried to shift around so that my neck wasn't craned so awkwardly and nearly vomited from the vertigo that the motion triggered.

"Ah, sorry about that. You've probably got a concussion. I'd offer you something for the pain, but again, I'm planning on torturing you, so that's kind of contraindicated. I have to hand it to you though, I never expected you to fight back, let alone that you'd be so good at it. Geoffrey sure does know how to pick them, doesn't he?"

Even through the pain, I knew that the fact she knew Geoffrey was important. It meant that she wasn't just some random psychopath, this was somehow personal.

"Look, I don't know what's going on, but if you're after money I'm sure Geoffrey can come up with whatever amount you need. Let's give him a call before you do anything hasty."

She smiled and even through my fear I wished that I could kick her in the teeth. Nobody should be that gorgeous. It was like the perfect protective coloration for someone who was little more than a human tiger trap.

"I'm not after money, love. This is strictly payback. I've known that something was up with Geoffrey for months now, but it took me forever to track him back to your neighborhood.

He always loses me when he goes down into the tunnels over by the park, even when he doesn't know I'm following him."

"I don't understand. I didn't have anything to do with whatever he did to you."

The blonde smiled again, but there was an absent feel to the expression. "I probably never would have found you if not for this backpack."

She held up my utilitarian black backpack, which technically wasn't even mine. I'd taken it out of Geoffrey's room back when I started leaving the apartment on a regular basis and realized just how inconvenient it would be to come back from the bookstore with my arms full of books. Geoffrey had a bunch of extra supplies cached in his room and I'd figured that he'd never miss one of the three identical backpacks in his closet.

"You see, this is a custom-made backpack that Geoffrey designed himself with a little bit of help from Vicardo Paseres. I called Vicardo after I saw you the first time and asked him if he'd sold any copies of Geoffrey's design to anyone else and he was quite emphatic about the fact that he'd only ever created a dozen or so of them for Geoffrey. You probably should have thought twice about using something that would connect you so obviously to Geoffrey to someone who knows him as well as I do."

The smile was back again, but this time it had a sick edge to it, like a kid who was about to kick a puppy just because they liked to hear it whimper. "Actually, you probably should have thought twice about getting involved with Geoffrey in the first place."

All of a sudden the fear that was foremost in my mind, and the anger that had been simmering in the background for more than a decade and a half, just boiled over. "I never had any say in whether or not I got involved with him! That's the way that families work, even dysfunctional ones. You don't get to pick them, you get stuck with whomever you get stuck with and then you just try to make the best of it until you can get away and actually pursue your own dreams for a change."

My captor, the cruel goddess who'd been prepared to use a knife on me slid off of the bed and onto the floor, only it was less like sliding and more like collapsing. The knife was still in her hands, but she seemed to have forgotten it as she moved towards me in what was almost a crawl.

"What did you say?"

"I said I didn't get to pick my father, I just got stuck with him like any other kid on the frickin' planet."

She seemed to deflate before my eyes. She was still beautiful, but now there was a timidity to her that was completely at odds with who she'd been a moment before.

"His daughter? He'll kill me and he'll be completely justified in doing so. What have I done?"

Chapter 3

June
Lucy's Age: 17

It was obvious that the girl was shaken up, but she managed to pull herself back together enough to tell me that her name was Venice and then she used her knife to cut me free of the web of ropes that she'd wrapped me in.

The abrupt transition from psychopath to normal person was more than a little troubling, but I was suddenly more concerned about the implications of what she'd said about Geoffrey. I'd long suspected that he was involved on the fringes of stuff that wasn't completely above board, but I'd never actually thought that he was a murderer. It took me a few minutes to get Venice calmed down enough that she was coherent, but gradually an understandable picture started to emerge.

"I've been working with your father for a few years now. He's the one who taught me nearly everything I know."

"Right, I get that, and judging by your display of jealous rage from a few minutes ago, you aren't just coworkers. How long have you been sleeping with him? You do realize you can do a lot better than an emotionless cyborg, right?"

At least I thought she could do better. If she was really as unstable as she was starting to appear then maybe she couldn't do better. Even when dealing with guys there was only so much craziness that a pretty face could compensate for. Once you got too crazy then even someone as good-looking as Venice would eventually start having problems keeping ahold of her conquests.

Venice blushed and looked away from me. Everything I knew about sex had come from movies or books. In fact most of what I knew about anything had come from those two sources, so I hadn't exactly known what to expect out of Venice in response to my painfully blunt question. I'd thought maybe that she'd tell me it wasn't any of my business. I hadn't expected for *her* to be the one acting like the bashful virgin.

"It's complicated."

"So tell me the backstory. You've pretty much just told me that my adoptive father is a much worse person even than I thought he was."

She nodded slightly as though filing away the fact that Geoffrey and I weren't blood relations and then sighed. "Geoffrey works for a very bad man named Imastious. It's a bit like working for the Mob, once you're in there's no leaving, no matter how badly you might want out. It means that Geoffrey ends up doing a lot of terrible things because he doesn't really have a choice."

I shook my head. "There's always a choice."

Venice wrapped her arms around herself and looked off into the distance for several seconds before shrugging. "That's what I used to think too. I'm not so sure now. There are things that nobody can be expected to withstand."

I didn't agree, but I motioned for her to keep going. She looked back at me and frowned, as though remembering that she was the one who was supposed to be in charge, but apparently she was still rattled by the revelation that she'd just kidnapped and threatened to torture Geoffrey's *daughter* rather than the rival lover that she'd thought I was.

"Imastious finds out what you love and then he uses it against you. He's really good at it. There's…well, there's no way to keep something from him, not forever. You might make it for a little while, but eventually he drags it out of you and then he'll threaten whatever it is you value as a way of making you do what he wants."

A chill worked its way up my back, but I tried again for nonchalance. It ended up coming out sounding like bravado.

"Well, Geoffrey doesn't actually care about me so I'm pretty sure I'm safe."

Venice shook her head. "You really don't get it, do you? Do you have any idea how much time and effort Geoffrey has expended to keep you a secret? Even I didn't suspect that Geoffrey was sneaking away for a *daughter*, and I know Geoffrey better than anyone else. He's spent hours watching his back trail each time he visits, just so he can make sure that nobody is able to follow him to you. Geoffrey isn't the kind of guy to just expend resources for no reason. He's not keeping you fed and clothed out of simple habit. Your very existence is proof that he loves you, that he'll kill to keep you safe."

The chill was back. I'd never viewed Geoffrey's actions in that kind of light. I guess I'd assumed that he was like all of the other dysfunctional parents that I'd read about, that he did what he did because he didn't know what else to do with me. It had always seemed like things had just kept going out of nothing more than inertia.

If Venice was right, if what I'd seen was Geoffrey's version of a concerned and attentive parent, then he was simultaneously more scary than I'd realized and somehow less scary all at the same time.

"Even if you're right, Venice, only someone really far gone would act like Geoffrey has towards someone they care about the way that you're saying that he cares about me."

Her smile was somehow vulnerable. "I never said that he was perfect, but when you consider where he comes from you have to give him a whole lot more credit than you would otherwise."

"This isn't just some kind of fling for you, is it? You really love him, don't you?"

"Yes. It's not like it's a secret. He's...well, he's done some terrible things to me and he's made me do some terrible things too, but he did a lot less than he could have, a lot less than Imastious did."

I looked back down at the knife in her hand and something finally clicked for me. "Your little torture bit from a few minutes ago, you weren't making it up as you went along, were you? Imastious did that kind of stuff to you?"

"Yes. I'm sorry by the way. I would have tortured you, but I wouldn't have enjoyed it. I just couldn't see any other way to scare Geoffrey off. I thought maybe if I hurt his human lover that he'd leave you, or at least you'd leave him."

"So he'd go back to you?"

"Yes, that's part of it, but that wasn't the only reason. Imastious has finally noticed how erratically Geoffrey has been behaving lately. I need to come up with a way to force him to start paying attention to his 'day job' or Imastious will pay him another visit. I don't want that...it's never a good thing."

There was a pause while we both thought about what she'd said and then I cleared my throat. "So let's come up with a plan where we can work together to get him to stop being so distracted all of the time."

Venice gave me a confused look. "You don't exactly seem like you'd care what happened to Geoffrey."

I shrugged. "If you'd asked me this morning I would have told you I didn't care. I'm not sure how you managed to change my mind so quickly, but you have. I guess...well, I guess that I'm curious. You've told me that there is a whole different side to Geoffrey...to my father...that I didn't even suspect existed. I want to see that side of him before I pass final judgment."

"I wish that we could do that, but it's not safe for you. I guess if I had to screw things up and get myself killed chasing down Geoffrey's imaginary lover then at least it's not all wasted if you're willing to give him a second chance as a result. I could have died for a lot worse ends any one of a dozen times over the past year."

She continued on while I was still trying to process the implications of what she was saying. "I'll make sure to tell Geoffrey before he snuffs me. I'll tell him that he should sit down and have an honest conversation with you, that you're ready to hear the truth he's been keeping from you."

I shook my head violently. "No, you're not going to sacrifice yourself over this. We do this together or we don't do it at all."

A DARKNESS MIRRORED

Venice looked as surprised as I felt. I was actually having a hard time explaining to myself why I was so opposed to the idea of her telling Geoffrey that she'd found me. Obviously it would mean that he'd know I'd been sneaking out, but it was a lot more than that. I think that it came down to the fact that Venice was the first person I could remember in a really long time who'd just come right out and told me the truth.

Even Renworst, with all of his curmudgeonly kindness, had still treated me like I was too young to understand what was going on around me. I stood and looked down at Venice. "I'm not kidding. You keep what you know a secret or I'll run away. I'm old enough now that I could swipe some cash and make it on my own. If you think Geoffrey is distracted now then you haven't seen anything. Just imagine what he'd be like if he was spending half his waking time looking for me."

It was a bluff, but it was a pretty good one. Venice looked at me for several seconds before finally nodding. "Okay. We'll have to come up with some kind of system that offers you at least a little protection. I can never know where you live, and if it ever looks like Imastious knows about you then you're going to have to make a run for it. In the meantime, I'll have to be a very good little soldier so Imastious doesn't suspect me."

"Great, it sounds like it should be easy."

It was like Venice wrapped herself back up in the psycho persona that she'd been wearing when she'd first attacked me. She slipped it on like it was a set of armor and then managed a smile that would have looked normal if I hadn't just spent the last half an hour interacting with her when she was more herself.

"Sure. Easy. I probably won't have to do anything that I haven't already done."

Chapter 4

August
Lucy's Age: 17

There were layers to Venice I was still discovering as time went by, but I was having the most fun I could ever remember having. Talking to her was opening up options and illuminating blind spots that I'd never even suspected were running around inside of my mind.

I had a phone now, and not the crappy handset that Geoffrey had given me ages ago so that we could coordinate our training sessions. Actually, there was hardly any reason to carry the old phone with me anymore. It had gotten absolutely no use since Geoffrey had taken Renworst away.

My new phone, however, was nothing less than awesome. Venice had suggested that I swipe some cash from Mrs. Phelps' household fund and use it to buy a smartphone along with one of the higher-end prepaid sim cards. I'd done exactly that the next day and it had been like tasting freedom and then being able to go back for seconds. I could call whomever I wanted to now and never have to worry that Geoffrey was monitoring my usage.

Once I had my phone we were better able to implement Venice's plan for keeping me safe. It was all a little convoluted for my taste, but she told me that she'd be texting me every four hours without fail and that if one of the texts ever arrived late she made me promise that I'd call Geoffrey immediately and tell him everything that had happened, including the fact that he needed to get somewhere safe with me.

Mrs. Phelps hadn't liked handing over some of the cash that Geoffrey had left us, but she still wasn't in any position to argue with any of my demands. No, that part had been easy. Even texting Geoffrey, from my old phone and old number, hadn't been all that hard, not compared to what I was about to do.

I checked my reflection in the mirror and then slipped my running shoes on and went out the front door. Muscles One and Muscles Two were still standing at their posts, but I had permission to be out today so they just nodded at me and then watched as I started off towards the stairs.

Geoffrey was waiting for me just outside the building. It felt odd to see him in workout attire again after so long. Venice had let enough drop for me to know that Geoffrey was even less of a stranger to violence than I'd thought, so I looked him over trying to find a hint as to where he'd secreted his weapons, but there didn't seem to be anywhere he could have possibly hidden anything even as big as a knife.

We started off at a slow jog, just to warm up, and then after we'd both stretched, I led off towards Central Park. Geoffrey didn't say anything, he just ran at my side, effortlessly matching whatever pace I set. We ran for nearly an hour before my out-of-shape body started complaining enough that I dropped down to a walk and turned back the way we'd come.

Geoffrey wasn't even breathing hard as he slowed down to keep his place at my side. "Why did you text me, Lucy?"

"So we could go running. It's been forever and I needed to get out of the house."

I looked over at him in time to see him shake his head. "That's not what I meant, and you know it. I fully expected that you wouldn't want to talk to me ever again after the last time we saw each other."

"You mean after you took away Renworst? After you took away the man who had more to do with raising me than any other single person?"

Geoffrey didn't flinch; he just looked at me, waiting to see what I'd say next.

"I didn't want to talk to you for a really long time. I was pretty pissed, I guess I'm still mad about it, but it's not like anything either of us says or does at this point is going to change what happened."

"So why text me then? Believe it or not, I wish things could have happened differently, but I was more or less resigned to the idea that I'd ruined things between us."

I'd figured that showing some anger was entirely expected, but I needed to steer the conversation away from Renworst or I was going to lose control of myself. There was no telling whether I'd break down into tears or just start yelling at him, but neither option would help the situation.

I needed to focus on the reason I was doing all of this. Venice was going to be the friend I'd never had and she cared about Geoffrey even if I didn't. Only that wasn't the right answer either. Geoffrey mattered to more than just Venice; he was my only remaining link to my past. He was a pretty bad link as links went, but Venice seemed to think that there were levels to him that I hadn't seen yet, levels that were worth saving.

"I texted you because I'm lonely and you're the only person I have left. Mrs. Phelps is a terrible harridan and I used to have…well, not exactly fun, but running and training with you was better than how my life has been lately. I guess I want to give you a second chance because I need you, I need *someone* at least, and you are pretty much my only option as things stand right now."

Geoffrey stopped walking and looked me in the eye. "I'm sorry about Mrs. Phelps. I never intended for her to be permanent, but the two of you seemed to be getting along, so I assumed that you'd want things to stay the way they were rather than changing yet again."

"You could have told me that months ago."

"I could have. I thought about saying something to that effect shortly after she moved in, but that would have put her in a difficult situation. No nanny would want a parent actively telling one of their charges that if the nanny didn't make the cut she was out. It's already implied in the very nature of the arrangement."

My laugh came out more bitter even than I expected it to. "Maybe it's implied for other kids, but it wasn't implied for me. I've never had even the slightest control over my own life, why would I think this was any different?"

Geoffrey looked away, focusing on the pond just visible from our place on the trail. "I've never done this before, so I didn't realize how some of the pieces would fit together. I'm sorry. You're right to hate me."

"I don't hate you, not really. Mostly I'm just disappointed. The only constant in my life has been you, and mostly you just make things harder."

Geoffrey ran his hand through his hair and for the first time I saw how gaunt he was looking. For the first time I could remember he really did look like the workaholic billionaire I'd so often imagined him to be.

"So where do we go from here? Do you want to try and start over and see if I can be a better parent than I've been so far?"

I shook my head and rolled my eyes. "Seriously? What teenage girl wants parents? No, I don't want a father, I just want a friend. I'd like to go running with you and get in some training on a semi-regular basis at least, and I'd like to have the house arrest restrictions eased up a little bit. It would be really nice to take up martial arts classes again."

"Okay, I think I can swing most of that. What about your tutors? You're learning stuff that most people your age don't learn until their second year of college. I can get rid of them if you want."

"No, it's nice having some other people around from time to time who aren't Mrs. Phelps. I'd like to keep studying if that's okay with you, I'd just like a little more latitude to pick my own subjects and tutors."

Geoffrey checked his watch and sighed. "Okay, that's fine. I'm on a deadline though today so we'd better head back to the apartment now if we're going to make it in time for me to give Mrs. Phelps her notice."

As quickly as that, my freedom to see Venice was in imminent danger of evaporating. Geoffrey was never going to give me as much latitude to move around the city as what I'd been getting out of Mrs. Phelps now that I'd caught her with her hand in the cookie jar.

"Let's leave Mrs. Phelps where she is for now. I pretty much hate her, but her replacement could always end up being worse. Besides, I didn't really like Renworst back when you first sent me to live with him. Maybe she'll grow on me too."

Chapter 5

September
Lucy's Age: 17

Venice was indulging in her usual cloak-and-dagger antics today. I'd texted that I wanted to go out earlier that morning, and she'd responded back at the regularly scheduled four-hour check-in with an address and a time that had been accompanied with a reminder that I was to hightail it out of there if she missed the next check-in or was more than fifteen minutes late.

I arrived at the address, a particularly high-rent area near Fifth Avenue, fifteen minutes early because I hadn't been quite sure how long it would take me to walk there from my apartment. Venice arrived five minutes early herself and smiled when she saw me. The expression started out cold and haughty and then warmed up as she shed her working persona and the girl who'd texted me a picture of two kittens yesterday peeked out from underneath the uncaring be-otch that Imastious had tried to turn her into.

"What made you pick this place? It's way on the other side of the island from where we normally meet up."

Venice shrugged, her bare, shapely shoulders moving as she pointed at a store across the street. "It's good to mix things up in case someone tails me partway to the rendezvous spot. Besides, you said you wanted to get out of the apartment so I figured I'd take you shopping."

I looked at the displays in the store. "There's only so much cash I can steal from the house fund before Mrs. Phelps starts threatening to just come clean to Geoffrey. She's bluffing, but it's pretty apparent that she views the house money as her own personal slush fund. There's no way that I've got enough cash to buy anything there."

Venice's smile was even warmer than it had been a few seconds earlier. "Don't worry about the cash, silly girl. Imastious is a complete lowlife, but working for him means that I've got a lot of cash that needs spent in some useless fashion or another. Clothing has the benefit of being not only non-threatening, but also fun."

I'd never really been shopping before. Food shopping with Renworst didn't count, and ever since I'd gotten access to the internet I'd just purchased all of my clothes online. I almost said as much, but stopped because I was worried that Venice would tell me that she'd already deduced as much just based on the state of my wardrobe.

I'd always thought that I dressed okay. Today I was in jeans and a short-sleeved polo, but Venice was a whole level above me. I stared at the store she'd pointed to for a couple more seconds and then shrugged and followed her across the street. It wasn't like she could dress me any worse than I was already dressed, not in a place as expensive as this was likely to be.

Half an hour later I was starting to wonder if I'd spoken too soon. The clothes were all expensive, not designer, more like an extremely high-end box store, but Venice had a distinctive style and it mostly involved, tight, thin, and short. My figure was still pretty good despite the fact that I hadn't been running as much lately, but I still wasn't sure that I was ever going to wear some of what she purchased for me.

I finally lured her over to the boys' section of the store by claiming that I needed to get some running clothes, not that I expected to find anything good in a store that seemed to cater to 'preppy slut,' if there was really such a thing.

There was a guy stocking the shelves over by the running gear and Venice gave him a slow once-over as we got closer.

"Now that is what you need, Lucy. Look at the way his shirt has to stretch to contain those shoulders, but don't spend too long staring though."

"Because we don't want him to see us drooling over him?"

"No, because you'd miss the amazing things his pants are doing for his butt!"

My face instantly heated up. I was pretty sure that he'd been able to overhear Venice, but she didn't seem to care. Instead she practically danced away from me with a twinkle in her eye. I was starting to suspect that she was extra childish when she was with me as a way of compensating for how controlled she had to be when she was working for Imastious.

Actually, it probably wasn't just when she was with me. The photo of the two kittens she'd sent me hadn't been professionally done, which meant that she'd been somewhere recently where she'd been able to snap it. A leisurely morning at the pet store was hardly in keeping with the image she gave off most of the rest of the time.

I rubbed my cheeks, wishing that there was a way to instantly eliminate a blush, and then I walked back over to Venice who was busy holding up a pair of boxer briefs and raising her eyebrows suggestively at me.

"Do you know how hard it is to tell where the act ends and the real Venice begins? The suggestive clothes, leering at boys, it's hard to sort it all out sometimes."

She shrugged, as though trying to dismiss the question, but I could feel her mood change. "It's probably hard for you to tell where the act starts and ends because sometimes I'm not sure myself. I'm not the oversexed whore that Imastious tried to turn me into, but I do still have a pulse. I can appreciate a nice set of shoulders or a tight butt and still be faithful to Geoffrey, not that he cares one way or another right now."

"Is that why you're into him? Just purely for physical reasons?"

"Who, Geoffrey?" Venice looked at me in surprise. "And here I thought you weren't paying any attention to Geoffrey's less subtle attributes."

I blushed slightly. I didn't think of Geoffrey as a father figure and there wasn't any blood relationship between us, so it wasn't like what I was thinking was tantamount to incest, but the tone to Venice's words still made it feel like we'd just crossed over in to awkward territory.

"I've got eyes and a 'pulse' like you. It would be hard not to notice the fact that he keeps himself in good shape."

Venice seemed to be waiting for me to say something else, but when I didn't volunteer anything else she shrugged and put the underwear back on the shelf.

"No, love, I'm not with Geoffrey just because he's got a killer bod and knows how to use it. I'm with Geoffrey because, despite all of the terrible things he does, he could be so much worse. He doesn't even realize just how hard he's trying to be good. He's rationalized away everything good he's ever done to the point where he thinks that it was all just about his own self-interest, but I know that's not the reason."

Venice absently reached out and ran her fingers over another pair of silk boxers. "I'm with him because he saved my life. I may not be entirely happy with who I've become in the process, with the things that I'm capable of doing now, but alive sure as hell beats dead."

"So you pretend not to care, wear the clothes that Imastious dresses you in, hurt whomever he tells you to hurt, but it's all an act to hide the fact that they didn't succeed, that you're still a decent person inside where it really matters?"

My question earned me a sad smile that reminded me of the first time we'd talked. "Honestly, I don't know anymore. There are days where I'm not sure which one is the act. Sometimes I wake up from nightmares where I'm doing terrible things and enjoying them."

She shook herself slightly, apparently having decided that she'd said too much, and shot me a smile that was much more chipper.

"Besides, this isn't Imastious' style at all, this is the kind of stuff that Geoffrey likes. Imastious runs much more to high-class prostitute than girl next door. Come on. It's time to get a couple more things for you. I actually wish I could be there to see his expression the first time he catches you wearing some of this."

"What makes you think I'll ever wear any of it, let alone somewhere that Geoffrey might see me in it?"

"Trust me, once you own this kind of stuff it's hard not to dust it off at least once in a while and see how many heads you can turn. You'll wear it sooner or later."

Chapter 6

December
Lucy's Age: 17

I texted Venice as soon as I got back from my run with Geoffrey. We'd layered up to brave the extreme cold, but that wasn't anything different than what we'd done dozens of times before. I'd been expecting for Geoffrey to crack a joke or two during the course of the run like he'd been doing lately, but he'd barely spoken two words to me the entire time.

I would have said that he was just preoccupied with whatever Imastious had him busy doing, but I'd seen that before and this wasn't it. It was like there was a different person walking around inside of his skin, a person who weighed every response and was considering each of our exchanges as if it was the first time he'd run into me.

It wasn't preoccupation, but it was something else, something I'd also seen before. I didn't know how to handle this, but I was hoping Venice did.

Venice texted back according to her usual schedule and agreed to meet me in a hole-in-the-wall restaurant eight blocks over from my apartment. I usually tried to make sure we met up further away from home than that, but by the time she responded it was starting to get late and I didn't want to walk halfway across the island to get back home, not in the dark at least.

I waited there for ten minutes with Venice's past warnings running through my mind the entire time. I must have checked the clock thirty times while waiting for the big hand to move from the six to the seven.

I knew it was too soon to panic, but I was terrified that something had happened to her. The Geoffrey whom I'd spent the last few months helping to loosen up a little—the one who'd joked around with me from time to time and who'd even been talking about taking me to the opera for my birthday— wouldn't have been too bad to talk to, but I was scared to death of this new Geoffrey.

I'd started to believe all of the good things that Venice had been telling me about Geoffrey, but with the way he'd been earlier in the day I was pretty sure that he'd kill me if he couldn't come up with an easy way to solve the problems Venice and I would be dumping on him.

A DARKNESS MIRRORED

I was freaked out enough by the time Venice finally arrived that I'd almost convinced myself to just leave even before the fifteen minutes were up, but she slid into my booth a few heartbeats before my courage would have failed me.

"What is it, Lucy? Do you have any idea the kind of hell I've been through over the last three hours?"

I'd been too wrapped up inside of my own worries to notice right off, but now that she'd shocked me back into reality I noticed that she had a massive bruise forming on one side of her face.

"Oh my gosh, Venice, what happened to you?"

"Imastious happened. He's got something in the works, so he stopped by to make sure that I still remember who's signing my paycheck."

I opened my mouth to say something reassuring, but nothing would come out. I'd hit Venice with an elbow to the face that would have broken two inches of pine and she hadn't had even the slightest mark just a couple of hours later. Imastious must have hit her with a baseball bat. I couldn't offer any reassurance because I wasn't sure there was any to be had.

"I went on a run with Geoffrey earlier today, but he was different. Not like a little different, like an emotionless robot who was trying to decide whether or not to just kill me and save himself the inconvenience of having to deal with me in the future. It was eerie, and it wasn't even the first time it's happened. I remember him getting like this a few times in the past."

Venice swore under her breath, but she didn't seem surprised, not really. It was more like she'd known it was coming and was just bent out of shape that it had happened now rather than later.

"Look, there's a lot I can't tell you, some of it because there are some things I don't fully understand myself, but Geoffrey does this sometimes. It's like he takes all of his emotions and locks them away."

"How is that even possible?"

"Look, it's not important how he does it—I'm not even quite sure how it happens, but it's some kind of defense mechanism against Imastious. The important thing is that we need to bring him back as quickly as possible. The more he interacts with people he cares about, or at least that he used to care about, the faster he gets back to normal."

I shook my head. Things were just getting too weird for me. Normal people couldn't just turn off emotions like she was describing. You'd have to be a full-blown psychopath to do something like that.

"You're not making sense. That's not even possible."

I stood up to leave, not sure what I'd do next, but positive that I needed to get away from Venice, but she grabbed my arm and pulled me back down.

"You're not just going to take everything I say on trust anymore, are you?"

"Not when you sound like you're living in some kind of fantasy world."

"Fine, hold still for sixty seconds and I'll give you the proof you're looking for."

Venice looked around, confirming that we were the only ones on this end of the restaurant, and then grabbed one of the paper napkins out of the dispenser on our table and tore off a corner.

"Watch the piece of paper."

I opened my mouth to ask her what she meant, but she'd already closed her eyes and it looked like she was concentrating extremely hard. A couple of seconds later the napkin corner shot across the yellow table.

I put my hand out to catch it, but then it suddenly darted back towards Venice. I waved my hand over the table, trying to see whether or not there was some kind of gust of air causing the paper to move around, but I already knew that there wasn't.

I watched Venice's prop skitter across the smooth surface of the table a couple more times before I grabbed her arm and told her to stop.

"Okay, you've got my attention, how did you do that?"

Venice rubbed her temples and for a moment she looked like she was second-guessing her decision to go forward.

"I guess I'm in as deep as I can get already. The truth is that I can do a lot more than just move a bit of paper around, but I'm not so good when it comes to fine control. I'm a telekinetic, it's one of the three main powers that…my kind of person can develop. Imastious and Geoffrey are both mentalists, so they can read people's minds."

Even with the proof of her unusual ability still fresh in my mind, it was hard to believe, but she was obviously serious. She waited for a second to see if I was going to say something silly about mindreading being impossible, but I managed to suppress the urge.

"That is why Imastious is so dangerous. He's extremely powerful, so if he decides that you know something important he's more than capable of just ripping the memory right out of your mind. You can train yourself to be harder to read, but if he wants the information bad enough then he can always just torture you until your mental defenses start to crumble."

Some of the pieces were starting to fit together now for me.

"So that's why you've been so paranoid about everything. You check in every few hours because you figured that you could hold for at least four hours if Imastious started torturing you."

Venice looked tired. She'd come into the restaurant battered and angry, but now she just looked like she wanted nothing more than to go home and fall into bed.

"Yeah, that's about the size of it. Geoffrey is operating on borrowed time now. He has been ever since I found out about you. I've been a very obedient girl when it comes to Imastious now that I know about you, but it's only a matter of time. Eventually he'll invade my mind and find out what Geoffrey has been up to for the past few years. I should have killed myself months ago."

My mind whirled as I tried to understand the implications of what she was telling me. "So Imastious will know about me, but I could lie low, which would mean that he couldn't use me against Geoffrey. This doesn't have to be an either-or situation, you don't need to do anything drastic."

Venice shook her head. "No, you're still not getting it. Imastious has been inside of Geoffrey's mind multiple times over the last few years, but he doesn't seem to have clued into your existence yet. That means that Geoffrey has found a way to keep at least some of his memories safe from Imastious, which shouldn't be possible, not considering how much stronger Imastious is than Geoffrey."

"So he'll kill Geoffrey just because he can't control him?"

"Yes. Imastious is terrified of someone from inside his organization taking it over and dethroning him. I don't know how Geoffrey is doing it other than that it seems to be associated with Geoffrey losing access to his emotions on a semi-regular basis, but if he's hidden your existence from Imastious then I can guarantee that he's got other plans in the works, plans which are a direct threat to Imastious."

I suddenly felt incredibly small. Venice had just thrust me into the center of an extremely dangerous world and the fact that I'd already been in danger and just hadn't known about it didn't do anything to alleviate my feelings of powerlessness.

"So what do we do? Can we just run?"

"I'm not sure. You could, but Imastious has done things to my mind. I tried to run away before and I just ended up in one of the locations he programmed me to go to. Geoffrey might be able to scrub my mind clean of Imastious' booby-traps, but with the way he is right now I'm not sure that he would agree to help me."

"But that's crazy, Venice. Surely he'd help you get away if it would mean that his secrets would stay safe from Imastious."

Venice shrugged uncomfortably in the way I'd started to realize meant that she was about to make reference to the aspects of Geoffrey's personality that she was least comfortable with.

"This version of Geoffrey isn't very warm and cuddly, Lucy. If I were to go to him right now and spill my guts he'd know that something would have to be done, but that doesn't necessarily mean that he'd decide to help. Geoffrey just loses the good emotions when

Imastious goes inside his mind. The guy you went running with today is nothing more than ambition and a pure hatred of Imastious. He might just decide that killing me is the easiest solution to the problem I created."

"So we don't tell Geoffrey now, we wait until he's back to normal and then we tell him."

Venice looked like she was nearly ready to cry. "Yeah, that's pretty much what I was planning on doing, but this isn't my first time trying to help him get back to normal. I've spent years trying to break down his barriers, but Imastious always makes another incursion into his mind at some point or another and I've never been able to change him fast enough to get him all of the way back before he flushes all of his emotions again."

"Get him back? You mean that he used to be better than this?"

"Yes. Nine or ten years ago. Things had been so bad for so long, and then Geoffrey and Imastious let me start running operations for them. We spent a ton of time together over the course of several months and I fell in love with him. He kept telling me that it was dangerous, that I shouldn't be trusting him, shouldn't be making myself vulnerable, but I couldn't seem to help myself."

Venice looked down at the table for several seconds before shrugging. "I think that I almost had him ready to make a run for it with me, but there was something holding him back. It turns out that something was you."

I'd only known Venice for a short time, but she'd gotten such a bad deal out of life that I couldn't help but feel bad about the fact that I'd been the one to ruin her chance to get away from Imastious.

"Okay, I'm in. How do we go about getting Geoffrey back to normal as quickly as possible so that we can all get away from Imastious?"

"Are you sure, Lucy? You're the one person who can walk away from all of this and never have to look back. It might not be a good idea to get yourself even deeper into the craziness of my world."

"I'm sure. How can I help?"

Venice took a deep breath and then started laying out her methodology.

"Mostly it comes down to human interaction. Just being around other people seems to help, but the more intimate the interaction the faster he tends to come back."

"So what, you want me to flirt?"

Venice shook her head. "No, at least not at first. He's not going to let anyone get away with that kind of stuff initially. He's going to be pretty standoffish and cold for the next little while, so you're going to want to start off with non-threatening interactions for the time being."

My jaw practically hit the floor. "Venice, I was joking. I don't really think of Geoffrey as my father, but it still would be really, really weird to flirt with him. Besides, he's yours. The last thing

I'd want to do is go up against you when it came to trying to get some guy's attention."

I felt my cheeks heat up as the blush worked its way up from my shoulders. "I...well, I wouldn't want to ruin our friendship, not that any guy would ever choose me over you in the first place."

The look that Venice gave me was indecipherable, but after holding it for a couple of seconds she just shrugged. "I value your friendship too, Lucy. I think you might be surprised just how many heads you turn over the next few years, but that's a conversation for a different time. You need to be careful though thinking of Geoffrey as the same person you were spending time with last week and the week before. The thing that is wearing his skin isn't him. It's got most of his memories and over time we should be able to help it uncover the underlying character traits that make Geoffrey worth saving, but that isn't Geoffrey, not really."

I hadn't forgotten the way that Geoffrey had looked at me earlier, but her warning was finally starting to sink in. He really had been trying to decide whether or not I was worth keeping around while we'd been running.

"I understand. Don't push him, because he doesn't have any of the normal attachment to friends or family that you'd expect out of someone."

"Exactly."

Chapter 7

January
Lucy's Age: 18

"Happy birthday, Lucy. Do you want me to get the employees to sing to you while we're there tonight?"

I managed not to blush, mostly because I was getting used to Venice's sense of humor, but it was a close thing.

"No, thank you. I'd rather just have a quiet, peaceful dinner. Besides, this place you're taking me to is supposed to be pretty high-class. I doubt they'd go for that kind of thing."

Venice shrugged. "We'll never know unless we ask, but it's your birthday so if you want quiet, then quiet you'll get."

It was only a short, albeit bitingly cold, walk from our meet-up point to the restaurant, so almost before I knew it we'd arrived. Despite the frigid temperatures, Venice's only concession to the weather was the long, green coat that she promptly removed as soon as we were inside. Her pants were fairly conservative, black slacks like you'd see on a bank teller, but her top was as tight as usual and more low-cut even than was normal for her. She used it to her advantage, as she talked to the maître d'. I watched his eyes linger for an extra couple of heartbeats as she leaned in and whispered something in his ear.

Despite the impressive line of people still waiting to be seated, less than fifteen minutes later we were being led to our table. I looked back to check on the maître d and saw that he was following her with his eyes as we walked away.

I waited until we'd been seated to ask the question that was burning a hole in my mind. "So what exactly did you say to him?"

"Who? Oh, the maître d'? I told him it was your birthday, but that you'd be more than happy to give *him* a spanking if he'd be ever so kind as to get us a table off by ourselves."

This time she did make me blush. "I'm serious, Venice. It wasn't all just the clothes, was it?"

She shrugged. "It depends on the guy. He was apparently extra susceptible to my charms. I had a twenty ready to palm, but he didn't need it. It's mostly about providing the illusion that a small favor now on their part will result in an increased chance of a favor in return on your part at some future date. They don't actually expect to cash in, at least not most of them, but the illusion helps make everything go better."

Her answer was tossed off with complete nonchalance as she thumbed through the wine menu, but she flagged the waiter down less than ten seconds later and ordered two bottles of wine. I knew next to nothing about alcohol, but that seemed like a lot of wine for one person to drink.

My suspicion that something was wrong was confirmed when she handed our waiter a fifty-dollar bill and told him that there was another one waiting for him if he could get the wine here within the next three minutes.

Venice drummed her fingers on the elegant red table cloth. "Wine goes better with food, Lucy. Hurry and pick an appetizer, I want to order as soon as he gets back with my fun-juice."

Our waiter must have run as soon as he was out of sight, because he made it back less than a minute later. I was still looking through my menu, so Venice handed him the promised fifty and then took both bottles off of his hands.

"Fine, I'll just have to get drunk without the food."

Venice popped the cork on the first bottle and poured a generous amount of wine into one of the largest glasses I'd ever seen.

I decided what I wanted to eat and then set my menu down. Venice was already starting her second glass, hardly pausing to swirl it around the clear crystal of her glass before tossing it back.

"What's going on, Venice? This isn't normal for you."

It looked for a second like she was biting back a nasty retort, but then she sighed and looked around to confirm that we weren't close enough to anyone else to be overheard.

"Our psychotic little friend just torched a building."

It took me a second to realize who she was talking about. I felt myself go white as I realized that Geoffrey was the one who'd started the fire that had been all over the news for most of the day.

"Are you sure?"

"Yeah. I suspected it was him, but when they released a partial list of people who were killed as a result of the fire an hour ago I knew my suspicions were right. Imastious assigned Geoffrey a target last week, but it wasn't just any target. This guy was a top-level arms dealer and he employs some of the best security around. Geoffrey and I went back and forth for a couple of days trying to come up with a plan of attack that would let us get in, kill the scumbag, and get back out without getting shot by his guards."

Venice started to pour herself a third glass, realized the bottle was empty, and popped open the second bottle.

"We couldn't come up with anything workable. I was starting to get worried because Imastious isn't the kind of guy to casually accept failure, but yesterday Geoffrey stopped by my apartment and told me that he had everything figured out."

The first half of the second bottle was now in her glass so she paused to drain the wine in one long draw.

"I was excited that he had a plan, right up until he told me that he didn't need my help. I should have known that he was up to something after that, but I couldn't get any kind of details out of him."

She looked down at the table. She'd been whispering so far, but the next sentence was so quiet that I almost couldn't make it out.

"He didn't tell me because he knew I wouldn't approve of a plan that involved waiting until our target was home and then torching the entire building."

I was still reeling, but had enough presence of mind to keep my voice down too. "He killed dozens of people just to take out one guy for Imastious? Are you really sure he's still worth saving, Venice?"

She refused to meet my gaze for nearly a minute, fiddling with her wine glass instead. When she finally looked up at me, I didn't see the raging drunk that I'd been expecting. Venice was stone-cold sober and the same worries I had were tearing her up too. It was bad enough for me, just knowing that I was enabling him in some small way. It would be even worse for her because of how much she loved him, or at least the man that he'd been.

"I think so."

"That's not a very strong response, not given what we're dealing with."

"I can lie to you if that's what you'd prefer, but the truth is I'm not certain right now. Each time Geoffrey does the scorched-earth bit on his emotions things get bad, but this is different. There was a pattern there before, but I refused to see it until now. He's getting worse. It's like the weight of all of the terrible things he's done makes it harder for him to come back to me each time and makes it easier for him to do even worse things."

Venice poured the rest of the second bottle into her glass, but she didn't drink it. "I know I'm not the most unbiased person right now, Lucy, but I still think he's worth saving. He didn't involve me in the operation because he was trying to spare me from doing something that bad. He could have started the fire at night, but he didn't. By nearly every measure I can think of, the fire would have been more effective at night, but he chose to do it during the day so that fewer people were around to be hurt. I know it may not seem like much, but there's still a core of goodness there that Imastious hasn't managed to completely corrupt yet."

I could feel a headache starting behind my eyes. I wanted to just put my head down on the table and wait for someone else to come deal with the mess that I'd jumped into feet first. Venice reached over and put a hand on my arm.

"I know I'm asking a lot, but I think this is my last chance. If we can't get him out this time I'm not sure that I'll get another opportunity. There are things you just can't come back from, and he's skirting around them already this time."

"What if he's already done something that he can't atone for, at least not all the way?"

"Then I guess I'll have to put him down and take my chances running away."

"Can you really do that?"

Venice shrugged, but I could tell that the motion cost her a lot more than she was willing to let on. "Not if he's expecting something like that, but maybe if I catch him by surprise. If he goes through another cycle like this and gets even worse before we manage to get him back to normal then I'll get him to trust me again. Once he's not expecting it, I'll stick a knife into him."

"That wasn't what I meant, and you know it."

Venice motioned with her head and I realized that the waiter's arrival meant that we were going to have to pause our conversation. The waiter introduced himself as Calum and flashed a very winning smile at each of us. Venice rattled off an order that included a bottle of vodka, I ordered with what I hoped was a bit more politeness, and then Calum disappeared back into the kitchen again in a flash of blond hair that was only a couple of shades darker than Venice's.

The silence between Venice and I stretched out for ten more minutes. Our appetizers arrived before Venice finally responded.

"I don't know, Lucy. I hope so though because if I can't then it means that *I'm* farther gone than I think I am. And not just where he is concerned."

Chapter 8

I still wasn't completely sure that we were pursuing the right course. There were so many ways that everything could come crashing down on us, but Venice was my friend and I wanted to help her. Not only that, Geoffrey had taken me in as a small child when he didn't have to.

Part of me suspected that he had some nefarious scheme behind his actions still, but the fact of the matter was that he'd provided for me for a decade and a half and never asked for anything in return. Even if he did have some crazy long-term plan to take advantage of me in some way, it was always possible that Venice was right and he'd used the plan in question as a way of rationalizing what he wanted to do in the first place, which was save a little girl from freezing to death.

A DARKNESS MIRRORED

Once Venice and I had agreed to go forward with our efforts to redeem Geoffrey, we'd spent the rest of the night trying to come up with a plan that would allow us to spend more time with him in an effort to speed up the process of re-humanizing him.

It sounded to me like Venice was already on unstable ground where Geoffrey was concerned though, so that meant everything came down to me, which I was okay with, but there were complications there.

Venice had a set of valuable skills and an iron-clad reason for interacting with Geoffrey. I, on the other hand, was a burden in every sense of the word. Training with me wasn't any kind of a stretch for Geoffrey because he was so much better than me in that area. Conditioning was a bust too. I was in a lot better shape now than I'd been a few months back, but I still couldn't push Geoffrey hard enough for the exercise to really be worthwhile for him.

Neither Venice or I wanted to risk tipping the set of scales inside his head over from the 'acceptable burden' side of things to 'time to cut my losses,' which meant that I needed to come up with a way to spend time with him where I'd actually be a help instead of just a hindrance.

Just before Venice had ordered dessert I'd finally come up with a decent, if still somewhat risky, option, which had left both of us in a celebratory mood, which had only been magnified when the waiter had brought over our check.

Actually Venice had been celebratory, I'd just been embarrassed. Flattered, but embarrassed. Calum had left his number in our bill with a brief note saying that he hadn't wanted to interrupt our conversation, but that he'd very much like a chance to take me out to dinner sometime.

It wasn't the first time that a boy had expressed interest in me, but I was understandably hesitant to use the number he'd left me. My first crush had gone really well, right up to the point where Renworst had threatened to kill him and Geoffrey had shipped us back to the city. The second experience hadn't really left me with a raging desire to try a third time. I wasn't particularly worried that Calum was going to try and rape me, but it just felt like the wrong time to be chasing after some random guy.

Once I made it home I slipped the piece of paper containing his number into my faded brown journal and then pushed him out of my mind. Geoffrey and I were supposed to go running the next morning and this particular run was more significant than most.

The next morning Geoffrey met me outside of my building just like he usually did. I pushed harder than normal, trying to give him a decent workout, but by the end I was gasping and wrung out and he was barely breathing hard.

We made it back to my building and Geoffrey turned to go, but around gasps I asked him to come upstairs for a minute. I could see him weighing me with his eyes, but after a couple of seconds he nodded and followed me inside.

"You pushed yourself a lot harder today than normal. How come?"

I made a mental note to ask Venice if she'd ever tried curiosity as a way of getting Geoffrey to engage as I shrugged.

"I think I just wanted a change. That was actually what I wanted to talk to you about."

I opened the apartment door and dropped my keys into the red cup on the ornamental table just inside of the living room. Geoffrey followed me in and folded his arms.

"I'm listening."

"A while back we talked and you said it would be okay for me to start picking my own tutors. Well, we never did anything there and I'd really like to get started."

"So pick them. I'll leave you the number for the company I use to run background checks on people. Do a search online to find some likely candidates, get references, run a background check on them and then hire whomever you want. You're an adult now; you don't need me to do some of this stuff for you."

It was looking like I'd caught him on an even worse day than I'd realized. I licked my lips, but it was too late to turn back at this point. If I didn't ask now it would be really hard to do it later.

"You're right, but I was thinking that I'd really like to learn more about business. I already purchased a couple of textbooks on the subject and I've been teaching myself a little, but I think a better way to learn would be by doing."

Geoffrey looked past me, glancing at the antique clock on the wall. "Is this your way of trying to get money out of me? Are you wanting to start up some kind of hobby business now?"

I shook my head quickly. It was starting to look like the only thing that had saved me before was the fact that we'd engaged so little during the blocks of time when he'd disassociated himself from me.

"I just wanted to see if you could use some assistance. You've got some kind of business presence, so I thought that I could help out. You wouldn't have to do much in the way of teaching me, just tell me what to go study and then give me a few tasks to do. I probably won't be much help to start out with, but I'd get better as time went on."

Venice had warned me that Geoffrey would be worried that I was trying to rob him, so I was already prepared to point out that he could just give me information-gathering jobs and keep me away from any of the real assets, but he didn't bring it up.

After several seconds he nodded. "Fine. For starters go off and learn everything you can about utilities."

"Okay. Why utilities though?"

"With all of the drilling going on in North America, there's been a real shock to the energy industry. Most people would agree that it's a good kind of shock, but anytime you introduce a significant new technology into a mature industry you end up with changes and if you understand the changes better than others do, then you can make money. It's too late to profit on the actual drilling side of things—that's probably where the biggest rewards would have been—but there's a chance that you can find something worthwhile in the utilities section of the process."

He'd just thrown me in the deep end of the pool without checking to see whether or not I could swim, but given that I was the one who'd initiated the conversation, there wasn't much I could do other than just nod and smile.

Chapter 9

March
Lucy's Age: 18

I'd only thought that I'd been lonely before. Not having anyone to talk to was pretty bad, but it was somehow worse when you had someone whom you should be able to talk to and couldn't for some reason.

Venice had pretty much dropped off the face of the earth. She still texted me every four hours to check in, but beyond that she might as well not have existed. I'd tried a couple of times to get her to tell me what was going on, but she just ignored my texts, that or told me that she didn't have time to talk.

I half wished that I could just go back to my old life, the one where all I did was read books and wish I had friends. It hadn't been any great shakes, but it was better than constantly worrying about whether or not the wheels were about to fall off of everything.

My internship with Geoffrey wasn't going very well either. I didn't know where to start when it came to finding a way to make money buying or selling utility companies, and I didn't even know where to go in order to start learning about that kind of thing.

After a couple of days of metaphorically running around with my head cut off, I decided I was going to just find out what utility companies actually did. I started reading up on power generation and before long I realized that what I was learning was actually pretty cool.

There was a Wikipedia entry on black starts that really got me interested in the subject. I'd never realized that it took power to start a generator, or that bigger generators can take a really long time to get up to where they are generating power like they are supposed to.

The concept of using a small battery to start a small generator, which would provide enough power to start a slightly bigger generator, which would turn on a bigger generator still, was fascinating. At that point I was hooked.

I read for hours every day, finding better and better sources for the information I was after. After a week of studying, I started feeling like a real expert on the subject.

Geoffrey showed up out of the blue two weeks after our run with an impatient look on his face. We hadn't run or had any kind of training sessions since I'd asked him to let me work for him. I hadn't been sure whether or not that was a good thing, but based on the way he held himself as he sat down across from me on the sofa, he didn't like the fact that he'd finally had to pay me a visit.

"So what have you learned?"

"A lot, I'm just not sure how it ties into the kinds of stuff that you want to know."

That earned me another frown, so I just started telling him everything I could remember. We ran through everything from the fact that currently only about five percent of the electricity in the United States was being generated via oil to rough estimates of the cost of deploying new generators to the fact that natural gas was now producing approximately as much electricity as coal.

Geoffrey's posture slowly relaxed over the course of my briefing. By the time I finished up, he was actually smiling.

"That's not bad. Let me go off and do some research of my own, and then I'll come back and tell you what I end up doing as far as my buy and sell positions. For now, I'm thinking that coal companies will come under some pressure, which will ripple through their entire supply chain. If I can find some equipment manufacturers whose stock hasn't started dropping yet, I can probably make some money by going short on it."

Geoffrey got up to leave, but turned back around when he got to the door. "I'm impressed. I never thought that this would work out, but if you can keep demonstrating this kind of dedication and smarts then we're going to be spending a lot more time together."

He was still smiling when he left. I collapsed back onto the couch as soon as the door swung shut, and started texting Venice the good news even before my butt hit the leather cushions.

I should have known that she wouldn't respond, that not even good news on this kind of epic scale would be enough to get her to break the veil of silence that she'd imposed on me lately.

I could hear Mrs. Phelps rattling around in her room, but she rarely came out other than to eat or use the bathroom, and even if she did come out, she was the last person that I wanted to go celebrate with.

Muscles One and Two were out as well, even assuming that I could convince them that it was okay for me to go out as long as they were with me. After two weeks of nearly solid studying I needed to blow off some steam and just going to the bookstore wasn't going to cut it. I needed more social interaction than that.

I sat on the couch for a few minutes before the perfect idea finally hit me. Calum's number was still in my journal, still waiting for me to get up enough courage or enough interest to call him. I went into my room and pulled the scrap of paper out of my journal. Several seconds of staring at the paper didn't help with regards to courage or interest either one, but ultimately my boredom was more than equal to the task.

I pulled my phone back out and dialed Calum's number. He picked up on the third ring.

"Hey, this is Calum."

"Hi, Calum. My name is Lucy, you might not remember me, but my friend and I ate at your restaurant a little while ago."

"Oh, hey, Lucy. Yeah, I remember you. Did you manage to get your friend home okay?"

It took me a second to figure out what he meant. It had been long enough that I'd forgotten just how much alcohol Venice had drunk that night.

"Yes, believe it or not she walked home the entire way under her own power."

"That's good, she's a good tipper. I'd hate to hear that something bad had happened to her."

I didn't know what to expect as far as my first call to a boy went, but this wasn't how these kinds of things seemed to go in the books that I'd read. I considered just waiting to see where he would take the conversation, but I didn't want to go out in a few days, I wanted to go out tonight.

I took a deep breath and just went for it. "Look, I've been super busy for the last little while, but I've ended up with an opening tonight and I want to take you up on your offer of a night out."

His chuckle practically reached out of the phone and caressed the side of my face. "I thought that you might be a take-charge kind of girl when I saw you. I've got to work tonight, but I can be free for lunch if you want."

"That sounds good."

"Cool, where do you want me to pick you up?"

I opened my mouth to give him my address and suddenly realized that more of Venice and Geoffrey's paranoia had rubbed off on me than I'd realized.

"I've got a couple errands that I need to run still today. How about if I just meet you?"

Another chuckle, this one even better than the first. "Take-charge and careful all at the same time. How about if we go up to the Gray's Papaya on Seventy-second and Amsterdam? We can have a quick lunch and then go up to the new film museum a few blocks over."

"That sounds good."

"Perfect, I'll see you there in two hours."

Chapter 10

March
Lucy's Age: 18

Calum turned out to be funny and carefree. Gray's Papaya wasn't the kind of place that Venice would ever approve of, but the hotdogs were tasty and it was amazing fun to watch the cooks as they fried up dozens of hotdogs all at once.

Calum seemed to know one of the employees because the guy took our orders and then handed us our food without any money changing hands. We ate our food while leaning against a long, narrow counter as people hurried past the window in front of us.

"So, Lucy, what exactly brings you to New York?"

I finished chewing and then shrugged. "Nothing actually brought me here, I was born here. We lived up in Yonkers for a few years, but the city is where most of my memories are. What about you?"

"I'm taking acting classes."

"I thought that Hollywood was the place to be for that kind of stuff."

"It definitely is if you want to do movies, but a lot of the television stuff gets filmed out here and television is a pretty good way to go because the stories tend to focus on more than just one or two characters. It's pretty hard to get noticed in a movie because you're either the star or you only get a couple of lines. Plenty of people start out in television though and build a fan base before jumping over to Hollywood."

It actually made a lot of sense, and I found myself wondering why I'd never made that connection before. It was amazing how the world was made up of a ton of small things that all came together to create order out of what looked like chaos, or sheer dumb luck, when you were looking at it from the outside. I'd just spent weeks learning about power generation, but there was a whole new world of rules when it came to acting that I didn't know anything at all about.

Calum interrupted my train of thought by waving a hand in front of my face. "Earth to Lucy. What do you do?"

"I'm a...student right now."

"What are you studying?"

I'd said that I was a student mostly because it was a safe thing to say, but I suddenly realized that it had been the truth.

"Kind of everything at some point or another, but currently I'm taking classes in business."

"Oh, no, a rabid capitalist!"

His tone sounded so serious that I looked over to check his expression. His face was so deadpan for a second that I wasn't sure how to respond, but he grinned a moment later and I felt my stomach unknot.

"Better a rabid capitalist than a layabout actor."

"Touché."

From there our conversation progressed through a relaxed, but fun, range of topics. I told Calum a little bit about how utilities worked and he talked about the different ways that posture or expression helped to sell a role.

Once we finished our hot dogs we walked over to the film museum that was a few blocks from Gray's Papaya. Calum was in heaven, but I'd seen so few of the movies that I didn't have much of a frame of reference for most of what he was talking about. The museum was nothing but a huge series of televisions each of which had a small plaque next to it explaining what was playing and why it was included in the collection.

Excerpts ranging from *Citizen Kane* to *Life is Beautiful* made up the displays and Calum seemed completely in his element. He claimed never to have been to this particular museum before, but he had something to say about each of the exhibits. His comments had a smattering of the discussion I'd expected about the craft displayed by the actors, but he spent even more time talking about camera angles, plot and lighting.

I was surprised by just how much he knew about so many of the different aspects of filmmaking, but when I expressed my admiration he just shrugged it aside.

"It's just part of landing a role. Craft is important, but knowing what's going on around you is one of the ways to help make sure you can deliver a good performance."

"Still, I'm impressed. I bet that there are a lot of aspiring actors in New York who don't know all of that."

"Yeah, you're probably right. Acting is one of those lucky break kind of professions. You do everything you can to be ready when your break comes along, but it can be hard to keep at it month after month when nothing happens for you. I guess I just figure that the more work I do now the better chance I'll have that I'll be able to recognize my break when it rolls around."

"You're pretty driven, aren't you?"

Calum looked down at his clothes with mock shock. "What gave me away? Was it the shoes?"

"No, silly. It was the fact that it sounds like you're working forty hours at the restaurant, another fifteen hours a week doing other odd jobs and you're still managing to take acting classes and study up on all of this director-type stuff."

"I would have said no, but it sounds like you've pretty much got me dead to rights after that. Yeah, I guess I'm pretty focused."

"So why hide it?"

Calum watched one of the monitors for a few moments before sighing. "I try to keep it on the down low because most people don't like driven individuals. Nerds get made fun of not just because they lack social skills, it's also because the other kids resent the fact that the nerds are working towards something more than just getting drunk or lucky, and their time horizon extends out to more than just what happens at the cool party this weekend. Nobody likes having it pointed out to them, however indirectly, that their priorities might be out of whack."

He'd provided a much more revealing answer than I'd expected to receive. I let it process for a couple of beats and then shrugged. "So you were a pretty big geek in high school then, I take it?"

"The biggest. Complete with double-bridged glasses and a year-round membership to the debate team."

"So why did you choose to pursue acting then?"

"The really good debaters have more than just facts to back up their arguments, they develop a kind of stage presence. I wanted to be a good debater, so I started studying anything and everything I could find that might help me get better onstage. I got contacts, changed my hairstyle, the whole nine yards. I was still planning on going to college until all of a sudden girls started hitting on me instead of the other way around."

"So you abandoned your college goals and decided to pursue acting full-time so you could get girls?"

"No, I realized pretty quickly that the girls who were hitting on me now were just interested in my looks. As soon as I started trying to talk to them about the kinds of stuff that I was really interested in, their eyes would glaze over. Once I was more attractive it became a lot harder to tell what girls were interested in me for who I was instead of just for what I looked like."

I was tempted to make a wisecrack about him having a big head or something like that, but it wasn't the right time for that. Besides, he really was extraordinarily hot.

"For a couple of days I was tempted just to go back to how I was before, but then I realized that that would just be putting the problem off. If I went to college and worked as hard as I could then eventually I'd have money and I'd just be looking at the same old problem. So I decided to just go off and do what made me the happiest."

Calum looked back over at me and gave me a wry smile. "So now I guess you know everything there is to know about me. Sorry, I don't usually info dump on people like that."

I put my arm through his and grinned at him. "I suspect that there is a lot more there underneath the surface than you've even hinted at yet. You're in luck though, I like driven people. By the way, when you agreed to have lunch with me I didn't realize just how precious your free time is. Thanks for this."

I actually managed to get a slight blush out of him. "So what about you, Lucy? What were you like in high school?"

His question was so unexpected that for a second I couldn't get a response out. "I...ah, I've never been to high school. I've just had private tutors ever since I was little. You're worried about people finding out how driven you are, well, I'm worried about people realizing that I have no social skills whatsoever."

Calum slipped my hand off of his arm and down into his hand, giving it a squeeze as he looked over at me again. "I think your social skills are just fine, Lucy. I hope that we can do this again sometime."

Chapter 11

May
Lucy's Age: 18

Geoffrey put his tablet down and rubbed his eyes. It was still before noon, but I'd realized a while ago that Geoffrey had a pretty inverted sleep schedule, so it was probably well past the time when he should be heading off to bed. I paused the slideshow on my tablet, which was currently mirroring onto his device, and asked if he wanted to stop.

"No, I only just arrived here half an hour ago. I appreciate all of the time and effort that you've put into pulling this presentation together. Quitting now and heading back home would be poor thanks indeed."

I shrugged. "The information will still be here tomorrow."

"I expect you're right there, but the real question is whether or not the opportunity will still be around then."

He had me there. I'd moved away from doing just background research and now my duties included a fair amount of investigation of actual companies. I'd found a very small company that created mounting kits that were a key component in putting up oil pipelines.

I'd also turned up some rumors indicating that the test drilling another small company had started to do in a previously unexplored section of Wyoming was going even better than their most optimistic assumptions.

The rumors were already pretty widely disseminated through the market, but based on the recent surge in the stocks for several refinery companies located in the general area, most of the market seemed to have decided that the most logical solution for the sudden oversupply of crude oil in the area would be for a new refinery to be put in.

It wasn't a bad conclusion all things considered, but I'd looked everywhere I could think, and all of the signs I'd turned up said that there was no way that anyone was going to manage to put a new refinery anywhere nearby. The entire area was swarming with environmentalists and there didn't seem to be a single piece of land within a hundred miles that was for sale, reasonably close to a road, and that looked like it would have a snowflake's chance of getting all of the relevant permits and approvals to even start a project of the scale needed for a new refinery.

I had, however, identified that the drilling company had a small corridor of land that they'd purchased under a shell company which could be used for a pipeline if they were willing to pony up the cash to install one.

All of the construction companies in that area of Montana that were large enough to take on a project of this size were all either privately held or trading at a definite premium as compared to where they'd been a couple of months ago.

That was my first sign that the smart money hadn't all just thrown itself at the refinery as being the only solution. I'd been nearly ready to quit until I found an interesting tidbit online. It was posted by an employee of one of the construction companies that had worked on the last major pipeline that had been built in Alaska.

The employee had been complaining about just how hard it was to get ahold of a tiny, but critical set of fasteners used in the initial stages of putting the sections of pipe together. A little more research turned up the fact that out of the four fastener manufacturers operating at the time of the posting, one had gone out of business, another had stopped manufacturing that particular fastener, and both of the other two were private companies.

One of the two private companies was a waste of time, but the last was an interesting proposition. All indications from the outside were that they had expanded much too quickly to meet the increase in the demand caused by two of their competitors leaving. They were running short on cash, and they'd lost a couple of key bids recently because the construction companies they'd been working with no longer had confidence that they'd be around long enough to complete the jobs in question.

After the quick and dirty finance course that Geoffrey had given me over the last few months, I'd known enough to realize that I needed to get him involved in this particular opportunity right away. All of which meant he was right. He needed to see this and he needed to see it right away if he was going to capitalize on it before someone else did.

I waited until Geoffrey had picked his tablet back up, and then started the slideshow back up. Half an hour later Geoffrey knew everything I knew about the target company and the overarching situation we were dealing with.

"That was very good, Lucy. I'll have to put in a call to the target's owner as soon as I make it back to my place. I guess that means I'm going to go without sleep for a few more hours."

I did some quick math in my head and the results weren't promising.

"Actually, if you wanted to you could just do the call from here. Your room is still empty and you've got your laptop. Once you're done with the call then you could just crash in your room. It would save you at least a couple hours of travel when you factor in the fact that you'll be checking your back trail on the way home. Not only that, it would mean that I would be nearby if something came up that you needed me to research or explain. It actually makes quite a bit of sense."

Geoffrey paused to consider the idea. A month ago he would have refused outright. Even now, after all of the time we'd spent together recently, I was pretty sure he would have vetoed the idea except for the fact that he really was exhausted.

"I don't want to put you or Mrs. Phelps out, Lucy. The two of you have had your own space for a really long time at this point."

It was a smokescreen, even I could see that, but the mere fact that he'd thought of it was a huge step up from where he'd been just after he'd gone all cold again. The old Geoffrey would never have thought about whether or not he was inconveniencing us, not even just in the context of needing an excuse not to stay around.

"You won't be putting us out. Mrs. Phelps mostly just stays in her room all day, and I can research as well from inside my room as I can from out here in the living room."

It was a lie, but I was pretty sure that Calum wouldn't mind me rescheduling our date. He seemed to get that I had commitments just like he had commitments, and if sometimes that meant that we didn't get to see each other, then at least we could spend a few minutes on the phone or texting every day.

Geoffrey looked at me for several seconds and then finally nodded. "You're right; my staying here today makes a lot of sense."

He stood up to go to his room, but there was an odd hitch to his movements. It reminded me a little of the way one of the assistant instructors back at my dojo had moved after having his ribs separated.

"What happened to you?"

Geoffrey tried for a casual smile. "Just a training injury. I pulled some muscles the other day. I'll probably be okay by tomorrow."

I'd seen Geoffrey take full-force kicks to the chest during our training sessions. I'd hit him hard enough to have broken a one-inch pine board and he'd never even flinched. There was no way I was going to buy the idea that a minor injury was the reason he was moving like that.

"I'm sorry to hear that. I hope you recover quickly; we're supposed to go on a run on Thursday."

This smile was much more relaxed. "I haven't forgotten. I'll come out and get you if I need anything, but I shouldn't need to interrupt you. These kinds of initial calls are usually pretty high-level."

I gave him a cheery wave as he disappeared into his room and then I retreated back into my bedroom and flopped down on the sea-foam green comforter. I texted Calum and got a response a few minutes later.

I'll miss you, but I understand that things come up. Hope you get a lot done, I'm excited to watch Castle *with you next week. We've got a lot of episodes to catch up on.*

I smiled and then dashed off another quick text.

You've got it. I can't wait to watch it too. I'll be thinking of you.

Venice's next check-in was nearly due, so I decided to ping her too.

Geoffrey is spending the day here. Seems like he's injured somehow. Things are progressing nicely though.

Venice's response arrived right on schedule, just like always.

Things are heating up lately. He took a sword to the chest, but he'll be okay. Glad to hear that he's relaxing a little.

My mouth practically hit the floor.

He got stabbed? I should get him to a hospital!

Calm down, Lucy. He'll be okay. Don't let on that you know how badly he's hurt or you'll blow everything.

She was right, there wasn't any way for me to get him to seek out some kind of medical care, at least not without clueing him into the fact that I knew a ton of stuff I wasn't supposed to know, but I still had a hard time calming down.

We were pretty sure that Geoffrey had decided not to invade my mind, although neither of us knew for sure why, but I wasn't confident enough in the mental exercises that Venice had shown me to think that it was a good idea to give Geoffrey any reasons to go poking around inside of my memories.

All of the logical arguments said that the best thing was for me to take Venice at her word and just assume that Geoffrey would be fine without any additional medical attention, but it was hard to force myself to just sit in my room and pretend like everything was okay.

I'd started out wanting to save Geoffrey for Venice's sake. That and a little bit out of gratitude for everything that he'd done for me over the years. More and more however, I was seeing the same kinds of qualities under the surface that made Venice love him.

I no longer had any doubts about whether or not Geoffrey was worth saving. Now it was just a question of whether or not we could pull it off in time or not.

Chapter 12

Calum pushed play on the DVR and then pulled me down onto the beat-up microfiber couch next to him. I loved being close to him, so I didn't protest when he put his arm around me. We watched the episode and then as the credits started to roll Calum leaned over and gently brushed his lips across mine.

I leaned into the kiss for a few seconds before pulling back.

"Tell me about your week."

He shrugged, nicely toned muscles rippling under his blue polo shirt. "Not much to tell. Lots of work, two more auditions that I'm pretty sure aren't going to pan out, and then a few idle hours looking forward to seeing you."

This was the part of our relationship that I didn't enjoy. Calum was attractive, and he was driven in his own way, but the things that he was investing himself in seemed so trivial to me lately. Sometimes it really did feel like we were from two different planets.

He seemed to sense my mood, leaning back and looking at me with more seriousness than was usual for him.

"I picked up a new technique the other day, but you don't care about that, so let's talk about your week."

Now I felt bad. "It's not like that, Calum."

"I think it is like that, Lucy. You're different lately. I like that you're serious, but you're serious all of the time now. Everything is high-stakes this and super-important that. It's like you don't know how to have fun anymore."

"I know how to have fun, but not everything is about having fun. Don't you ever wish you were making a difference?"

Apparently I scored a solid blow with that one because Calum stood up and backed a couple of steps away from the couch. "We can't all be playing with million-dollar investments out of the gate, Lucy. I'm doing what I want to be doing. I'm learning the stuff that I want to be learning, and I'm putting myself in a position where someday I will be making enough money to make a difference, and it will be my own money, not somebody else's."

I opened my mouth to respond back with something petty and spiteful, but his last comment managed to shut me up. He was right. I was putting in a tremendous amount of work and Geoffrey was making a ton of money off of the things I was helping him find, but it wasn't my money and I had no control over what use it would ultimately be put to.

It was something that had been worrying at the back of my mind for weeks now, and it showed how well Calum knew me that he was able to identify what was bothering me like that. I'd been taking my frustrations out on him.

"I'm sorry, Calum. You're right. I shouldn't be busting your chops like that."

I held out my hand and when he took it I tugged him back down onto the couch.

"I don't like fighting with you, Lucy."

"I know. I don't like fighting with you either, it just seems like it's all the two of us seem to be able to do lately."

Chapter 13

September
Lucy's Age: 18

Venice and I had finally managed to get back together for dinner. We'd eaten out at some pretty lowbrow establishments lately, but this time she'd insisted on somewhere nicer. Thankfully she'd picked a new restaurant this time, so we wouldn't be eating at Calum's restaurant.

Not surprisingly, she beat me there. I looked her over through a window as I hurried to the door. She was tapping her hand against her thigh, indicating that she was getting tired of waiting for me, but that wasn't what caught my attention first.

The entire right side of her back was the angry red of a major sunburn. For once I was pretty sure that the thin, silk tank top she was wearing was more about trying to be comfortable than about her undeniable need to be sexy.

Venice had already worked her magic on the hostess, so we were seated within seconds of my arrival. I watched as Venice settled back into her chair with a grimace of pain.

"What happened?"

Venice did a quick check to make sure we wouldn't be overheard and then just gave up trying to get comfortable with her back against the chair and leaned forward.

"Imastious put us up against one of our own kind. A pretty powerful chick whose gift happens to be lighting things on fire. You should have seen me a few days ago, it wasn't pretty."

There was something about that statement that didn't add up for me, but I'd learned that there were things that Venice invariably refused to talk about. Besides, she'd already started moving on.

"I thought I had her dead to rights and then suddenly my whole side of the room went up in flames. I kept her busy for just long enough for Geoffrey to worm his way inside of her mind though and he put his sword into her a second or so before she would have burned me to a crisp."

Venice took a long drink of water and then held the cool glass against her right arm. "I can't even begin to explain how good that feels."

"Does it still bother you?"

"What, nearly getting killed while doing Imastious' dirty work?"

Even as the words had left my mouth I'd realized that I was headed towards treacherous ground, but it was too late to take them back now. Venice wasn't a mentalist but she was incredibly good at telling when I was lying to her.

"All of the people you kill."

Her jaw clenched slightly, but she took a deep, calming breath before responding. "Every damn day, but not this one. She was bad to the core. The world is a better place with her gone."

I nodded, but she could tell I wasn't convinced. "Look, Lucy. I have a very good idea of just how many people she's killed over the years and the number would shock you. There wasn't a single redeeming quality about her, trust me on this one."

I held my hands up and made a calming motion. "I'm sorry, Venice. I do trust you; it's just still a little hard for me to adjust to. I've led a pretty sheltered life up to this point."

She rubbed the side of her head like she was starting to get a migraine or something and then nodded. "Yeah, I know. Geoffrey has kept you wrapped in cotton for the last decade and a half. I'm sorry too. I didn't mean to bite your head off, I'm just not always comfortable with my actions either."

"That's a good sign, Venice. You don't have a choice about all of this right now, but you will someday soon. We'll get you and Geoffrey out of this and then you'll never have to kill anyone else ever again."

She gave me an odd look, but as well as I knew her I apparently still didn't know her well enough to be able to interpret all of her expressions. "Yeah, that will be nice."

She took another drink of water and then shrugged. "That's all for a future day, though. What about you? How are things going with your boyfriend?"

I once again wished that I'd never told her that I'd gone ahead and gone on that first date with Calum. Even after so many weeks of teasing I still blushed every time she brought him up. Venice took in my red cheeks and smiled even wider.

"Hmm, that's an even better reaction than normal. Did you guys finally get horizontal?"

I hadn't thought it possible for my cheeks to get even hotter. "No! Calum has been a real gentleman. I told him that I wasn't ready for any of that yet and he's respected my wishes."

Venice rolled her eyes at me. "Fine, fine. Have you at least started wearing something more exciting than jeans and a tee-shirt on your dates? I mean, really, the boy has needs."

I actually had started breaking out some of the clothes that Venice had bought me. Only the tamer stuff, but still, it had been nice to see Calum's eyes light up a little when I'd shown up in something slightly sexier than my normal attire. I wasn't going to admit that to Venice though, not when it would just mean I was setting myself up for more teasing down the road.

"No, I haven't. Calum likes me just fine how I am, thank you very much."

It was a lie, but only the first part. Calum wouldn't have stopped dating me because of what I did or didn't wear. He really was amazing in so many ways, which made me feel all the guiltier since I wasn't enjoying being with him as much lately.

"If that's true then Calum is even more boring than you've made him out to be."

Venice had been picking at her food when she'd said it, but she looked up quick enough to catch my expression, which apparently wasn't as controlled as I thought.

"Uh-oh. What's wrong?"

I shrugged, but I knew that I couldn't just leave things there, not after making Venice mad at me earlier.

"It's hard to describe. I guess I'm just not as into Calum as I was back when we first started dating."

Venice nodded gravely. "Does he seem concerned with boring, unimportant stuff? Do you feel like he wastes all of his time?"

I nodded, almost in spite of myself. Her level of insight was astonishing. She'd just nailed the heart of my problem with Calum. It wasn't his fault, not really, which was probably part of why I'd had such a hard time being honest with myself about why our relationship had been off lately.

"I guess that really is the main problem. I don't understand it though. My entire life I've been taught that he's the kind of guy I should be interested in. He's nice, he's thoughtful, he's driven, and he's talented. The goals he's working towards aren't anything earthshattering, but they are perfectly acceptable compared to the kind of things that most everyone else wants to accomplish. I shouldn't feel this way."

Venice's smile was sad. "The heart wants what the heart wants, Lucy. The world is made up of all kinds of people and sometimes you're surprised by who you turn out to want."

It was the kind of metaphysical doubletalk that my sensei used to spout as an explanation for what was right or wrong with the world. I'd hated it then, and I didn't particularly like it now. Apparently my unhappiness showed through because Venice patted my hand and shrugged.

"Now that you've identified the cause of your unhappiness you have a couple of options you should consider. You can ignore the fact that you're unhappy and try to make the relationship work despite the fact that you want something different than him. You may tell yourself that you can change, that you can get to the point where he doesn't bore you to tears, but I'm not sure that's possible."

I wanted to object. Everything we were doing with Geoffrey was based on the idea that he could change, either for the better or the worse. It didn't seem fair to just blithely assume that *I* couldn't change. I opened my mouth to tell Venice she was oversimplifying things, but the words wouldn't leave my throat. As much as I wanted to believe otherwise, something inside me seemed to agree with her, seemed to think that I wouldn't ever be able to reach a point where I wanted Calum in the way that I should want him.

"Ah, good. I thought maybe you'd put up more of a fight than that. Now that we've got that rather stupid option off of the table, we can move onto options that are at least marginally better. You could try to change Calum, try to make him over to something that's more appealing to you."

I shook my head. "I don't think that would be fair to Calum, even assuming it's possible. He likes who he is right now, it seems pretty selfish to try and make him into a new person just so that I can be happy."

Venice tapped the table a couple of times and then nodded. "I have to agree with you, at least about it not being possible to change him. You wanting to avoid being selfish probably rules out the next possibility though."

"What's that?"

"Don't try to change him, don't try to change you, just enjoy the relationship for what it is, or what it could become."

My ears heated up at what she was implying, but I shook my head. "You know that's not me, Venice."

She shrugged. "Then your only real remaining option is just to call it quits. You can be nice about it or you can be mean, but if you're not going to change or try to change him, then eventually you're going to break up, it's just a matter of time."

I put my face in my hands and sighed. "You're right. Why does dating have to suck so bad?"

"You haven't seen anything yet, love. At least this time you're the one in the driver's seat. It sucks a lot worse when you find the one you want to be with but they aren't so sure they reciprocate the feeling."

"Geoffrey still not progressing very well?"

"He's coming back to us and he's doing it faster even than what I've seen in the past, but he still doesn't seem very interested in me. I've done everything but strip down naked and wait in his bed for him to get home."

I forced myself not to blush this time, which still seemed to amuse Venice. She watched for a couple of seconds to see if I'd lose my inner battle and then made a throwing away gesture.

"I tried that a few years ago and it didn't work then, so there doesn't seem much point in trying it again now."

"I'm sorry, Venice. I wish there was something else I could do. I can't exactly push him in your direction given that I'm not supposed to even know you exist."

"I know. It's just one of those sucky things that I'm going to have to deal with for the time being. I'm trying to just focus on the fact that he's progressing in other areas so well. Tell me some good news so I don't feel like throwing myself off of a building."

I frowned at her joke, but she waved my concerns away. "Come on, spill it. I really, really need to hear about some positive developments."

"Well, I'm not sure that there is much to tell. It's mostly just a slow, steady change without much in the way of big developments to talk about. He's more relaxed around me, and I don't get the feeling that he's still trying to decide whether or not to just abandon me to save himself the hassle of dealing with a daughter that he wasn't sure he still wanted."

Venice raised her glass in a mock toast. "Hear, hear. I'm all for him keeping you around. What else?"

"I don't know, he laughs more than he used to and he smiles when he sees me. You know, just the same kind of stuff that you'd expect out of a normal person."

"Anything else? Anything at all?"

Venice looked almost like she was going to cry, which in another girl wouldn't have been unusual. Tears are always a cause of concern, of course, but with Venice it was practically a sign of the apocalypse. Desperate for some bit of news that would cheer her up, I cast about through my memories of the last few days and suddenly I remembered the really odd gift he'd given me just a little while ago.

"Ah, I almost forgot. He gave me a present. It was the oddest thing he could have possibly given me, but he said something about wanting to reward me for all of my hard work lately."

Venice had been shifting around in her seat, leaning back until her skin actually touched the dark wood of the chair and then sitting forward again as the pain reminded her of the burns on her back. She went instantly still at my announcement.

"What was the gift?"

"He gave me an old samurai sword. It had a certificate of authenticity and everything."

"It wasn't any kind of gag gift if that's what you're thinking, Lucy. A sword like you're describing is worth millions of dollars and in fact it may very well be priceless."

I felt like I'd been hit. Somehow I'd never realized the sheer value of what Geoffrey had given me.

"Why a sword? If he was going to spend that kind of money on me why didn't he just buy me a car or something else more practical? I know that we've been studying kenjitsu together, but I still don't understand why he'd give me a priceless sword."

"Think of it as being a kind of odd graduation present. It means that he thinks you're accomplished enough with a blade to avoid hurting yourself, but more importantly it means that inside of his head you've moved out of the liabilities column and into the assets column."

My earlier words to Venice came rushing back at me and I looked down and realized that I was shaking.

"I don't want to kill anybody, Venice. All of the unarmed combat is okay because I can defend myself in such a way as to not kill my opponent. The kenjitsu is okay when it was just learning in the abstract, but I don't want to be dragged into your world, not like that."

Venice gave me a reassuring smile. "You're not in any danger yet, at least not in any more danger than you've been in all along. I expect he's viewing you as more a financial asset than a combat asset. I've been through the process Geoffrey uses to turn someone into a fighter and you are still only skimming the surface."

A part of me wanted to ask her what she meant, what kinds of things Geoffrey would expose me to once he decided to start preparing me for combat operations, but I already knew. She'd avoided getting into the specifics on a lot of things, but I had a pretty good imagination.

I was still shaking, but Venice reached across the table again and took my hand in both of hers. "You don't have to keep doing this, Lucy.

You could walk away tomorrow if you wanted to. Take whatever money he's left there at the apartment and just disappear. I've got some money saved up that Imastious doesn't know about that I could give you too. Odds are that Geoffrey never implanted the kind of captivity protocols in your mind that Imastious put inside of mine."

"What if you're wrong? What if I run away and then just go exactly where he programmed me to go? He'll find me in a matter of days."

Venice bit her lip. "It's a possibility. I don't think it's likely, but things could happen that way. Even if he did find you again though, I don't think that he'd be nasty to you, not if you played things like you were just some troubled teen who wanted away from home."

"That's predicated on him still caring about me. If he has to sanitize his memories for some reason then all of that would go out the window."

Venice's nod was slow, like she wished that she didn't have to agree with me. "Yeah, there is that. Look, I don't think that you need to be worrying right now anyways. This present is a good sign; it means that Geoffrey is trying to reconnect with you in a whole new way. I was actually starting to worry that he hadn't given one of us a gift before now."

"What do you mean?"

"Geoffrey tends to come back from being a cold, emotionless bastard in a regimented set of steps. One of the milestones is a gift to someone he cares about. Usually he finds a way to rationalize it away as something non-sentimental, but the fundamental truth is that he wants to connect with people. It's his basic nature, and even after his emotions have been wiped away he still finds ways to continue to interact with people, he just justifies it all as being pure self-interest."

Venice let go of my hands and gave me a smile that did a good impression of being heartfelt, but wasn't quite convincing enough, not to fool me.

"This really is a good thing."

Her words and her expression didn't quite match up. It took me a couple of seconds to put together the pieces that had been there staring me in the face during the entire conversation.

"He usually connects with you. You're the one he should have given this gift to, not me. I'm so sorry, Venice. I'll go home and get it right now. It should be yours, not mine."

Venice grabbed my arm, pulling me back down into my seat in a casual display of strength that still seemed unnatural regardless of how many times I'd seen her do something similar.

"Sit down, Lucy. You need to keep that present and you need to display it prominently somewhere in your apartment so that Geoffrey knows that you still have it and that you value it."

She let go of my arm and looked away from me for a moment. "Look, I'm not going to lie to you and say that I'm overjoyed at the fact that Geoffrey is so much closer to you than he is to me, but the truth of the matter is that I want him out from under Imastious' thumb and if that means that he bonds with you instead of bonding with me, then that's a price that I'm willing to pay."

"What if I'm not willing to pay it?"

"I'm not asking for you to sleep with him, Lucy. Just keep doing what you're doing. Interact with him, help him with his business ventures, be someone he can trust. I really should have seen this coming. Geoffrey's need to be close to someone is so intense that it is sufficient to even overcome his inherent distrust of anyone who's a...anyone who's in our line of work. It only makes sense that this time around he's going to become closest to you. He can trust you. Becoming close to you is straightforward and uncomplicated. "

She looked back at me and I saw utter conviction in her eyes, but there was nothing inside of me that even began to approach her level of certainty. I couldn't help but feel like my whole world was balancing on the edge of the precipice. I couldn't stop moving, but each step carried with it the chance that everything I knew would come crashing down.

Chapter 14

November
Lucy's Age: 18

The weather was cold enough that I'd donned several layers, but Geoffrey was only wearing running tights and a light gray jacket when he met me in front of my building.

"Are you ready for something a little more challenging today, Lucy?"

I started to say no, but by the time they made it out past my lips the words had turned into an emphatic agreement.

Geoffrey smiled at my excitement and then headed off at something only slightly faster than his usual pace, trusting that I'd be able to keep up. We covered the first mile before I was able to put my finger on why I'd agreed to a route that was even more punishing than what we usually ran.

A DARKNESS MIRRORED

I needed a distraction, and it was more than just Geoffrey's lycra-covered legs and butt that I needed to be distracted from.

Venice's analysis of why I was unhappy with Calum had been spot on, but it had missed one hugely important detail. The reason that Calum was coming up short was that I kept comparing him to Geoffrey. In any kind of sane universe I would have stuck with Calum instead of breaking up with him a few days after Venice and I talked.

Calum had been nice and safe, but both of the times that I'd seen him before I broke things off I'd just kept thinking that things would have been so much better if he were a little more dangerous. It wasn't until I'd broken things off with Calum and then went and sparred with Geoffrey the next day that things finally clicked for me.

It wasn't just that I didn't want Calum, it was that I wanted Geoffrey. We'd been in the middle of practicing knife techniques and I'd feinted to the left as a precursor to trying to run my pot metal practice blade along the inside of Geoffrey's right arm.

In a real fight that would have helped start bleeding him out and made his knife slippery, only my knife never actually managed to connect with his skin. Geoffrey had captured my right wrist and hit me in the ribs hard enough to knock the wind out of me.

I'd sat there wheezing for half a minute as I'd tried to get my breath back, and all I could think about was the fact that it was nice to be around someone who expected me to be able to take whatever they could dish out.

Being wrapped in tissue paper and treated like a porcelain doll might be nice from time to time, but in order for me to be okay with a guy treating me like that he'd have to have proved that he could tie me up in knots if push came to shove.

I managed to succeed in my attempts to pass my sudden awkwardness off as nothing more than the last effects of how hard he'd hit me, but the truth was that the blow that had put me down this time wasn't physical.

Since then I'd tried everything I could think of to convince myself that I didn't like Geoffrey. He was the closest thing I had left to a living father figure. He had tortured people, including Venice, and he had killed dozens, maybe even hundreds of people.

Every logical piece of my being said that I needed to root out any attraction for Geoffrey, but I just kept thinking about how far he'd come in the last few months.

The situation was rapidly becoming intolerable. I needed to put some distance between us if I was going to be able to keep my feelings under control at all, but if I did that it would just set back his progress.

A DARKNESS MIRRORED

Venice had been this close a couple of times before, but both times Imastious had been circling Geoffrey for one reason or another and he'd erased his emotions. Every time I was tempted to get out of a run or plead ill to avoid a business briefing, I'd think about just how much time and energy had gone into getting Geoffrey to the point where he would joke with me. I'd remember the way that he'd been coldly weighing my value the first few times that we'd interacted after he'd lost all of his feelings.

Most of all though I'd remember the fear in Venice's voice when she'd first told me that she wasn't sure that Geoffrey would be able to come back from the edge of the void again.

I'd done the best that I could to keep things the same between us, but I wasn't succeeding very well. My attraction for Geoffrey continued to grow, and there had been an odd strain to our conversations lately.

All by itself that would have been enough to make me miserable, but there was Venice to consider as well. Venice and I had talked a couple of times over the last few weeks, but those conversations had felt forced. On her part, it seemed to mostly be about the fact that things were getting more hectic on the operational front, but on my part it was sheer guilt over the fact that I was slowly losing my battle to remain disinterested in the man that she'd loved for the last several years.

I'd tried to tell Venice what was happening, but I hadn't been able to make myself do it. Instead of clearing the air and just dealing with the consequences of my feelings, I'd let it sit there, festering between us. I was a terrible person and a worse friend.

Geoffrey poured on a little more speed as we got clear of the traffic and entered Central Park. I'd been outside of my comfort zone, running wise, for the first part of the run but now I was flirting with the upper edge of my aerobic capacity.

My breath was coming harder now and I could feel the first signs of lactic acid buildup in my legs, but I grinned and just pushed through the discomfort. In a few minutes the discomfort would turn into pain, but for now I could lose myself in the task of simply keeping my legs moving fast enough to stay within a dozen feet of Geoffrey.

We started up the slight incline that would take us to the top of the great hill and I crossed over fully into an anaerobic state. My lungs were screaming now and I was gasping for air, but I kept pushing. We made it to the top of the hill and my body gave out on me. I made it over to a park bench before collapsing, but it was a close thing.

Geoffrey ran for another fifty yards before he looked back, realized that he'd lost me and jogged back in my direction. He pulled down the swath of fleece covering his nose and mouth as he got closer.

"Sorry. It didn't look like that much of an elevation increase, but I should have realized that it would push you over the edge."

I waved away his apology. I'd been demolished, but I at least had the satisfaction of seeing that Geoffrey was breathing hard this time.

"It's not your fault; I could always have just slowed down a little as I started up the hill."

I'd stretched out on the black iron bench within seconds of reaching it, but Geoffrey just lifted my legs up and slid under them so that he was sitting on the bench with my legs across his lap. As far as physical contact went it was about as casual as it came, but it was all I could do to tear my thoughts away from the feel of having his rock-hard quads under my trembling calves with nothing more than a few millimeters of material between us.

"You're getting faster."

"Yeah, but still not fast enough. I swear, you're practically a machine. How many years will I have to train before I can keep up with you?"

He'd gone slightly stiff at my comment, but it was the kind of thing that I'd only recently come to know him well enough to catch. As always, the signs that something had put him off balance were gone almost instantly. He turned slightly more in my direction and then shrugged as he put an arm across my legs.

"Lots of years, but don't let that bother you. The important thing is that you're improving."

As my breathing started to slow back down, I closed my eyes for a second and just drank in the sensation of his touch on my legs. I knew it was a bad idea even while I was doing it, but I couldn't seem to stop myself. I tried to keep my feelings off of my face, but I must not have entirely succeeded because when I opened my eyes back up Geoffrey was staring at me with an odd expression on his face.

His face snapped back to the normal, semi-guarded expression that he wore most of the time, and I realized that he knew something was up. His half-poker face was infinitely better than the rock-like mien he used whenever the two of us weren't alone, but I relished the few infrequent moments when his guard seemed to come down all of the way.

My lack of self-control apparently hadn't just tipped him off as to the fact that something wasn't quite right between us. It had also deprived me of the chance to see him at his most vulnerable. Things could have become awkward, but Geoffrey demonstrated more of the smooth conversational footwork that had become second nature for him as he'd left behind the cold cyborg he'd been, and regained some of his humanity.

Geoffrey casually slid out from under my legs and off of the bench. I was pretty sure that it was my imagination, but the motion had seemed almost *too* casual.

"Come on, we need to get you up and moving again or you're going to get cold and stiff."

I took Geoffrey's hand and allowed him to help me to my feet. Part of me wanted to keep ahold of his hand even after I regained my balance. It would force the issue and bring my feelings out into the open, but I knew it would be one of the most selfish acts I could pursue.

I didn't want to devastate Venice, and I didn't want to freak Geoffrey out, so I forced myself to let go after only a second or so. It was still a half-beat longer than I should have maintained the contact if I'd wanted to keep the appearance that things were normal, but it was the best I could manage.

I silently cursed myself as Geoffrey started back down the hill. I knew the complications that my feelings would create, but I couldn't seem to help myself. Even the knowledge that Geoffrey would be freaked out if he knew what his 'daughter' was thinking didn't seem capable of curbing my desires.

"Do you want to run back home?"

I shook my head. "Not yet, I don't think I could make it five minutes, even at our normal pace. You can run on ahead if you want. I just need to walk for a few minutes."

I expected him to head back home without me. Lately he was even busier than normal, but instead he just nodded and waited for me to catch up.

"You don't have somewhere you need to be?"

"Honestly? Yes, but it can wait. I'd rather not leave you alone out here."

"If you're worried about me being tailed home I can take extra precautions."

Geoffrey shook his head and kept walking. I knew I should find another reason to send him on without me, for both our sakes, but I was out of ideas. We walked in companionable silence for several minutes before Geoffrey looked over at me and sighed.

"I'm sorry if I'm being overly paranoid, the less desirable elements of my work have started to heat up lately and sometimes that makes it hard not to see bad guys behind every tree and rock. I'll go if you want me to."

My common sense was yelling for me to send him off, but my unhealthy obsession with him had one benefit. I could read him better than I'd been able to even just a few months ago. I wasn't anywhere near as good at it as Venice was, but this felt like one of those turning points.

Even now, it was so rare for him to volunteer anything about his life that I couldn't bring myself to waste the opportunity he'd just handed me. I shook my head and then cleared my throat.

"What's going on that's got you so worried?"

Geoffrey reached over and took my arm as we got to a patch of ice on the sidewalk. I'd just hurdled it on the run earlier, but ironically now that we were moving at a more sedate pace it represented more of a danger than it had before. We crossed the ice and then Geoffrey let go of my arm. My disconnect from reality was so bad that I fancied that he'd held onto me for a split second longer than he'd had to, but I knew that was nothing more than my illness talking.

"I've got a…competitor who's been sniffing around more than normal. A certain amount of that is unavoidable, but there are things that I have to make sure I keep secret from him or the consequences could be severe."

"You're not talking just about money this time, are you?"

Pumping him, however subtly, for information was risky, but I had a suspicion that I already knew who the 'competitor' was. If I was right then Venice needed to know.

"No, not just money. Don't get me wrong, there is a lot of money at stake as well, but he's incredibly dangerous and he doesn't operate by what you would call civilized rules of engagement."

"You don't usually compete with people directly. Usually the market itself helps shield your identities from each other. Who is this guy and why can't you just fade back away so that the two of you aren't in direct conflict anymore?"

The risk level had just shot up again, but I'd managed to set the bait with this comment. All that remained was to see whether or not he would bite.

"He...his name is Imastious. I wish that I could just walk away, but the situation is complicated. He's not the kind of person to just let an issue drop."

For a second it looked like Geoffrey was going to say something else, but then he looked off to the left and I realized that I'd pushed him as far as I could go for today. I debated the proper response for a couple of seconds and then grabbed his arm and hugged it in what I hoped was a familial manner.

"Just be careful, Geoffrey. Don't do anything hasty. It sounds like you and this...Imastious have been rivals for a long time. Maybe the situation has changed slightly and you haven't realized it because you're still operating under your initial analysis. Maybe you have more options now than you did way back when."

Geoffrey gave me an odd look, but he didn't say anything. I tugged him into a jog and then let go of his arm. I needed to get home as soon as possible. Venice needed to know about this.

Chapter 15

December
Lucy's Age: 18

Venice had put me off for a couple of days. After my third text all but begging her to meet with me, she'd finally told me that she just wasn't going to be able to see me any sooner than she'd already agreed to.

It wasn't a situation designed to calm me down. On the one hand I had Geoffrey, who might decide to scrub his emotions at any point, and on the other I had Venice who already seemed pissed at me and I hadn't even told her about my feelings for Geoffrey yet.

The nightmares came back with a vengeance and made me wish for the days when I'd wanted to see the face of the nebulous figure who'd always been so central to them. He was still there, still shrouded in shadows, but the blood and flames had taken center stage in my dreams. I got the feeling that I was trapped somehow, that I wanted to move but couldn't as the flames got closer and closer. It made for restless nights which in turn made me even more jittery and nervous about what was going to go wrong between now and whenever I finally got Venice up to speed.

When the day of our meet finally arrived, I pulled myself out of bed earlier than normal, showered, and then hurried off to the designated spot more than three hours before our scheduled time. I watched the empty bench in the park for twenty minutes before I finally realized what I was doing. Apparently I was channeling even more Geoffrey than normal because I was casing out the meeting spot.

Everything about this discussion with Venice was fraught with risk, and it wasn't just being driven by the fact that I had feelings for Geoffrey. That was an obvious problem, but from what I knew of Venice so far, she wasn't going to take the fact that Imastious was sniffing around again very well.

Honestly I wasn't taking it very well myself and this was really just my first attempt at bringing Geoffrey back from the abyss. For Venice, who'd already tried and failed so many times before, this was going to be enough to send her into a screaming rage unless I handled things just right.

A DARKNESS MIRRORED

Geoffrey, even the new and improved version, probably would have brought a weapon to the meet, but I didn't go that far. No matter what happened, this was at least mostly my fault. I wasn't going to kill Venice, even assuming that was possible given how much better she was than me at unarmed combat. No, I didn't want to fight Venice. I'd do the best I could with my words and then accept the consequences of having betrayed her.

Apparently I wasn't the only one who was feeling unsettled. Venice arrived twenty minutes early and looked like she was about to take up a surveillance position herself until she saw me. She gave me an odd look and then waved me over to the bench that I'd just spent the last few hours watching.

"All right, Lucy, what's got you so worked up?"

"I talked to Geoffrey on Friday and he said that Imastious is sniffing around. It sounded like Geoffrey was worried about the things that Imastious might find out."

Venice looked away from me for several seconds, and then when she looked back in my direction she was obviously not happy.

"This is what you dragged me out here for? Why didn't you just text me, Lucy? Hell, even a phone call would have been better than waiting three days to pass that kind of information on."

"I tried to tell you. Usually you can meet up with me the same day or at least the day after I contact you. This is too important to just leave to a text. We need to figure out what we're going to do."

"No, *we* don't need to figure anything out. I need to go find a way to pull Imastious off of Geoffrey's trail, preferably one that doesn't end up with me being bled out so that Imastious can figure out why I'm suddenly so interested in his comings and goings."

"Why are you acting like this?"

Venice didn't answer, at least not immediately. Instead I watched as she visibly tried to get ahold of her emotions.

"Geoffrey came to me a few days ago. For months now I've been hoping that he'd act on the memories of all of our time together and that he'd decide that he wanted to have that again with me. You have no idea how excited I was. I wanted to scream for joy right up until I realized that he didn't want me, he just wanted someone to take his mind off of the person he actually did want to be with."

I'd known for more than a year that Venice and Geoffrey had been together in the past, but somehow I hadn't anticipated that he might go back to her again now, after all of the time that had passed without him evidencing that kind of interest in her. I wanted to back away, to stand up and put more distance between the two of us, but I knew that would be a mistake. As tightly as Venice was strung right now there was no telling how she'd react.

"So the two of you are together again now?"

I'd done my absolute best to keep my voice from showing the raging torrent of emotions washing through me, but Venice still saw through me.

"Don't give me that innocent act, Lucy. I know. I've known for weeks now. I even tried to give you a heads up of what you were in for the last time we went out to eat, but you weren't ready to hear it. I thought that I could deal with this because I saw it coming, but I also thought that you'd come tell me when *you* finally realized that you had feelings for Geoffrey."

"You knew all along?"

My voice came out as something less than a whisper, but Venice nodded. Some of the tension seemed to have gone out of her now that the issue of her, Geoffrey and I was out in the open finally. She was feeling better, but my sense of betrayal, of me having betrayed her and of Geoffrey having betrayed me, hadn't vanished.

"Yes. I knew it was a possibility all along, but the last time we sat down together it was obvious to me that you weren't interested in what's-his-name precisely because of your feelings towards Geoffrey."

I knew I was close to tears, but apparently Venice could tell too. Moving carefully so as not to startle me, she reached over and patted my arm.

"I didn't sleep with him, Lucy. I wanted to. You have no idea how badly I wanted to, but I didn't because I knew how it would make you feel."

Her admission pushed me over the edge and I started crying. "I'm so sorry, Venice. I've tried not to fall in love with him. I've tried so hard because it's wrong on every level. He's not just some random guy, he's yours. Not only that, he's what? My dad?"

Venice pulled me into a hug. "I told you already, Lucy. The heart wants what the heart wants. You can't help that any more than I can help *my* feelings for him. As for the other, Geoffrey isn't your father, not really. There's no blood relationship there and you barely saw him at all growing up. Besides, the Geoffrey you're falling in love with now isn't really the same person as the one who paid Renworst to raise you."

"I know. It just still seems wrong to have let myself get to this point. How are you handling all of this so calmly?"

Her shrug was eloquent all by itself, but she took pity on me and answered my question. "I'm not, not really. I may look serene on the outside, but I'm probably just as big of a mess inside as you are. It gets a little easier with time. Like I said, I saw this coming a while ago. I thought about all kinds of things that I could have done to try and head it off before it got to this point, but ultimately it comes down to the fact that you are good for Geoffrey."

I tried to shake my head but she stopped me. "It's true, Lucy. He's coming back to himself much faster now than he ever has before. I'm kind of a selfish be-otch, but if I have to choose between a dead Geoffrey or a live Geoffrey who's with someone else then I guess I choose to have him be alive and happy with someone else."

I wiped the tears away from the corners of my eyes and shrugged. "I don't know why I'm such a baby. It's not like anything has been decided. With Imastious looking like he's going to cause problems, there's not even any guarantee that we'll get him out."

"There's no guarantee, but there's still a chance. I meant what I said earlier. I'm going to go back home and spend some time thinking about ways that I could distract Imastious. With a little luck I should be able to buy us some more time."

I felt the tiniest ray of hope start to shine forward into the future, but Venice held up a warning hand before I could get carried away too far.

"One thing needs to be clear between us, Lucy. I'm not giving up on Geoffrey. Not on getting him out from under Imastious' thumb, or romantically either. Right now we both have roles to fill, but if we get him away, take him somewhere safe where he can start to trust me again, then I'm going to do everything I can to win him back. I consider you to be a friend, but the heart wants what the heart wants."

"I understand. That might even be for the best, all things considered."

Venice nodded. "You're more right than you know. There are lots of dark places inside of Geoffrey that you're not ready to become acquainted with, Lucy. I'm not saying that to hurt you, but because you need to know what you're setting yourself up for. Geoffrey isn't an easy man to love, not even when he loves you back."

"Do you really think he does? Love me back, I mean."

It wasn't a very fair question, not considering what it would cost Venice to give me an answer, but I needed to hear it. She waited for several seconds before sighing and nodding.

"Yes. He's of two minds about it or he would have already acted on his attraction to you, but he is falling for you. That much was obvious to me the last time I saw him."

Chapter 16

December
Lucy's Age: 18

Geoffrey wasn't kidding when he said everything was heating up. Things were still a little tense with Venice, but she kept me in the loop enough for me to know that it looked like Imastious had done a very bad job positioning himself in his current attempt to take over whatever criminal enterprise had caught his eye. The target that Imastious had picked out was actually much bigger and tougher than he'd originally thought and it sounded like a real dogfight was in the works.

With how hard Imastious was running Geoffrey, I'd only seen him once since our run up to the great hill. Nothing particularly important had happened, but I'd made sure to tell him how much I appreciated him coming on runs with me. It was a small thing, but I was grasping at straws now. I didn't know how close he was to deciding it was time to protect his memories from Imastious, but I figured the more appreciated he felt the more likely he'd procrastinate implementing his defense mechanism.

Of course the downside to all of that was if I somehow managed to convince Geoffrey to delay too long then I'd end up as the recipient of a visit from Imastious. Everything that Venice had let drop about Imastious made my skin crawl, but it was a risk I was willing to run if it meant that I'd be able to get Geoffrey away from him. Everything I was risking was stuff that Venice and Geoffrey had already been through and I couldn't in good conscience back out now, not given how little I had at stake compared to how much they had on the line.

Venice had been really vague about her plan to distract Imastious, possibly because she didn't want there to be any evidence, electronic or otherwise, but on a couple of her regular check-in texts she'd indicated that she had a workable idea and that it was progressing about as well as could be expected.

All I could do was sit on the sidelines and hope that her plan worked and that it wouldn't expose her to too much extra danger.

I was sitting on the couch trying to decide whether to dive into another round of researching as a way of getting my mind off of everything or just go to bed instead when I got a really odd text from Venice.

I'm hurt, I need your help. Geoffrey will have a couple bags of blood somewhere in the apartment, probably hidden somewhere in the freezer. Bring them. Hurry, I'm in a service corridor off of Grand Central Station. GBP42C14

The string of numbers and letters on the end of the text was incomprehensible, so I decided to ignore it for the time being and focus on the parts that I understood.

Venice hadn't been scheduled to check in for another hour still, which meant that the text was probably legit unless Imastious had thought to look through her phone before he started torturing her. Everything Venice had said seemed to indicate that Imastious had a slight blind spot for some reason when it came to technology.

The chance that this was a trap was remote, but there was still a chance and I needed to understand that if I was going to try and help her. It only took me a couple of seconds to decide. Our recent friction didn't change the fact that we were friends and I couldn't just leave her injured and helpless somewhere because I was afraid that Imastious *might* be using her to lure me out of hiding.

The part of the text about bringing blood bags was odd to the point of creepy, but I opened up the freezer and once I was actually looking for it, I found the false panel in the back in less than half a minute.

There were actually four bags hidden inside of the freezer, along with a small bag that had some tubing and needles in it. The needles actually made me feel quite a bit better because I realized that Venice must have known that Geoffrey cached bags of both their blood in the apartment along with the equipment needed to do a blood transfusion.

I shoved the blood inside of my backpack and grabbed a coat as I headed towards my window, but then paused just before I opened it. I was going into this understanding the risks, but that didn't mean that I should go completely unarmed.

Geoffrey had given me a fixed-blade knife as a kind of graduation present a few weeks before when I'd finally demonstrated what he considered to be basic proficiency in knife fighting. It was a four-inch beauty of a blade with a non-reflective surface and a drop point.

I debated for only an instant before picking it up off of my dresser and sliding it free of its sheath. It was just as slender and deadly as I remembered, so I threaded my belt through the sheath and then pulled my coat back on so that it wouldn't be visible to anyone I walked past.

I hadn't climbed down the fire escape in the dark during winter before now, and the trip to the ground was just as nerve-wracking as I'd expected it to be, but I made it down without falling and then flagged down a cab.

It was too far to walk very quickly and I'd started mirroring some of Geoffrey's investments with the funds I'd pried out of Mrs. Phelps' skeletal fingers—I didn't have hundreds of thousands of dollars yet, but my nest egg was growing—and I could easily afford to take a cab given that Venice was probably bleeding to death in some dark corner of the station.

It was late enough that traffic wasn't as bad as normal, but I still tapped my feet restlessly the entire way to Grand Central. I threw a handful of bills at the cabbie as soon as the car stopped and then ran down the stairs into the station two at a time.

I'd texted Venice on the drive there, telling her I was coming and asking for more specific directions, but she hadn't responded, which meant that I was on my own. I started through the station at a quick walk so as not to attract unnecessary attention, but I was up against a clock and I had a lot of ground to cover since I was pretty much going in blind.

I'd only been walking for five minutes before I saw the police. There were more than a dozen of them blocking off a corner of one of the concourses, but there was just enough of a space between two of them for me to make out the fact that there was a body bag behind them and that the entire floor there was covered in blood.

It wasn't much to go on still, but at least now I knew I was in the right section of the station. The police were giving me nasty looks that told me at the very least that they didn't want me rubbernecking. They were obviously keeping an eye on the tiny crowd that had formed around them. I wasn't a criminal returning to the scene of the crime, but I wasn't much better than that given that I knew the criminal, so I kept moving and tried to avoid looking suspicious.

I did look around as I walked though and I noticed that there were three separate security cameras that had been ripped free of the walls where they'd been mounted. None of the cameras were easily accessible, so either Venice had used her power to put them out of commission, or she'd been up against another telekinetic.

I pulled my phone back out and looked at the gibberish on the end of her message, only it wasn't gibberish anymore, at least not completely. The GBP at the start of the string probably referred to Graybar Passage, which was where she'd left the body. That meant that the 42 was probably another location.

Feeling like an idiot I headed towards the 42nd Street section of the station. Less than two minutes later I was hurrying down a dingy yellow and white corridor with my eyes peeled for any service doors. The second one I saw was the one I was looking for. It had a plate bolted to the door that read C14.

A DARKNESS MIRRORED

The door looked like it was shut and locked, but the knob turned freely and when I put my shoulder into it the door slowly slid open. The room inside was like something out of a slasher movie.

There was more space than I'd expected to find. It looked as though the Metropolitan Transit Authority had planned at one point on putting another store here but they'd abandoned the plans and put some kind of electrical substation in instead.

Counting the corpse that had been holding the door shut, I could see three bodies just from where I was standing. The lights were on, but their flickering illumination didn't do very much to calm my nerves.

Conscious of the fact that I'd been incredibly lucky so far not to have had someone come walking by, I pushed the door far enough open to slip inside and then used my backpack to hold it shut so that nobody else would get curious and stick their head inside the room.

Once the door was shut, I looked down and noticed that I had my knife out already. I slowly worked my way past the first two corpses, taking care not to step in any of the puddles of blood so that I wouldn't be leaving a trail back here once I left the room.

Venice was hanging several feet up in the air, impaled through the ribs by a shard of metal. I wanted to run to her, but I kept my pace very slow and measured as I tried to piece together what had happened.

The room was in shambles, which I would have attributed to Venice's telekinetic gift except for the fact that none of the bodies were close enough to her to have impaled her like that with their hands. All I could figure was that one of the others must have been a telekinetic as well.

I checked the bodies one by one, figuring out cause of death and confirming that I didn't need to worry that one of them was suddenly going to jump up and attack me.

The guy next to the door had a length of steel pipe through where his heart otherwise would have been.

Another guy had had his throat sliced open, and the third guy looked like he'd been in the midst of killing the second guy when a piece of machinery had fallen from twenty feet above him and broken his neck.

It was all I could do to keep from throwing up, but I still made myself get close enough to the last guy to make sure that he wasn't breathing before I turned my back to him and started making my way towards Venice.

I was half-expecting to find out that she was dead too, but her eyes fluttered open when I touched her arm.

"Lucy, where's the blood? Did you bring it?"

"Yes, it's over by the door. I'll go get it as soon as we get you down from there."

I knew enough first aid to know that it was a bad idea to pull something out of someone who'd been impaled, but it looked like she'd been lucky enough to have it miss her heart and I didn't know the first thing about running an IV, so I needed to get her to the floor so that she could help me start the blood transfusion.

"No, get the blood first."

Her voice was weaker than it had been a second ago, and I realized that I was starting to lose her. I wrapped my arms around her thighs and steeled myself for what I had to do next.

"What happened here, Venice?"

It felt like it was important to get her talking, so I waited a second for her to respond to my question.

"It was a double-cross. I lured a rival group here by using myself as bait."

She paused for breath and I made my move, lifting her up and away from the wall with all of the force that my frame could muster. I could hear the metal grate against her ribs and based on Venice's hiss, the pain was intense.

I worried for a moment that she wouldn't be able to muffle the scream that was building in her throat, but she kept herself together enough to keep from making any noise loud enough to alert the cops that we were only a few hundred yards away from where she'd killed the first guy.

"Aren't you supposed to count or something before you do that?"

"No, the whole point is for you to be the one talking. Stop complaining and finish telling me how you got hung up on the wall like a side of beef."

"The target was Jackson, the guy with the broken neck. He's way out of my league, but I've been working on turning some of his grunts. It hasn't been too hard because the guy's a complete ass. The other two guys agreed to help me take Jackson down, but there was a complication."

She'd relaxed a little, so I lifted her up and back again, gaining another couple of inches, and then shifted my grip on her legs as she swore at me and tried to stabilize her breathing again.

"Keep going, Venice. I'm still listening."

"Right, complication. Jackson brought a third guy, one I hadn't turned yet. I lured him away from the others and killed him, but it alerted Jackson to my presence. I didn't make it here fast enough and he threw me into the wall before I could hide."

The metal rod she was hanging from angled up as it moved away from the wall, which meant that it was getting harder and harder to move her, but I thought I could get her free in two more surges.

"I thought I was dead. If Jackson's people had been using their brains they would have just let him kill me. Instead they went crazy and attacked him. It was a complete massacre, they were totally outclassed."

I lifted again and this time she did scream. "Damn it, Lucy. Just get me off. Don't drag it out."

"I'm trying. I'm not strong enough to do it in one go, though."

Venice was shaking now. I suspected that the blood loss and pain was sending her into shock. It was actually pretty amazing that she'd held it together for this long.

"Jackson forgot about me while he killed his guys, which gave me a chance to drop that chunk of metal on his head."

I adjusted my grip again so that I was holding just above her knees and lifted. This time I managed to get her clear of the metal, but the leverage was all wrong. I nearly impaled her again, and my desperate attempt to keep her away from the wicked spear of metal resulted in both of us crashing to the floor.

Venice landed on top of me, pinning me between her legs and some of the scrap metal that littered the floor. I hit my head pretty hard, but Venice's near scream distracted me from my own pain. I started to carefully roll her off of me and then stopped as I saw the way that her legs flopped as I tried to move them.

"They're broken, just move them all at once and be done with it."

I looked at Venice, unsure if that was a good idea, but she was right, her chest was bleeding again. There wasn't very much time before she'd bleed out and I couldn't afford to waste precious seconds trying to baby her legs out of the way.

I put a hand on her hip and pushed, rolling her up onto her side. She whimpered, and it looked like she almost passed out, but it was enough for me to get back up onto my hands and knees.

My coat was probably shredded, but it seemed to have saved me from the worst of the damage, as far as my back was concerned at least. My hands hadn't been as lucky. I noticed that my left hand was dripping blood as I grabbed one of my gloves and held it against the hole in Venice's ribs.

"Lucy, get the bags of blood for me."

"In a second. I have to get some pressure on your wounds or the blood will all just leak out as fast as it drains into you."

"No! Get it now, Lucy."

I jammed my second glove between her shirt and her skin and then rolled her body back onto it so that her weight would hold it in place. I was just about to stand back up and go get my backpack when I saw her shudder.

It was the most eerie thing I'd ever seen. One second she was sitting there, panting in agony as her life slowly leaked away, and then the next she turned on me with speed that was quite literally inhuman.

The only thing that saved me was the fact that her legs were broken. The pain didn't seem to deter her, but neither limb was able to support her weight which meant that she wasn't nearly as mobile as she should have been. Even so, she grabbed ahold of my left hand in a single lightning motion and pulled me towards her.

I was surprised, but I still managed to get my feet up, one on her stomach and the other at the base of her neck almost directly over her collarbone. My reaction was pure reflex, it wasn't until I saw the expression on her face that I realized how much danger I was in.

She looked like some kind of feral animal. There wasn't anything even remotely like intelligence behind her eyes. It was obvious that she was operating off of nothing more than pure, bestial instinct.

Venice pulled on my arm with her right hand and all of a sudden I realized just how much stronger than me she was. I'd always known she was more muscular than me, despite having a frame that didn't look it, but she was pulling my arm towards her despite my best efforts, despite the fact that I was resisting with the more massive muscles of my legs.

I had all of the leverage on my side, but it didn't seem to matter and in fact I was starting to wonder if she'd end up ripping my arm free of my shoulder.

"Venice! Let go of me."

She'd been staring at my bloody hand with an unsettling focus, but my words made her look up at me and I got an even bigger shock. Her canines had lengthened somehow and she was licking her lips in anticipation as my hand inched ever so slowly towards her mouth.

My legs were burning. I tried to shift my right foot over slightly so that it was pressing more on the front of her throat, but her left hand was stopping me from adjusting my footing. The leverage was too bad for her to move my foot, but she'd turned the struggle into a slowly eroding stalemate.

She'd started bleeding more profusely now, but it didn't seem to be affecting her strength. All indications were that she could continue on for however long it took my muscles to turn to jelly.

Panic was starting to steal my ability to reason, but then I remembered the knife that I'd secreted underneath my coat. It came free of its sheath without a hitch, but Venice didn't react to the sudden appearance of a weapon. She was looking at my left hand again and if anything her teeth looked like they were longer than they'd been a couple of seconds before.

My legs started shaking, which meant that I was out of time. I debated targets for a split second and then slammed the knife home in her forearm in a bid to sever the nerve that controlled her ability to contract her fingers. I didn't want to leave Venice paralyzed, but the alternative would be killing her, so I stabbed her in the arm and when that didn't succeed in making her let go of me I adjusted my aim and stabbed her again.

The second time did the trick. Her right hand flopped open and the tension holding me against her was suddenly gone. My legs straightened out in an explosive movement that threw the two of us away from each other and sent us both sliding along the filthy, bloodstained floor.

If I'd been by myself I would have just lain there, but Venice started dragging herself towards me even before she stopped sliding. Her progress was a jerky, painful series of motions, but she was still moving faster than I'd have been able to if our positions had been reversed.

I didn't have time to watch her pull herself forward with her left hand; I'd just realized that there might not be any way short of killing her that would stop her from coming after me. I pulled myself back to my feet and backed carefully away from her. She was between me and the door, which wasn't a very promising situation, but I felt the beginnings of a plan start to form when I noticed a metal pipe that had been ripped free of the ceiling at some point during her fight with the others.

Venice was moving more quickly now. She'd started using her right arm to prop herself up as her left hand shot forward for another handhold. The way her right hand hung limply from her wrist was enough to turn my stomach, but I told myself that I hadn't had any other choice and hefted my four-foot length of pipe.

I waited until Venice was only a few feet away from me and then I swung the pipe at her head. Not hard enough to break her neck, although I did put a little extra force into it since I was pretty sure she wasn't actually human.

The blow didn't put her down, but I hadn't expected it to. It did, however, stun her, which was what I really needed. I followed up with a second blow from the other direction and then stepped on her so that I'd pinned her left arm under one foot and her right shoulder under the other.

I wedged one end of the pipe into a hole in the wall and then forced the center of the pipe up tight against her chest, pushing until I was able to fit the other end underneath a heavy piece of machinery. I heard her ribs creaking as I finally got the pipe wedged in there good enough that I was confident that it wouldn't just come undone the first time she thrashed around.

I had my knife in my hand again as I stepped back and let her test my impromptu restraints, but they held. I backed away, still keeping an eye on her as I tried to clear my head enough to come up with a plan.

She was dangerous, even like this there was a chance that she'd get free and hurt someone, but I couldn't bring myself to just kill her. She was some kind of psycho animal, but she was also

Venice, she'd helped me get Geoffrey to reconnect to me, she'd taken me shopping and somewhere along the way she'd become my best friend.

In the end there was really only one course of action open to me, one option that I could live with. I got my backpack and pulled out the four bags of blood that I'd brought with me from the apartment. I wasn't sure whether or not she'd be able to control herself well enough to avoid just shredding the bag and getting the blood everywhere, so I only tossed one to her to start out with.

It landed on her chest, but she grabbed it with her left hand in a lightning-fast motion and raised it to her lips. She watched me the entire time as she drained it dry, like she was worried that I'd try to steal the blood back from her.

Once the first bag was empty I threw the rest of them to her one at a time, watching until she'd finished all four, and then I found her phone and gently kicked it over to where she could reach it. It wasn't much, but at least it gave her a possible way out if she came back to herself enough to remember how to use it.

Chapter 17

January
Lucy's Age: 18

"Lucy, are you paying any attention at all?"

"Hmm? Sorry, it's getting late enough that I'm starting to get a little punchy. What was it that you asked?"

It wasn't a bad excuse as things went even if it *was* a total lie. Geoffrey and I were running through possible investment targets again, but this time we were meeting during what was late evening for me and early morning for him.

I actually was tired, but it had less to do with the lateness of the hour and more to do with the fact that I had just spent the last hour on high alert, all the while trying not to let on to Geoffrey that I was on high alert.

It was pretty obvious that Venice was a vampire, maybe not in the traditional sense of combusting in sunlight or turning into a bat, but she was faster and stronger than any human and her first instinct when she'd been injured had been to try and feed from me.

If Venice was a vampire then Geoffrey almost certainly was one too. It explained so many things that I'd never thought to question. Venice didn't look any older than me, but she talked like she and Geoffrey had a really long backstory. I'd always assumed that she was just exaggerating slightly, but for all I knew she was thousands of years old and they'd been together for centuries.

Venice's powers as a telekinetic and Geoffrey's powers as a mentalist weren't because they had some unique ability present in small quantities among the general population, it was because they were vampires.

Even the fact that Geoffrey didn't look any older than when I'd been a kid made sense now. I'd never really thought about it because we'd never had pictures of each other around the house, but I should have noticed some gray hair and wrinkles somewhere along the way.

"I asked you what you want for your birthday next week."

I shrugged. "I'm actually not feeling very excited about this birthday. Maybe we should just skip celebrating it this year."

Geoffrey shook his head at me. "We're celebrating it and that's final. You only turn nineteen once."

"We never celebrate your birthdays."

I'd caught him by surprise, I could see that much, but I wasn't sure what was going on inside of his head. It was stupid to do anything that might tip him off to the fact that I knew about him and Venice, but I couldn't seem to help myself. The effort of trying to stay on a hair trigger for so long was taking even more out of me than I'd realized.

It was a pointless thing to be doing anyway. Based on what I'd seen out of Venice, Geoffrey was so much faster and stronger than me that nothing I could possibly do would save me. I took a deep breath and forced myself to relax as I waited for Geoffrey to respond to my last question.

"You're right, Lucy. It's a bit hypocritical for me to insist on celebrating your birthday when we don't ever celebrate mine. To be honest, I don't even know when mine is."

There was a level of vulnerability there that two days ago would have made me jump for joy. Geoffrey was more in touch with his humanity than I'd ever seen before, but I couldn't seem to muster any excitement over that fact.

"I haven't had a very good life, Lucy. My childhood and the years that followed were...difficult. I've got a lot of sins hanging over my head that I rationalized away at the time, but which I regret now. I can't go back and fix any of those things, but maybe I can redeem myself a little bit through my actions with you."

"Is that all I am to you? Am I nothing more than a ticket up to the pearly gates?"

Geoffrey shook his head. "You're not any kind of ticket, you're Lucy. You're someone I care about deeply, you're...well, you're my daughter."

There was something else there that he'd been about to say, but he didn't give a chance to dwell on that fact.

"What's gotten into you, Lucy? This isn't like you."

I opened my mouth, not sure how I would respond, and words just poured out. "I don't know how I fit into the world. You took me in, saved me from freezing to death, but then I hardly saw you for years. You'd show up for a few months and then just as I'd start to feel close to you, you'd leave."

Geoffrey tried to interject something, but I barreled right on through, determined to get my say in.

"I've hardly ever even been allowed to leave the house. You've paid a small fortune educating me, but now I don't even know what to do with myself. Most kids my age are headed off to college, but I don't even know if I'll ever even be able to leave the apartment!"

Geoffrey's mouth snapped shut in shock. Silence hung in the air for nearly a minute before he nodded. "You're right. I've never been there for you when you needed me."

He paced over to a window and looked down at the people on the street below. "I'm sorry if I've smothered you. I've seen so many bad things happen that I've had a hard time letting you go out there and be exposed to them. Do you really want to leave? I thought you were enjoying the work we do together."

I wanted to be angry, wanted to yell and scream at him, but seeing him like this, completely vulnerable, thawed something inside of me. He wasn't pretending—I knew him too well for that. No, he was genuinely sad at the prospect of me leaving, and it wasn't because of some ulterior motive, it was because he would miss me.

There wasn't any way for me to be certain of that, but somehow I knew it was the case. A part of me argued that Geoffrey's vulnerability shouldn't be any more valuable than anyone else's vulnerability, but somehow it *was* more important. The very fact that I knew what he was capable of—that I knew of some of the terrible things he'd actually done—made the fact that he was standing there, waiting for me to crush him, intoxicating on levels that I'd never even known existed.

"I do enjoy it, Geoffrey, I just wish I felt like I had a choice in where I went and what I did."

He nodded. "I can understand that. I guess I didn't keep up. For so long you were a child who needed protecting, but now you're an adult and you need to be able to go your own way."

He took a deep breath, like it was costing him more than I could understand to make his next statement. "I'll need a couple of weeks. Given the way that you came to live with me, I don't exactly have your real birth certificate. I have a set of good forgeries put together for you though, they just need some updating. You'll need to take one or more of the standardized tests and then get your applications into your top couple of choices. I don't know when any of the deadlines are, but you'll want to move quickly on everything. Most kids your age are already in their first year of school. I'm sorry I've put you a year behind everyone else."

I shook my head at him and willed the tears that were waiting in the wings not to make an appearance. "You haven't put me behind everyone else, not in any way that matters. I won't be leaving tomorrow or the next day, or even next month, but I do appreciate you giving me the option."

"You're welcome."

Geoffrey's motions were jerky as he gathered up his things and placed them inside his backpack. "I need to be going actually. I'll see you next week."

Chapter 18

February
Lucy's Age: 19

Every single aspect of my life seemed to be defined by how conflicted I was about the things that were the most important to me. Venice had completely disappeared. I'd gone back to Grand Central Station, but the door to the room where Venice had tried to kill me was locked now. I'd tried texting her and calling her, but her number was disconnected now, which just made me feel even worse.

I couldn't just forget the look on her face as she'd tried to kill me, but I likewise couldn't stop missing her. Part of me was convinced that I'd gone too easy on her, that I should have just killed her while she was vulnerable, before she could hurt someone else, but mostly I was just worried that I hadn't done enough, that I should have helped her more than I had.

My feelings for Geoffrey complicated the situation even more. It was impossible for me to think of Venice as some kind of animal that needed to be put down and yet remain convinced that Geoffrey was redeemable.

Either they were both worth saving or neither of them was.

My birthday came and went without another appearance by Geoffrey, which was both good and bad. It was good because I'd realized that I needed some time and space from him if I was going to be able to sort out my thoughts, but bad because I missed him even more than I'd expected to.

I was flying completely blind now. I didn't know if Venice was dead or if she was alive and Imastious was only seconds away from breaking her and setting out to find me. For all I knew Geoffrey was the one on Imastious' torture table.

The only communication I got from either of them arrived the day of my birthday and consisted of a card from Geoffrey. On it he wished me a happy birthday and then at the bottom of the card it had an account number, a password, and a single word of explanation, 'college.'

The account turned out to be one that Geoffrey had set up in my name, and it had half a million dollars in it, which was more than enough to see me through graduate school at any institution I might want to attend.

The money had just muddied the waters for me even more, but I knew that I needed to get some clarity around my situation soon, so I'd done the only other thing I could think of. I'd withdrawn thirty thousand dollars from my secret bank account, the one that Geoffrey didn't know about, and hired a private investigator.

I'd actually considered trying to hunt down Mrs. Agosti before, but had always shied away from the idea for multiple reasons. The payment to the PI nearly wiped out the balance in my account, which was part of it, but mostly it came down to the fact that I was worried I wouldn't like what I'd find out.

Geoffrey had always told me that Mrs. Agosti was alive and happy somewhere else. I was about to find out whether or not he'd lied to me. There were two things that he'd done to me so far that I'd never been able to quite forgive him for. Taking Renworst away from me was the most recent, but it was the one that I already knew I couldn't get resolution on. Renworst was dead, and nothing I could do would bring him back, but Mrs. Agosti was another matter entirely.

She might be dead too, but if she wasn't then I wanted to find her and ask her what Geoffrey had offered her to keep her away from me for all of these years.

The PI found her after only a couple of days. He sent her address over and then all that remained to be done was for me to make the trip.

A DARKNESS MIRRORED

My freedom to come and go wasn't what it once was, not since Geoffrey had started coming by the apartment so regularly to review the results of my research. Mrs. Phelps had standing orders to tell him that I was in my room napping if he stopped by while I was out, but there was still a pretty good chance that if he did come by unexpectedly that he'd knock on my door and then figure out that I'd gone out the window.

I'd risked a few quick trips lately, but nothing more than an hour or so, nothing even approaching the eight-hour trip that would be required to make it to Mrs. Agosti's house in upstate New York and then return home.

I delayed the trip for two whole days after I knew where she lived. I told myself that I needed to arrange a car, but the truth was that I was scared. Not just of Geoffrey visiting my apartment and figuring out that I was gone, but scared of what I'd find at Mrs. Agosti's place.

The fact that the PI had found her seemed to indicate that she hadn't been killed. That in turn begged the question as to why she'd moved away from the city and never even tried to look for me.

On the morning of the third day I rolled out of bed, told myself to suck it up, and called the car service. Less than an hour later I was on my way upstate.

The drive up took nearly four hours, but I spent the whole time wishing that there was a way to prolong it and put off the time when I'd actually have to confront her. My wishes were just as ineffective as they usually were, and a little after noon the driver dropped me off in front of her house.

Her place was comfortable-looking. It wasn't overly ritzy or ostentatious, but it had a nice feel to it. I knocked on the door and then braced myself when I heard her footsteps make their slow way towards me.

"Yes? Can I help you?"

It was her. She was older than I remembered, in fact it looked like there wasn't much more than willpower and inertia keeping her moving, but it was her. I stared into her eyes, but there was no sign of recognition there.

"You don't recognize me, do you, Mrs. Agosti?"

"No, I'm afraid I don't. Should I?"

My bottom lip started to tremble and there were tears gathering in the corner of each eye, but I shook my head. "No. I don't suppose that you should recognize me. I'm sorry to have bothered you, Mrs. Agosti."

I turned to go, but she reached forward with surprising speed and stopped me. "What's your name, young lady?"

I didn't want to answer her. I had my answer. She hadn't come looking for me because she hadn't remembered me. Geoffrey had destroyed her memories of me just like he destroyed his own emotions whenever they became inconvenient.

A DARKNESS MIRRORED

From Geoffrey's perspective he'd probably been pleased that he'd been able to keep her alive and yet avoided the complications of having her looking for me at some later date.

From my perspective it still felt like he'd killed her. Her body was still walking and talking, and she probably had the same kindly, stubborn nature, but she didn't have any memories of me. The person who'd been my mother for those first few years after Geoffrey had taken me in was dead.

"My name is Lucy."

I tried to pull free of her grasp, but she held on with astonishing strength. "Your name is Lucy? Can you tell me your father's name?"

"It's Geoffrey, his name is Geoffrey."

Her eyes went wide in astonishment and she released my arm, but I no longer felt any inclination to leave.

"It is you. After all this time, you're really here on my doorstep."

"You remember me then?"

She shook her head and then looked past me as though worried that someone would see us together. "Come inside, dear. Come inside where it's safe and I'll tell you all about it."

I followed her into her front room and took a seat on the cream-colored couch as she disappeared into what looked like a bedroom.

"I don't remember you, Lucy. There is a period of approximately three or four years where I don't remember anything from my life. I essentially woke up in a hospital one day and realized that I didn't know how I got there or what I'd been doing with myself for months."

She came back out of the bedroom with a thin, leather-bound book in her arms. "I was able to track down a few old friends and a niece who said that I'd talked to them during the block of time that I no longer remembered, but they weren't able to tell me much other than that I'd taken a job caring for a young girl and that I'd been more secretive than normal."

I accepted the book as she handed it to me, but didn't open it, instead waiting for her to finish talking.

"The doctors told me it was possible that I might regain some of my memories as time went by, but I knew that wouldn't be the case. Even back then I knew that something outside of the normal had happened to me."

She looked incredibly sad. I started to reach out to comfort her like she'd comforted me, but then I remembered that she didn't know me anymore, that she wouldn't welcome comfort from a stranger who had just shown up on her doorstep out of the blue.

"I thought that I'd go through my life without any additional clues as to what had happened during those missing years, but then a few weeks after I got out of the hospital, that book was left on my doorstep. Go ahead, open it."

A DARKNESS MIRRORED

I wasn't really sure what to expect, but the book still somehow managed to surprise me. It appeared to be a journal, one that was at least a couple of decades old. I flipped through the first half of the book or so, unsure what to expect, and then realized that there was a huge chunk of missing pages in the middle of the book.

"What you see there is how it was delivered to me. I haven't removed those pages, someone else did."

I looked at the last of the entries from the front and did some quick math. Someone, Geoffrey almost certainly, had left the pages from before Mrs. Agosti came to live with us, but had cut out the pages that had covered the time that she had been taking care of me.

I looked at the jagged forest of paper protruding less than a quarter of an inch from the binding and felt tears start to try and work their way free of my eyes again. He might not have meant his gesture to be a quiet form of torture, but it had been. To return Mrs. Agosti's journal after excising all of the sheets that had talked about me was cruel. He'd shown her that there had been written records of her missing time, and then in the same motion he'd snatched those records away.

I flipped to the back third of the journal, expecting to find nothing but blank pages, but there was a single entry just after the section of the book that had been destroyed.

I no longer know what day it is. Sometimes I'm not even sure that I'm still alive. It seems inconceivable that a loving God would let a monster like Geoffrey continue to starve me, to torture me, and to violate my mind like this, but I gave up denying what was happening to me a long time ago.

Geoffrey has stolen Lucy away from me and locked me up, but my efforts to sneak this journal into my cage with me have paid off handsomely. He's doing something to my mind, making it harder and harder to remember her, but I've stretched that process out for weeks by poring over my journal entries whenever he isn't around. Reading about her has helped keep my memories of her alive, but I fear that even so I won't last much longer.

Geoffrey's anger grows in step with the passage of time. He won't release me as long as I can still remember Lucy, and I won't stop fighting his efforts for as long as there is still breath left in my body. At some point in the next few days I suspect that he'll abandon his attempts to wipe out my memory and he'll just kill me. Heaven knows I never expected for him to wait this long.

It strains the limits of believability to think that an inhuman monster like Geoffrey could have any part in raising an angel like Lucy, but I was there and I saw it. As much as I'd like to take all of the credit for Lucy, I can't. Some of her goodness was an inherent part of her nature, and there was some small part that I helped nurture, but she was always happiest and best behaved when Geoffrey spent time with her.

Of all of my regrets in life, taking this job isn't one of them. I only regret that I wasn't able to get Lucy out when I started to suspect just how terrible Geoffrey could be when angered.

I may not get the chance to write another entry, and even assuming that Geoffrey doesn't find my journal after I'm dead, there is still little chance that this book will ever make it into your hands, but if by some miracle it does, know that I loved you.

You were the daughter I never had and I couldn't be more proud of the strides you made during the time you were under my care. It was obvious that you'd suffered a terrible tragedy, but you never let that stop you from loving.

Your innocent heart is your greatest strength and I hope that you grow into being a woman without losing your ability to love, even those who may not deserve it, even tired old women who take nanny jobs with no intention of ever loving another child. You redeemed me, and for a brief time I thought you might even redeem your father.

I looked up from the page with tears in my eyes and found matching drops of moisture running down Mrs. Agosti's cheeks.

"Did I get my wish? You're a beautiful young woman, but have you retained your ability to love?"

"I'm not sure. I think so, but how do I know whether or not it's right to love somebody?"

She shrugged and smiled. "I don't know you anymore, Lucy. All I know of you is what's found on that one worn-out, tired, old page. I don't know your situation, and anything you could tell me would only be colored by what you want to believe."

I opened my mouth to argue with her, to plead for her advice, but she shook her head at me. "I do know this though, Lucy. In all my years, this cynical old woman has never written in such a fashion about anyone or anything else. If Michelangelo walked up to you and asked whether or not it was a good idea to begin a certain project, it would be the height of hubris to tell him yes or no. There is a level of genius that defies any mere mortal to instruct the holder in their use."

She reached out and took my hand in one of hers as she reached into her pocket with the other and pulled out an envelope which she pressed into my fingers. "Take this home with you. As much as I'd love to stay and spend more time with you, I've got somewhere I'm supposed to be soon. You'll know your path as it's placed before you; and like all great artists, you'll create something exquisite where others see nothing but the mundane. I can't direct you in your efforts any more than I would want to distract you from them."

Chapter 19

February
Lucy's Age: 19

I went back home in a daze. I was so far gone that I didn't think to look inside of the envelope until after I'd climbed the fire escape and was back inside my room. The envelope proved to be a veritable smorgasbord of financial information.

There was everything from lists of offshore, numbered accounts with distressingly large approximate balances next to them, to bus lockers and bank deposit boxes that seemed to contain everything from gold coins to guns.

The key to the whole arrangement, quite literally, was a thin key buried in with all of the paper that provided access to a storage unit that held the keys for the rest of the secure locations she'd detailed out.

The last sheet of paper had a cell phone number on it that was listed as Mrs. Agosti's. By the time I finished working my way through everything else in the envelope it was too late to call, but the next day I bounced around the house until I decided that it was late enough to call without running the risk of waking Mrs. Agosti up.

Someone picked up on the third ring, but it wasn't Mrs. Agosti who answered.

"Hello, this is Clarissa Agosti's phone."

"Um, hi, is Mrs. Agosti there?"

It was obvious from the pause in the conversation that whoever I was talking to had bad news that she didn't want to share with me.

"I'm sorry to be the one to tell you this, but my aunt Clarissa was involved in a hit-and-run accident last night. She...well, she didn't survive. The police are pursuing a few leads, but they don't seem to have much hope that they'll manage to track down her killer."

I felt like my whole world had just been upended. I'd only just found Mrs. Agosti again and now she was gone. The silence dragged out for several seconds before I was able to get control of myself enough to speak again.

"I'm sorry for your loss. Mrs. Agosti was a great woman."

I hung up the call and then collapsed onto my bed. She'd handed me her entire life savings just a short time before she'd been killed. It all seemed too bizarre to be an accident. She'd somehow known that she was going to be killed.

I wanted to leave the apartment, drive up to her town and start hunting down her killer, but I didn't know anything about her current life. I didn't know who might have motive, I didn't know anything.

It wasn't until I heard the apartment door open that I realized that I didn't necessarily need to know anything more than I already knew in order to find Mrs. Agosti's killer. I knew one person who had motive, who'd always had motive.

Geoffrey knocked on my bedroom door, but I didn't tell him to come in, instead I opened the door and looked up at him defiantly.

"You killed her. You killed Mrs. Agosti just because I visited her."

"You visited Mrs. Agosti?"

"Don't play dumb, Geoffrey. I don't know how you found out, but you found out and then you killed her."

"Just be quiet for a minute. I didn't kill her."

I opened my mouth to really let him have it, but the expression on his face told me that I'd pushed him as far as I could. With a normal person I might have kept pushing anyways, but I knew what Geoffrey was capable of.

I watched as Geoffrey walked over to Mrs. Phelps' room and knocked on her door. "Mrs.

Phelps, would you be so kind as to take a trip to the store for me? I think we're running low on pasta."

Mrs. Phelps was a nasty old woman, but she wasn't stupid. She looked at Geoffrey and then she looked at me, but I waved for her to leave. Whatever benefit she thought she might gain by staying and hearing Geoffrey and I air our dirty laundry wasn't actually going to pay off for her, not given the fact that Geoffrey was more than capable of just killing her to make sure there weren't any loose ends wandering around.

The two of us stood in silence as Mrs. Phelps pulled on her coat and scarf. Once she was disappearing down the hall, Geoffrey sent the two muscle-head guards off too.

"Okay, now we're going to discuss this like two sane individuals. That means no yelling."

"Fine. I know everything, Geoffrey. Venice tracked me down months ago. She found me and almost killed me because she thought I was your human lover. Only she found out that I wasn't your lover and somehow we became friends."

Geoffrey's eyes had gotten big. In someone else it would have been an indication of mild surprise, but for him it was the equivalent of falling off of a chair. He opened his mouth to ask me a question, but I just kept right on going.

"She told me that you and Imastious can read minds and she said that you have some kind of defense mechanism that allows you to stop him from getting at the important things inside your mind, but that is why you go all cold and calculating occasionally. She wanted to get you out, wanted to convince you to run away, but she knew you'd never go for it unless we managed to get you to reconnect with us first."

"So you asking for extra training sessions, you helping with the utilities analysis, it's all been a ploy to manipulate me?"

"No, not manipulate you, to save you. It was working too. You were the most normal I'd ever seen you be up until a little while ago when you started worrying about Imastious. So Venice came up with a plan to distract Imastious only everything went sideways and she ended up bleeding to death down in the subway. So she called me for help. I grabbed the four bags of blood that you'd hidden in the freezer and went to try and help her."

Geoffrey's jaw clenched. "Only that went sideways too, didn't it? Did she attack you?"

"Yes, she tried to kill me, tried to drain me dry. I put a knife through her arm and then pinned her to the floor with a metal pipe. By the way, it was obvious at that point that she wasn't human, which means that you aren't human either, are you?"

"No, I'm not. May I ask how you're managing to be so mobile?"

"Sure. Mrs. Phelps has been stealing from you for years. I caught her at it right after she moved in and have been blackmailing her not to say anything when I go down the fire escape. Are you going to kill her now too?"

"No, I'll simply put the fear of God into her and then I'll fire her. I don't kill people as casually as you seem to think I do."

"But you do kill them, don't you. You kill for Imastious, and you kill to protect your interests, financial or otherwise, and you probably kill to feed too, don't you?"

"Yes on all counts, but I didn't kill Mrs. Agosti. In fact, I went to a rather unusual amount of trouble to avoid killing her back when she first defied me."

"I saw her journal, Geoffrey. She showed it to me yesterday when I went to her house. I know that you tortured her and then you wiped her mind. I know what you're capable of. Hell, I've known what you're capable of this entire time, but for some reason I still trusted you. I think that is the part that is the hardest for me to accept. I trusted someone who is fundamentally untrustworthy."

Geoffrey pulled his phone out of his pocket and tossed it to me. "Venice is in my contacts. Call her and ask her where I was yesterday. I'm not proud of most of what I've done in my life, but for years I've done nothing but try very hard to do right by you."

He turned around and walked out of the apartment while I was still looking down at the phone. I stared at the door he'd closed behind him for several seconds before looking up Venice's number and dialing it.

"What's up, love?"

"It's me, Venice, not Geoffrey."

"What are you doing with his phone, Lucy? Put it back before he finds out that you've swiped it!"

"He already knows. I confronted him with everything I knew. Just now, this morning. He handed me his phone and left."

"What the hell were you thinking?"

The rage in her voice was unfeigned, but I didn't care anymore. No matter how much of a monster Venice was she couldn't hurt me because she didn't know where I was. Geoffrey had left assuming that I wouldn't be able to get very far before he came back to carry out whatever plan was hatching in the back of his mind. He didn't know about the money that Mrs. Agosti had left me. I would be gone by the time he returned to the apartment, and I would never even look back.

"I wasn't thinking, Venice. I was reacting. I was reacting to the fact that you're some kind of monster and that last night Geoffrey ran down one of the only two people who've ever really loved me."

Venice took a deep breath. Even over the phone I could tell that she was doing her absolute best to master her rage.

"I don't know what you think happened, but Geoffrey was with me from yesterday morning until a couple of hours ago. My plan to rattle Imastious' cage worked and he's had us running hits on rival assets almost non-stop for days now. There's no way that Geoffrey has had the time and energy to plan anything untoward over the last few days."

My head was whirling. Despite everything else that had happened, when Venice had said that they'd spent the night together, I'd felt my heart constrict almost to the point of breaking. Apparently I was still more conflicted where Geoffrey was concerned than I'd realized. Even knowing that he was a monster, even mostly believing that he'd killed Mrs. Agosti, still hadn't cured me of my desire for him.

I tore my thoughts away from Geoffrey and focused back on the call. The silence stretched out for nearly half a minute as the two of us played a kind of conversational chicken. I was the first to break.

"Why didn't you tell me?"

"That I'm a vampire?"

"Yeah, that would have been a good starting place."

Venice's sigh tugged at my chest. "I made sure that you knew I was a monster in other ways, maybe I thought that would be enough of a heads up for you."

"Maybe, or maybe you were worried that if I knew the truth then you wouldn't be able to convince me to help you try and redeem Geoffrey."

"Yeah, there was probably part of that in the mix too. Don't get too high and mighty though. You left me for dead in that rat-infested hole in the ground."

"After you tried to kill me!"

"I told you to get the blood bags, but you refused to listen."

I wanted to hit something, but I wasn't immature enough to go around destroying the apartment just because I was pissed.

"That whole situation went wrong because you refused to tell me the truth. If you'd told me you were a vampire I would have grabbed the blood right away because I would have known that you wouldn't bleed out like a human."

"Yeah, but if I'd done that would you have even been there to save me in the first place? I'm a vampire, but that doesn't make me that different from you, Lucy. I'm scared of dying as much as anyone else. More maybe because I know just how long I could live if I manage to make sure that nobody sticks three feet of steel through my chest. Would you have really acted any differently if you'd been the one in my place?"

She was right, that was the real question. If I'd known what I was getting into back when she'd first approached me about trying to redeem Geoffrey I probably wouldn't have helped. The thought of saving someone who killed people for nourishment went against everything I believed in, but now that I was this involved I was having a hard time not coming up with justifications for everything we'd done so far.

"I honestly don't know. I'd like to say that I would have, that if I'd been the vampire I would have told you and let you make your own decision, but who knows what I would have really done."

"Sucks to deal in grays instead of black and whites, huh?"

"Yeah, I guess it does at that. This doesn't mean that I've forgiven you."

There was a trace of the normal Venice back in her response. "That's okay, you've taken away the only thing that I care about, and you're not even really sure that you want him. You may have just ruined everything we've been working for these last few months and it was all because you were too much of a child to deal with the world as it actually was. In case you didn't get the gist of all of that, I'm not sure that I've forgiven you yet either."

The sheer venom in her voice by the end of her response practically knocked me back on my heels. She'd always acted so calm about our situation that I'd forgotten sometimes just how much she had invested in Geoffrey.

The silence grew again, but this time it was Venice that blinked first. "I didn't sleep with him last night. I'm still painfully celibate, have been since before I met you."

"Thank you. For telling me, and for not capitalizing on any opportunity that might have been there."

"Yeah, whatever. Look, I need to go see if I can track down Geoffrey and undo whatever damage you've just done. Assuming that I survive the experience, you need to spend some time deciding whether you're still interested in him. The important stuff hasn't changed yet. I still want him out from under Imastious' thumb, so if you're the best chance of making that happen, then I'll stay out of the middle of things."

Chapter 20

I didn't hear anything from Venice or Geoffrey either one for a while after that, but true to Geoffrey's word, Mrs. Phelps was fired. The two bodyguards from the hall escorted her out of the apartment shortly after she got back from running the errands that Geoffrey had sent her on while we argued.

Half an hour after Mrs. Phelps disappeared, one of the muscle-heads knocked on the door and told me that I was free to come and go as I desired and that they'd be happy to accompany me wherever I wished to go.

For all that we hadn't interacted very much, the apartment felt incredibly empty now that Mrs. Phelps was gone. I rattled around the house unsure of what to do with myself.

A DARKNESS MIRRORED

I'd been planning on taking the money from Mrs. Agosti and running, but somehow my conversation with Venice had changed all of that. Geoffrey hadn't killed Mrs. Agosti, which meant he was pretty much the same person I'd thought he was for the last little while. The fact that he was a vampire, that he needed to feed on humans to survive, was still possibly a deal breaker, but I felt like I needed to give him a chance to explain himself before I passed final judgment on him.

My thoughts went round and round inside of my head but they didn't really make any kind of progress when it came to solving my problems. Somewhere after the second day I started to lose track of time. I wasn't sleeping very well, so my days and nights slowly got changed around. I got the impression that the nightmares had gotten even worse again, but I'd wake up with no recollection of having dreamed at all.

I woke up one afternoon, having gotten the first decent span of sleep in days, and went out into the living room to find Geoffrey waiting for me.

"I had a long talk with Venice after I left here the other day."

I nodded. "She thought you would probably go discuss the situation with her. Is she okay? Did you hurt her?"

He shook his head. "I can see that you're still assuming the worst about me. No, I didn't hurt her."

There was real sadness in his face. It pulled at my heart in ways I thought I'd armored myself against. I took a deep breath and reminded myself that Geoffrey had fed off of dozens of people each year for decades, possibly even centuries, and held my ground.

"I'm not sure what to believe where you're concerned, Geoffrey. On the one hand you took a helpless child in and cared for her the best that you knew how, but on the other hand you've killed an almost unimaginable number of people."

"I don't enjoy the darker aspects of my life, Lucy. You and Venice were right. I've been sanitizing my mind to keep Imastious from finding out about you, about my efforts to eventually kill him, and that process has removed most of the emotional overtones that a normal person would have. You and she have changed that over the last few months though. I really am a better person now than I've ever been before."

It was like he'd read my mind and was telling me exactly what I'd hoped to hear, but I'd been concentrating on visualizing a solid brick wall around the inside of my mind since I'd first realized he was in the apartment, so I knew he wasn't actually invading my thoughts.

"What about the people you feed on? Has that changed?"

"I am what I am, Lucy. I can't change that, but I've made an effort over the last few weeks to kill only those deserving of death."

"Deserving according to what set of rules?"

"The same set of rules that the world uses. I go inside of their mind, I find out that they've killed someone, or that they've done some other great wrong, and then I use them to sustain myself so that I can continue to work towards bringing down Imastious."

"Is that really the whole purpose of your life, Geoffrey? To bring down Imastious regardless of the cost?"

He was getting mad. I could see him fighting to try and keep his temper under control, but he succeeded in mastering himself and responded to my question in a tone that was very nearly normal.

"You don't have any idea the amount of damage that he's done over the years. Bringing down Imastious is a worthy goal."

"You're right, I don't know anything about Imastious other than that he's bad, but do you really think that he won't just be replaced by someone else? Someone equally as bad?"

"I didn't come here to fight with you, Lucy."

"Then why did you come here?"

He took a deep breath and then ran a hand through his hair. "I talked to Venice. She filled me in on some of the particulars, but the most interesting piece of information she shared with me was the fact that you are in love with me."

I felt my cheeks flush. "She had no right to tell you anything of the sort."

"Is it true?"

I shrugged, trying to keep my face from betraying my feelings. "What if it were, Geoffrey? It wouldn't change anything. We'd still have the same problems we're dealing with right now."

"It matters because it's wrong, Lucy. I remember you as a child."

"Don't play the father card with me, Geoffrey. You were hardly ever there when I was growing up. Renworst was a much better father to me than you ever were and that's saying something because we hated each other until right before he got sick and you took him away from me."

My response came out louder than I'd meant it to, and Geoffrey stepped back slightly as though I'd just thrown weapons at him rather than simple words.

"If you were able to forgive me for what happened with Renworst, would it change things between us?"

I shrugged. "What happened with Renworst isn't the problem, Geoffrey, it's just a symptom of the bigger problem."

"What would it take for things to be better, for you to get past your concerns?"

"Why are you asking me that? Why does it matter?"

It was one of those moments where I could feel our lives balancing on the edge of a razor. It seemed almost as though Geoffrey could feel it too because several seconds passed before he answered me.

"It matters because I have feelings for you too. I've tried to fight them for months now, because they were wrong, because I didn't want to drive you away, but they are there. When Venice told me that you felt the same way about me that I feel about you, it was like a ray of sunlight broke through the clouds that have covered me for all of these years."

"A few months ago I would have been thrilled to hear you say that, Geoffrey. Now I'm not so sure. I can't just make my concerns disappear like that."

I'd only thought I'd seen him vulnerable in the past. There was a whole new level of openness to him now that quite literally took my breath away.

"I'm honestly asking you, Lucy. What do I need to do to make things better between us? Do you want me to run away with you and leave behind my vendetta against Imastious? I'll do it, even though it means never being sure that any given thought in my head is really my own rather than a construct Imastious buried in my mind. It will mean that I can never trust myself to make plans about where we go or how we hide, but I'll do it if that is what will convince you to put aside your doubts."

It was like having the door to heaven opened up a crack, not wide enough for me to enter, but plenty wide enough for me to see what it was that I was missing.

"I...well, I appreciate the fact that you are willing to do that, Geoffrey. I have at least some idea of what it would cost you to walk away from Imastious. What about your need to feed on people?"

"I'm not sure. There are a few possible solutions, but they all require time to implement. In the short term, until I could implement something that would sustain me, I'd probably have to kidnap a couple of people and take just enough to sustain me without killing them. Once I have another method of supply established then I could wipe their memories clean of the experience and send them on their way several hundred thousand dollars richer than when I first found them."

I forced myself not to let my feelings make it to my face. Geoffrey was trying to come up with an option that I would find acceptable, which was so much more than I'd expected out of him when we'd first started talking.

"I don't love it necessarily, but you could argue that there are plenty of people who would sign up for that knowingly if you offered them enough money. So two people for you and another two to sustain Venice until you can set up your more permanent blood supply solution?"

Geoffrey shook his head. "No, if we leave Venice won't be coming with us."

"What do you mean she won't be coming with us? We've talked about it; she'll definitely want to come with us."

"I know that she'll want to come, but we're not bringing her."

"Why not?"

Geoffrey stood and paced. "I know Venice much better than you do. She's got places inside of her that are every bit as dark as the things that make you uneasy about me. I know because I helped put them there. She may have told you that she's okay with the idea of you and me, but she's not, not really. Once we're away from here there's no telling what she'll do to you."

"Venice is my friend!"

He cocked his head slightly at me. "Is she? Is she really? She tried to kill you the other day in the subway, didn't she?"

"Yes, because she was starving. Your plan will keep that from being an issue."

"No, my plan would mean that I would be on starvation rations myself. I've got access to a little bit in the way of bagged blood, but it's not going to last for very long, especially not if there are two of us consuming it. Honestly, we may get to the point where I have to feed from you to help keep the hunger at bay. I'm old enough that I can do that without killing you, but Venice isn't. Whether she kills you because she loses control of the hunger or she kills you out of a simple jealous rage, the result is the same. She will kill you if she comes with us."

It was like the doorway to heaven had been shut. The room seemed to be spinning around, but I closed my eyes and tried to think. Geoffrey returned to the couch and placed a hand on my shoulder.

"Once we're somewhere safe I can make arrangements for Venice. I'll set her up somewhere far away from us; somewhere she can be safe from Imastious."

"But she'll have the same problem you'll have. She'll be doubting every action she takes, worried that it is part of the programming that Imastious put inside her to keep her from getting away."

"She'll just have to deal with that for a while. It's no worse than what I'll be going through and the risk of her leading Imastious back to us if I go there to try and clean her mind of any conditioning is just too great. Maybe in a few years I can figure out a way to meet her for the few days that would be required to address any programming, but not right away."

I was still punch-drunk, it was hard to think, but that felt like a better option—not perfect, but better. Geoffrey correctly read my silence as a kind of stunned inability to decide and pulled me to my feet so he could give me an awkward hug.

"Just think about it. I'd tell you to take as much time as you need, but we don't have very much longer. Imastious is getting very close to figuring out my involvement in something that I shouldn't have been involved in. I don't have much longer before I'll be forced to move my memories of you into a safe spot in my mind. If I do that I'll lose all of the emotions associated with the memories."

I was conflicted and confused about so many things, but there was no doubt that I didn't want to see Geoffrey return to being the emotionless golem that was capable of committing any atrocity without even a second thought.

"Don't wait then! If Imastious is that close then don't wait for me to decide anything, just get away. Once you're safe then we can figure out stuff with Venice."

Geoffrey shook his head at me with a sad smile. "I can't get out, not on my own at least. The key to all of this is you. If I'm on my own it will only be a matter of a few days before I blunder into some collection point that Imastious programmed into my mind decades ago."

"There's got to be a way. I'll pick a location for you and then you can go there and just not leave it until we can make other arrangements."

Geoffrey looked off into the distance for several seconds before shaking his head. "I tried something like that a few years after Imastious turned me. I picked a random person on the street, gave them a map, and then asked them to point to a spot on it. I only lasted three days before the doubts got to me."

"What do you mean?"

"The programming is incredibly detailed and robust. I became obsessively concerned that Imastious would find me. By the end I was relocating my hiding spot every two or three hours. At first I was having other people choose my new locations, but then I became convinced that everyone I met was working with Imastious. I stopped having random people point to spots on my map and just picked random locations myself. The third location turned out not to be random. Imastious picked me up a few hours after I arrived there."

"So don't do that this time, Geoffrey. If you know how the programming works then you can break it."

He looked tired all of a sudden. "It doesn't work like that. He doesn't program me to stop trusting people after being gone for a day. Instead, he programs a powerful but subtle need for me to go to one of a series of locations. It becomes the overriding imperative inside of my mind and my own subconscious finds ways to make Imastious' outcome happen."

"So there's no way out?"

"Not that I've been able to find, not after decades of trying. The only thing that makes this work is you. I know that you won't betray me so I won't let the conditioning force me to turn on you. You'll make all the decisions with regards to where we go and since you haven't been conditioned you'll keep us safe."

"I...I'm going to need some time, Geoffrey. You've dumped a lot on me that I'll need to work through before I can make any kind of decision."

"I know. I knew that would be the case even before I came here today. I know you much better than you realize, Lucy."

Chapter 21

April
Lucy's Age: 19

It had taken a lot of work to get Venice to agree to meet me, but I'd been persistent because I didn't feel like this was just my decision.

She'd finally agreed to meet in a secluded spot in Central Park. Nothing was ever guaranteed there, but we stood at least a decent chance of being undisturbed.

I headed to the spot more than half an hour early, braving the lunchtime crowds in an effort to arrive with plenty of time to spare so that I could marshal my thoughts. I walked around a bend in the path and found that Venice was already sitting on the bench that had been my intended target.

"Wow, and I thought that I was early. How long have you been here?"

Venice shrugged. "I don't know. A few hours at least."

With someone else that statement wouldn't have been significant, but for Venice to have said it threw me for a loop. Venice had always been a barely-controlled bundle of energy. The thought of her sitting aimlessly in a park for hours was so alien that I never would have considered it before today.

We sat in silence, she with her concerns and me with mine, for several minutes before she looked at me and arched an eyebrow.

"You were the one that used who Bat-signal. What did you want to talk about?"

"Geoffrey. He came back by my apartment a few days ago and he wants to leave New York."

She nodded. "I thought he might. I worked pretty hard the last time I saw him to convince him that you cared for him and that getting out was the best option for the two of you to be happy. It's good to know that my plan worked."

Her tone didn't match her words. She didn't sound happy about the prospect of achieving the goal that we'd been working towards for months and that she'd been pursuing for years.

"You know already, don't you?"

"That Geoffrey won't be bringing me along with the two of you? Yes, I've suspected as much for weeks. For the longest time I thought that he'd want me along, but it's become apparent that he hasn't bonded with me enough to even consider the possibility. Before this we've always been able to work around the distrust that is a natural part of two vampires interacting, but not now. He's got you so he doesn't need to work around the fact that I'm a vampire."

"I'm sorry, Venice. I didn't ever mean for things to happen like this."

I got another shrug from her, this one not quite as indifferent as she meant for it to appear. "You did exactly what we discussed. You made him reconnect with his humanity, with you."

"What should I do?"

"What do you mean what should you do? You need to call him as soon as we are done talking and you need to tell him that you want to go with him."

"What about you?"

"I'm a dead woman. I took chances I shouldn't have taken in my efforts to buy Geoffrey more time. Once Geoffrey disappears Imastious will pillage my mind and he'll know that I triggered this little brushfire war that's caused so much damage to his operations. Between that and the fact that I helped, even indirectly, in getting Geoffrey out from under his thumb, Imastious won't have any choice but to kill me. That kind of disobedience has to be punished or it takes on a life of its own."

"I don't want you to die, Venice."

"I'm not so keen on the idea myself, love, but there aren't really any other options out there."

She sighed and then motioned at the park, seeming to take in everything with a broad, sweeping arc. "There's a lot of stuff that I never got a chance to do, but the important thing is that Geoffrey is going to get out and at least the two of you will be happy together."

Something on my face clued her into at least some of my doubts.

"You're not seriously considering refusing him, are you?"

"I don't know, Venice. There are just so many complications to the situation. It was easier somehow before. I knew he was out of reach so it was fine for me to want him and all of the things that made it wrong just made it more forbidden."

Venice gave me a cold look. "After all of this time and you still haven't realized how amazing he is. You're such a child. Now that the shiny toy you've been pining for is in your hands, you've lost interest."

I opened my mouth to protest, to tell her that it wasn't that simple, but she talked over the top of me.

"You're going to go with Geoffrey and you're going to do it soon because if you don't, if your stupid inability to decide gets Geoffrey killed or backs him into a corner so that he ends up dumping his emotions again, then I will hunt you down and I will kill you."

It was the kind of threat that I'd always thought someone had to be really angry to deliver, but Venice wasn't angry, not really. There was a pale shadow of rage underneath the surface of her words, but mostly she just seemed tired. I got the feeling that Venice was exhausted, that she'd spent the last few months fighting against an outcome that she'd finally come to believe was inevitable.

"Would you really kill me, Venice?"

"In a heartbeat. I'm dead no matter what else happens, so this is really just about Geoffrey. If you take my sacrifice and invalidate it, then I'll kill you and never even look back. I've done much worse things than that over the last few years."

There was a hint of tears in Venice's eyes as she continued. "I haven't had the benefit of just turning off my emotions like Geoffrey does. I've felt every step in my descent into depravity. Killing you would be just one more tiny step along the way. Don't think that I'm joking here, Lucy. If you screw this up, after everything that I've put into it, then you're a dead woman."

Chapter 22

April
Lucy's Age: 19

I'd given Geoffrey his phone back the last time I'd seen him so the act of contacting him was as simple as sending a text. Once the easy part was done I was left with nothing to do but stew over what I was going to say to him once we actually saw each other again.

As the hours dragged by it was tempting to text Geoffrey a second time and tell him that I'd changed my mind, that I wouldn't be able to make our running date, but Venice was right that I needed to move quickly. I didn't know about the rest of what she'd told me, but it really would be a waste if Imastious tortured Geoffrey and found out about everything simply because I took too long to decide what I was going to do.

Apparently April was coming in like a lamb because I woke to one of the most beautiful days I'd seen in months. The sky was clear and it was warm enough that I opted for shorts and a light jacket rather than running tights.

Now that I had no other companionship at the apartment I'd finally learned the names of the towers of muscle that had spent so many months standing outside my door. It turned out that there were actually four of them, two pairs of brothers, which helped explain at least part of why I'd never realized that there were more than two of them.

Hal walked me down to the street and waited while I started stretching. Hal was ostensibly there just to keep an eye on me until Geoffrey arrived, but I caught him watching me out of the corner of his eye and there was a glimmer of appreciation there that made me blush.

Geoffrey's recent protestations of love notwithstanding, it had been a long time since someone had noticed me like that. I hadn't picked the shorts out because I'd been trying to look sexy. I'd picked them out because they were the most comfortable pair of running shorts that I owned, but it was true that they bore an awful lot of resemblance to some of what Venice wore. They weren't tight, but they were definitely short and the way that they fluttered around as I moved probably exploited one of Venice's other secret weapons that I'd finally clued into after so many months.

Clothes didn't actually need to come off for guys to get hot and bothered, they just needed to look like they *might* slip at some inopportune moment and reveal more than the girl had intended.

I wasn't the slightest bit interested in Hal, but it felt simultaneously nice and wrong to have someone looking at me like that. Nice because even when he was professing his love to me Geoffrey hadn't looked at me like that, wrong because I'd spent so long now focused on Geoffrey and not even noticing other guys.

I moved slightly, angling my body such that Hal wouldn't get quite such a show as I finished stretching, and saw him smile guiltily. Apparently I'd managed the right balance there. He knew I'd noticed him watching and I'd communicated the fact that I wasn't interested in it continuing, but I'd done so without making him feel too bad about everything.

As I finished the last of my stretching routine I looked up to find Geoffrey leaning against a mailbox waiting for me.

"Sorry, have you been waiting there for long?"

"No, just a couple of seconds. Are you ready to start then?"

I nodded my assent and he led off, picking a pace that was pretty fast, but still comfortable. I caught up to him half a block in and then stayed with him as he led us around a long loop of the city. It was a different route than we'd taken before. Instead of going straight to Central Park he took us over and then up Columbus.

Despite the fact that I still hadn't decided what I was going to do, what I was going to say, I managed to lose myself in the run. The blocks rolled past and I found a measure of relief in the feel of the pavement beneath my feet.

I didn't even realize how far we'd gone until Geoffrey slowed down as we came up to a park that I didn't recognize.

"Where are we?"

"Morningside Park. There's a cathedral up here that I come visit from time to time. I can't really explain it, but it's comforting to sit in the park and look up at the cathedral."

"You've never struck me as being particularly religious."

"I'm not. It would be pretty hard to reconcile my actions with any of the recognized major belief systems. The comfort isn't religious, not really. Maybe it's as simple as being around something that's older than I am. It just feels right for me to be here."

We lapsed back into silence as Geoffrey led me deeper into the park. A few minutes later he stopped and pointed. "There. There it is. This is where I come when I want to just sit and watch the cathedral for a while. I think this spot has the best view of anywhere in the park."

"It's beautiful. Thanks for bringing me here. I think I needed that run this morning. It's odd how something so mind-numbingly repetitive can help push aside worries of the future."

Geoffrey nodded. "Before we started running together I would have said that I would never come to enjoy running, but for months now I've looked forward to our runs. You have no idea how often on the days when we ran together that I was silently wrestling with the fact that I was attracted to you."

A half-grin snuck onto my face. "Probably about half as often as I was running next to you worrying about whether or not it was wrong for me to be feeling the same kinds of feelings."

Despite the seriousness of our situation, Geoffrey smiled back at me and shrugged. "I guess we'll never know."

We stood next to each other, close enough to touch but not quite making contact, for a minute or two and then Geoffrey pointed at a bench.

"If you'd like to stay here for a few minutes, that bench is the best sitting view out of anywhere in the park. You may want to go ahead and stretch first though if we're going to be here for a while."

I nodded and started stretching, more out of habit than anything else, and then as I looked up I saw that Geoffrey was watching me with the same kind of appreciation that Hal had shown at the start of our run. I felt myself start to blush and then I realized that saying the two looks were the same was like comparing a flashlight to a forest fire.

A flashlight created light and probably a miniscule amount of heat as well, but it was nothing compared to the heat and light given off by a forest fire. Geoffrey wasn't just appreciating the lines of my legs; he was devouring the very sight of me.

Part of me wanted to turn away much as I'd done with Hal, but I forced myself to complete my normal routine without acknowledging his stare and then I looked up and met his gaze squarely.

"You don't usually look at me like that."

"I always look at you like that, Lucy, I just don't usually let what I'm feeling inside make it out to my face. I've spent a lot of years dealing with people who take advantage of any emotions displayed in their presence. That's part of what I love so much about being around you. I don't have to worry that you've got some scheme simmering away in the back of your head. The only thing unusual about the look you just got was the fact that this time there was less guilt in the mix than normal."

"You say that I never have a scheme that I'm working on, but that's not the case. Venice and I have been working on a scheme for months that was designed to manipulate you into regaining enough of your emotions to be willing to run away from Imastious."

Geoffrey nodded, but shrugged at the same time. "You've been scheming, but your scheming was only ever meant to help me. I'm not sure that a person can get away from scheming totally. I've been inside enough minds to have seen that most people scheme, even with regards to their loved ones. The best anyone can hope for is to surround themselves with people who will scheme *for* their benefit rather than *against* them."

"This wasn't my plan, Geoffrey, this was Venice's plan. She is the one who was so focused on making sure that you were able to escape Imastious. Don't get me wrong, I'm totally onboard with getting you away from this place, and I have been for months now, but Venice was the catalyst, she was the one who got the ball rolling."

Geoffrey sighed. "I understand why you want to save Venice. To be honest, I wish there were a way to bring her along with us, but I just can't see how it could work. There are complications to the situation simply because she's a vampire."

"I don't understand, Geoffrey. So much of the good that you want to attribute to me is all coming from Venice. How can you doubt her like this?"

"Lucy, have you considered the fact that she might be doing all of this just so that I'll go in and free her mind of any programming put in there by Imastious? A telekinetic who is turned by a powerful mentalist is invariably faced with decades, if not centuries, of servitude before she'll have even the faintest hope of freeing herself from any programming input by her master. Venice has been working on this plan to get me away from Imastious for less than two decades. If my getting out from under Imastious' thumb results in her being deprogrammed after such a small investment in time and effort, she'll have pulled off what most would consider to be a masterstroke."

I shook my head, frustration growing, but not sure how to get Geoffrey to understand what I'd seen in my various conversations with Venice.

"There is nothing to indicate she's ever even thought in those terms, Geoffrey. The only thing that Venice has ever wanted out of all of this is for you to be free. She's practically pushing the two of us together despite the fact that she'd much rather be with you herself than see me with you. She's not as calculating as you're making her out to be."

Geoffrey's fists had gone white, but his voice came out completely controlled, calm, almost emotionless. It was the way Geoffrey talked when he was trying very hard not to betray just how much something was costing him.

"Venice has considered doing exactly what I've just described to you. I know because I'm the one who explained to her how things like this are normally done among vampires. You want to believe the best of Venice because you've only known her for a few months. I don't have that luxury, not just because I've known her for years, but because I know what Imastious and I did to her. I know what went into turning Venice into a cold, calculating weapon while still maintaining an exterior that would make people trust her."

"If that's true, if you really did turn her into a heartless person, don't you feel some kind of obligation to help make sure that she comes back from that?"

"Yes, I do. I'm not going to let that ruin everything else though. You've done more to make me want to improve in the last few months than Venice has in all of the years I've known her."

"She was being who she thought you wanted her to be."

My voice came out soft, little more than a whisper, but Geoffrey didn't have any difficulty hearing me.

"Even if that were the case, can't you see that the situation will be better if it's you and me rather than Venice and me? You were a strong enough person to stand for what you believed regardless of what you thought I might or might not want. With Venice I'm much more likely to backslide than I'd be with you."

There was nothing particularly significant about what Geoffrey had said, but it suddenly crystallized something that had been lurking in the back of my mind.

"This isn't all because you can't see a way to be with Venice, it's because it has to be an either-

or decision for you. You either escape with me or you escape with Venice, but you can't take us both."

Geoffrey opened his mouth to say something, but I didn't let him get it out.

"It's an either-or decision and you're basing your reasoning on the wrong things, Geoffrey. It isn't that I'm a stronger person, it's that Venice loves you more than I do. Ever since I found out what you and she really were, I've been coming up with rationalizations to justify the kinds of things the two of you do. I'm not strong, I just didn't really care before. The more I care about you the more I'm tempted to bend on stuff that should never be negotiable."

I felt a headache building. "Venice was never operating under that kind of advantage, was she? She loved you almost from the very first and that is why she finally agreed to do the things that you and Imastious wanted her to do, wasn't it?"

Geoffrey nodded and I felt my decision make itself.

"If it's a question of either or then it's no question at all. Go, go today if you can make the arrangements that quickly, but go and take Venice with you."

"Taking Venice with me would complicate things incredibly. With two of us there is almost no chance that we'd be able to make it the weeks it would take to set up a long-term blood supply.

We'll end up feeding on people and killing them simply because we won't be able to kidnap and keep quiet the five or six people it would take to sustain us."

"I think you'll find a way, but even if you can't, I still want you to take her. I guess when all is said and done, it's better for you to be out from under Imastious' control and killing rather than his slave and still killing."

Geoffrey went to grab my arm but I was off the bench already. It was a sign of just how stunned he was that I'd managed to move faster than him.

"Think about what you're saying, Lucy. This isn't something that can be undone later. If I take Venice then I'll have to clean her mind and just put myself completely in her hands. I won't be able to make any calls or pick a destination or a route, there won't be any way for me to get ahold of you, not when every action I take could be Imastious' conditioning trying to assert itself."

"I know, and it's not like Venice will make the call for you. This is the end. Make the right decision, Geoffrey."

I turned and ran away from him. I knew I couldn't outrun him if he really wanted to catch me, but somehow I was sure that he wouldn't follow me.

Chapter 23

April
Lucy's Age: 19

Geoffrey's text the next day wasn't necessarily a surprise but I found myself wishing that there was a way to avoid talking to him. I could always refuse to see him, but then he'd just stop by the apartment. Leaving town would be a simple thing now with all of the money that Mrs. Agosti had left me, but while that would solve the problem of having to talk to Geoffrey, it would mean that I'd given up on trying to convince him to take Venice and leave town.

I couldn't do that, at least not as long as there was any kind of chance that I could still succeed.

It wasn't a running date this time. This time we were meeting in a café a little ways off of Central Park. When I stuck my head into the hall and told the guys that I was going to meet with

Geoffrey, Hal said that he'd go with me, which was how I found myself sitting in the designated spot with Hal sitting a few tables away, unsuccessfully trying to blend in with the rest of the clientele.

I half expected for Geoffrey to show up early for some reason, but I sat undisturbed for the entire fifteen minutes it took for the clock to finally advance to the actual meeting time. I'd flipped open the magazine that was already at my table to distract myself, but with each minute that passed by I got more and more antsy. I finally looked up five minutes after Geoffrey was supposed to have arrived and realized that he was sitting four tables over.

"How long have you been there?"

Geoffrey shrugged as he stood and moved over to my table. "Maybe fifteen minutes. You looked like you were pretty absorbed in your magazine so I chose not to disturb you."

He was lying, but I didn't understand why. Geoffrey waved Hal away, and once he turned back to me I decided to ask him.

"So why did you just lie to me?"

"It wasn't a complete lie. I really didn't want to disturb you."

"You were watching me, weren't you?"

"Would you deny a starving man one last meal?"

I shook my head. "You're hardly starving."

"Ah, but I am, just not in the way that the expression is normally used. I've gone without nourishment for so many years that I almost didn't recognize it when I came across it."

He was getting too metaphysical for me. I tried to steer the conversation to more familiar, if still uncomfortable, waters.

"Did you decide what you were going to do? Are you going away?"

"Yes to the first question and in a manner to the second."

"What do you mean?"

Geoffrey sighed and then looked around the café almost like he expected never to see it again. "This is my other favorite place here in the city. I stumbled upon it almost by accident twenty years ago. The pastries are really quite good. I don't indulge in sweets that often, but this is one of my favorite places to come and celebrate a special accomplishment."

He arched an eyebrow at me, almost like he was inviting questions, but I just motioned for him to proceed. I had no idea how any of this tied into anything.

"Sorry, I'm rambling. I've considered your terms. I could force you to come with me, but I have no desire to compel you because I know that I can't compel your feelings. You've rather expertly tried to box me into a situation where the only acceptable solution would be the solution you desire me to choose."

"So you're going to do it?"

Geoffrey shook his head. "No, I've come up with a third option, one that, although it is odious to consider, still represents the best route remaining me."

Geoffrey gave me a sad smile. "You will never really accept me in my current form, and yet I can't stand the thought of being separated from you for the rest of my days, even if it were to mean gaining my freedom."

"So what are you going to do?"

"You're right that Venice is in no small degree of danger because of her efforts on our behalf, so I've spent the last few hours implanting a series of false memories in people who were peripherally involved in this last skirmish. Imastious will eventually find those memories and he'll become convinced that it was me who caused him so many problems rather than Venice."

"So you're committing suicide? That's your solution?"

"No, this body won't die."

"What does that mean?"

Geoffrey pointed to his head. "I'm going to wipe all of my memories. I won't just move them to a safe spot inside my mind, I'll dissolve them. With a clear trail of evidence pointing at me, but with the me that committed the crime already gone, Imastious is unlikely to kill me. As long as Venice is careful to follow Imastious' orders to the letter, he's unlikely to scan her mind with any regularity, and even if he does ransack her mind he's unlikely to be looking for anything tying her to the events of the last few weeks. She'll be safe."

I could feel tears starting to pool in my eyes. "She'll be safe, but the two of you will still be under Imastious' thrall. I don't see how this is a solution."

"It's a solution because it gives me a fresh start. The person who has done so many terrible things will be gone. I'll truly be a new individual, and that means if you see me at some later point that there will be a chance for the two of us. You'll be able to love me without all of the complications that exist between us now."

The tears were flowing freely now, but I didn't care who saw me crying. "You'll be gone. The person you'll become won't recognize me, won't love me."

"No matter what happens to me, no matter what I become, I'll always fall for you, Lucy. All you need to do is spend some time with me. It's inevitable."

"Don't do this, Geoffrey! Please don't do this. Just run away with Venice, it's the better solution."

"I'm sorry, Lucy. You can't compel me in this any more than I can compel you to leave with me. I would rather face an eternity of slavery with the tiniest possibility that we might someday be together again than spend an eternity free but with a sure knowledge that you will never love me as much as I love you."

Geoffrey pulled a felt jewelry box from a pocket and slid it across the table to me. "Something to remember me by."

I tried to grab ahold of his hand as he stood, but today he was the one moving too fast. My hand caught only air as he backed away from the table with a smoothness that hinted at his supernatural speed.

"Goodbye, Lucy."

I must have gone into shock because I seemed to have lost time. I wanted to get up and chase after Geoffrey but I knew that doing so would be futile. He was faster and stronger than me and he knew the city much better than I would probably ever know it.

Instead of chasing after him I sat there at the table and cursed myself for being so practical, for not making the useless, grand gesture that the situation seemed to demand.

The black jewelry box contained a silver necklace with a clear crystal that was shaped like a tear. It was incredibly beautiful, but it didn't break the numbness that had overtaken me.

Hal carefully touched my arm sometime later. It didn't feel like much time had passed, but the length of the shadows out on the street seemed to indicate that it had been hours since Geoffrey had left.

"I'm sorry, Lucy, but it's almost to the end of my shift. Do you want me to have one of the other guys come here or are you ready to go back?"

"You can just leave, Hal. I'll be fine here."

"Geoffrey wouldn't like that. If you want to stay here then I really need to get someone else on their way over."

"No, that's okay. Let's go back to the apartment."

I couldn't help Geoffrey now, but I could at least make Hal's life a little easier today. It was a small thing to balance against all of the damage I'd done to Geoffrey's life, to Venice's life, but maybe a lifetime of small acts could begin to atone for my sins.

Chapter 24

May
Lucy's Age: 19

Venice's text wasn't exactly a surprise. She'd been texting me every four hours like clockwork since just before the last time I'd seen Geoffrey. I should have known even back then that her resuming her old check-in schedule meant that something monumental had changed, but I didn't understand any of that until it was too late.

I'd spent weeks running through memories of my last few moments with Geoffrey, examining them in an effort to figure out what I should have done different to convince him to leave with Venice rather than destroying himself.

Each morning Venice would include a request to meet with me along with one of her check-in texts, and each morning I deleted the text without sending back any kind of response and then went back to wallowing in my despair.

This morning though I realized something new. Venice had promised to kill me if I did anything to stop Geoffrey from getting away from Imastious, with or without her. This was my chance, not only to see someone who still had some kind of tie to Geoffrey, but to have my suffering ended. Geoffrey couldn't bear the thought of going an eternity with no chance of ever being together with me, but that was exactly what he'd sentenced me to.

In a way Geoffrey had reset the clock back to when he'd first been made a vampire, but unlike him I didn't have any faith that things would turn out differently this time around. Imastious had dragged Geoffrey down into the depths of depravity the first time around, back before his soul had been weighed down with all of the murders he'd committed just in the last few years. If anything I suspected that Imastious would find it easier to corrupt Geoffrey a second time.

So Geoffrey had created an illusion of hope for himself, but he'd stolen all hope from me.

I punched in a time and a place that was dangerously close to the apartment, and then sent the text to Venice.

It felt odd to be leaving the apartment again, odd to be sneaking out of the fire escape instead of going out the front door, but I couldn't risk

Hal or any of the others being hurt trying to protect me from Venice.

The day had started out gloomy, but it took a turn for the worse as I walked to the tiny park that I'd chosen for our rendezvous. By the time I arrived it had started raining, big, fat, driven drops that soaked me through almost instantly. It was the kind of monsoon-like downpour that seemed to blow through the city a couple of times each spring. It was cold enough to be uncomfortable, but not cold enough to be life-threatening, so I ignored it, picking out a bench that put my back to a neighboring building. I wanted to at least be able to see her coming.

Venice arrived exactly on time and took in my bedraggled state with a shake of her head. In contrast to my soaked t-shirt and jeans, Venice was dressed in a thin, clingy sundress and had a large white umbrella angled to keep the rain off of her.

All of Geoffrey's work had started to pay off. I recognized that the umbrella was too sturdy to be just a normal umbrella. The long central shaft wasn't collapsible, which meant it probably concealed a substantial stabbing blade of some kind. I knew how she was going to kill me, but strangely even that didn't seem to break me free of the malaise that had entrapped me.

"So you're pretty pathetic-looking."

"That's fine, I feel pretty pathetic so it suits me."

"You know you're taking all of the fun out of this. I thought I'd get more a response out of you than I'm getting."

I shrugged. "Sorry, I'm all out of tears and begging. Just end me and let's be done with things."

"I always pegged you as a fighter. I didn't think you had it in you to just give up like this."

"The funny thing is that I always thought I was a fighter too. I guess that was just one of those self-delusions that needed ripped away before I could accept the way things really are."

Venice looked at the bench next to me, grimaced at what the water on it would do to her dress, and just settled for leaning her bare shoulder against a light pole.

"Would you like to hear about Geoffrey?"

"No, Geoffrey might as well be dead. The thing walking around inside of his body isn't him. It doesn't have any of his memories or feelings."

"You're right...and you're wrong, all at the same time. Geoffrey's memories are gone, but before he went he came to my apartment and we talked, I mean really, really talked. For hours. It was like things used to be between us years and years ago."

"I only got a couple of minutes. Just long enough for him to tell me that he was leaving. I guess I should be jealous, but I'm just glad that the two of you got to reconnect, at least a little, before things came to an end."

"Lucy, I'm telling you, he isn't gone, not really. The memories aren't there anymore, but he's still the same person inside. The way he reacts to things, the way he moves and talks, it's all still Geoffrey."

"I'm glad, for your sake, but I don't think that it will matter for me, not in the long run. It's only a matter of time before he ends up just like the old Geoffrey, and if I couldn't bring myself to run away with him before I won't be able to do it later either."

Venice looked at my bench again and then just shrugged and sat down next to me. Once her umbrella was put up her dress soaked through in just a few seconds, but she didn't seem to care.

"He doesn't remember raising you, Lucy. He's even less of a father to you now than he was before."

"I know, but that doesn't change my memories of him. Is he happy at least? Now that he's not burdened by any of his past actions."

"I don't know. He's so disoriented that it's hard to read him in some ways, but in others he's like an open book. He really did love you, you know."

"I know. I loved him too, but it wasn't right for the two of us to run off and leave you here to die. I thought that I had everything figured out, thought that I'd mousetrapped him into leaving with you, but he just dashed all of my plans and went his own way."

"Yeah, he tends to do that. I think that's part of why Imastious is so fascinated with Geoffrey. He has a way of finding unorthodox solutions to problems that can be really enlightening. He told me what he was going to do even before he told you, but I almost didn't believe that he'd really go through with it until I got the text to come pick him up."

My questioning look must have conveyed more even than I'd realized because Venice nodded and pointed off to the west.

"He rented an apartment over on that side of town, but all I knew at the time was that I'd gotten a text from his phone with an address and a plea to come get him. He'd given me a copy of the key before he talked to you, so I went there and found him in one of the bedrooms."

Her knuckles tightened on the umbrella. "He'd locked himself inside with nothing but a cot, and a handwritten sign instructing him to text my number when he woke up. He was crying when I arrived. I don't think I've ever seen anyone so glad to see me in my entire life. He didn't recognize me, but he was so grateful that I'd come and let him out of that room. It felt nice, like we were just two normal people for a few minutes. He didn't remember me again when I saw him next, but at least I got a few minutes with him where all he felt was good stuff towards me."

Venice tapped her umbrella against the pavement a couple of times and then looked up at me, meeting my gaze directly for the first time since she'd arrived.

"Aren't you going to ask what we talked about?"

"No. I honestly came here expecting for you to kill me. I'm not really interested in taking a stroll down memory lane with you, Venice. I'm glad you and Geoffrey have another shot. It's what I was after, if not in the way that I wanted it to happen, but that's all over for me."

"No, Lucy, it isn't. Geoffrey came to visit me so that he could tell me how much he loved you. He told me all about your efforts to throw him and I together again, he told me about all of the little ways that you made him feel human again and then he asked me not to hurt you. I opened my mouth to tell him to go to hell, but then I realized that you were a much better girlfriend to him than I ever was."

"Yeah, some girlfriend. I convinced him to go off and commit some exotic form of suicide."

"No, I'm serious. You wanted what was best for Geoffrey in ways that were somehow higher than the things I wanted for him. I'm not used to taking second place, Lucy, but I took second place to you and it wasn't just because you're a human instead of another vampire."

"I'm sorry, I never meant for any of this to be a competition."

"I know, but I realized that I can either get mad, or I can learn from it. You have a gift that I didn't ever even know existed and I'm going to study you. I'm going to learn from you so that, however all of this turns out, I can be a better person than I have been."

"You're not going to kill me?"

"No. I never really wanted to. Don't get me wrong, I was mad at you and the situation in general, but I do consider you a friend. Besides, I'm going to need your help to figure out how to manage Geoffrey. We need to get him through his first few months with Imastious with the minimum amount of damage possible."

Chapter 25

June
Lucy's Age: 19

It was well and truly summer outside, but it felt like my heart had just started into spring. The desolate weeks after Geoffrey had left me and before I'd talked to Venice had left my insides feeling raw and frozen, but each time I talked to Venice things got a little better.

I could tell that Venice was self-editing a little as she told me about her interactions with Geoffrey, but I couldn't blame her, not really. There by the end I'd started doing a little bit of the same with regards to my time spent with Geoffrey. Our friendship had survived and we'd settled into a more or less restful truce where Geoffrey was concerned, but I was pretty sure that things had gotten better primarily because I wasn't as attached to Geoffrey as I'd been before.

He was slowly taking shape again for me through Venice's stories, but he still wasn't the vivid, living person to me that he'd been before. Even if I'd been under any illusions otherwise, the sheer self-doubt evidenced by the Geoffrey that Venice described would have told me that we were dealing with a different person than we'd been dealing with before.

It was obvious that Venice was frustrated with Geoffrey's early refusal to bend to Imastious' will. She was convinced that Imastious would kill him if he didn't do at least some of Imastious' dirty work, but I'd silently held out hope that Geoffrey would simply refuse to descend into the kind of darkness he'd participated in before.

As the weeks went by and Geoffrey completed not just one, but several hits our roles reversed. Venice became all but ecstatic over the fact that Geoffrey was finally 'seeing the light' while I became sadly certain that he'd begun the first few steps back down the path that had led him to so much unhappiness before we'd met.

I held out a little hope though that not everything was as it seemed, despite the steadily-mounting evidence to the contrary.

Given Venice's generally jovial mood these days, I was surprised when I finally got to our latest meeting place in the Bronx Zoo and saw just how unhappy she looked.

"What happened? Is it Geoffrey?"

The rising panic in my voice roused her enough to really look at me. "Yes, it's Geoffrey, but it's not that he's hurt or in trouble or anything like that. What's gotten into you?"

It took me a second to realize she was asking about my choice in clothes and then I felt my face heat up slightly. With no Geoffrey around to monitor my comings and goings I was spending a lot more time outside this summer than I ever had before and the days were getting so hot that I'd started choosing clothes primarily for how cool they were. My shorts and tank top were actually a pretty close match for what Venice was wearing.

"Nothing's gotten into me; it's just so stinking hot now. It's like the city boils all day and then we have those freak storms come in and the temperature plunges in the evening."

"Yeah, it's been an off summer. The worst I remember, which goes back a few years." Venice kicked at the asphalt underneath our feet. "All of the concrete and steel seems to just keep the heat in, even at night."

"So what's going on with Geoffrey?"

"He's falling in love."

Something wasn't adding up there for me.

"That's a good thing. Why are you so bummed?"

"Because he isn't falling in love with me; he's found someone else."

"Are you sure? I didn't even think he'd had a chance to meet anyone else, let alone start falling for them."

"Yeah, you and me both, but I'm sure. All of the signs are there. It's just like when he started falling for you, only this time I don't even know who it is."

"So what do we do? Follow him and find out who he's got his eye on?"

Venice shook her head, defeat evident in her posture. "Good luck with that. I've tried following him a few times over the last couple of weeks and he's still as paranoid as always. He doesn't have the same knowledge of the city that he used to have, but he's still too careful to trail for very far without getting caught."

"So we just have to watch from afar while someone else captures his heart and not be able to do anything about it?"

"I thought you didn't care about him anymore." I frowned at her and she held up her hands in a mock surrender gesture. "Fine, you don't care about him, but you still sort of do." Venice kicked a small rock across the blacktop. "Yeah, that's about the size of things. Welcome to my world, Lucy. Fair warning, it completely sucks."

"You don't think that you can steal him back?"

"No, not at this point. I underestimated just how much damage I did by pushing him to make those hits for Imastious. Geoffrey doesn't trust me and even if he did, once he gets his sights set on something he's unshakable. He probably doesn't even realize how hard he's falling yet, but it's pretty much a done deal at this point."

"I guess at least it means that he's happy, right?"

"Probably. It's hard to tell given the way that he freezes up around me, but he's probably happy when he's thinking about her at least, but it won't last. For people like him and me there isn't any happily ever after. He's either with another vampire, in which case she'll eventually stab him in the back at some point, or he's falling for another human, who won't be able to deal with the realities of his life."

"I'm sorry, Venice."

She shrugged. "It's water under the bridge now. I'm not holding a grudge or anything, Lucy, but we're not doing anyone any good if we ignore the world as it is."

Chapter 26

June
Lucy's Age: 19

New York had been in a state of panic for days. Everyone seemed to think that it was just gang warfare that had gotten out of control, but Venice had told me that it was actually a massive fight between nearly every vampire elder inside of the city. The gangs were just pawns and camouflage to hide the fact that some of the kills were being made by vampires.

Venice hadn't needed to tell me to stay inside because anyone with half a brain knew that the city turned into a war zone as soon as it got dark. Even during the day people walked around with more of a hurried, furtive feel than was normal for New York. As odd as that was, it was downright eerie just how quickly the streets emptied once the sun went down.

A DARKNESS MIRRORED

I waited for days for the violence to peter out, but although Venice had indicated that Imastious was running out of targets, it seemed like normal human looters were picking up some of the slack. I looked forward to each of Venice's regularly-scheduled texts, hoping that she'd tell me that the city's reign of terror was at an end, but if anything she seemed to be getting more skittish as time went on.

When the violence did stop, it was with an abruptness that left me feeling like something worse was about to happen. It seemed impossible for so much killing and arson to just stop in the course of less than twenty-four hours.

Venice's latest text was more verbose than normal.

Lucy, you need to stay inside as much as possible for the next little while. The legends about vampires are real, but so apparently are the legends about werewolves. Geoffrey and I have killed a couple of them, but they are the reason the fighting has ground to a halt. None of the others like us are willing to go out by themselves, so Imastious and the other elders have organized groups to try and hunt them down.

It was absurd for me to doubt the existence of werewolves after I'd faced off with telekinetic vampires, but I still had a hard time believing that there were hairy half-men running around New York at night. Still, as hard as it was to believe, I wasn't about to go outside at night and risk something bad happening to me.

I made my decision to play it safe as soon as I read Venice's text, but it became harder and harder to stick to it as the day wore on and the city started to take on all of the various signs that business was back to usual.

The morning rush of people commuting from home to work was just as scared and hurried as it had been all week, but by midmorning the number of people out on the street had doubled as compared to what I'd seen the day before. It was as though people had needed a couple of hours to process the severe drop-off in violence the night before.

By noon I could see bike messengers back out on the road, and the first few brave souls had come out for the lunch rush hour. I spent half an hour watching the streets from my window and then forced myself to turn away and go back to my laptop.

Part of the problem was that my heart wasn't really into what I was doing. I'd been fascinated by the opportunity to watch Geoffrey work the market and I'd really enjoyed the specific research tasks that he'd assigned me, but I didn't have the same love of the game that he'd had.

Still, I knew that the money that Mrs. Agosti had left me wouldn't last forever, not if I wanted to live in the same style Geoffrey had kept me in. I'd decided to start relatively small, investing no more than a hundred thousand dollars spread out over three or four different opportunities, so that I could start learning the kinds of things that had allowed Geoffrey to make obscene amounts of money. I had a plan, and it was a good plan, but now I needed to start identifying opportunities and I was finding that I just couldn't muster up the kind of excitement required to really make a go of things.

Back when I'd been working on projects for Geoffrey a knock on the door would have been greeted with frustration that someone was interrupting my work, but today I felt nothing but relief when I heard Hal knock on our heavy metal door with his characteristic three-knock pattern.

"Hi, Lucy. A delivery service just dropped this off for you."

"Thanks, Hal. I've got it."

I'd only thought that I'd had it. The box was big, so it was unwieldy, but it was also a lot heavier than I'd expected it to be. Luckily Hal hadn't taken me at my word and he'd kept a single hand under the box so that he was able to help support it when I nearly dropped it.

"Wow, it must be full of books or something."

"Yeah, sorry. I probably should have said something before I let you take it."

"No harm, no foul. Can you just put it there in the center of the living room?"

Hal nodded and carefully made his way around the couch. He was kind of slow leaving the apartment after he put the box down and I suddenly realized that this was the first time Hal had ever been inside my apartment. He'd stood for days just outside my door, but he'd never entered before now. I hadn't forgotten the way he'd looked at me back on the day that Geoffrey had taken me to the cathedral, but I knew Hal wasn't my kind of guy. Honest and painfully loyal, good to his core, but safe where I needed dangerous and bland where I needed the unexpected.

Still, I appreciated everything that he and the others had done to keep an eye on me over the years and I decided it was time to address something that had been worrying at the back of my mind.

"Hal, I don't know what kind of compensation arrangement you all had with Geoffrey, but he's moved on now so we'll need to discuss that here in the next little while. I've come into some money, but I don't know how long I'll be able to keep a protective detail onboard. I'll probably have to cut back coverage at the very least."

Hal shook his head. "I don't know anything about that, Miss Lucy. Geoffrey told us he'd made arrangements a little while ago. We got a four-month advance last month and then last week the normal amount for the month came through as well, so right now you're paid up for the next five months and Mr. Geoffrey didn't say as though we should be expecting anything different."

"Oh, well, that's a pleasant surprise. I guess please just let me know if anything changes in that regard."

"Yes, ma'am."

I closed the door behind Hal and then grabbed my knife off of my dresser and set about opening up the box. It was indeed full of books, but it wasn't just any random set of books, it was a series of black, leather-bound journals.

One volume, slightly newer than some of the others, caught my eye. It was resting across the top of the rest of the books and there was a note underneath it.

Lucy,

I'm not sure how long this will take to get to you. I had to arrange for some unorthodox pickup and delivery methods given the circumstances and my desire to make sure that it couldn't be traced to you at some future date.

These are the journals from the long years of my imprisonment to Imastious. The journal on the top is the most recent and contains a current overview of my finances. Given the timescales, I've been unable to shift all of my assets into your name, but I've also left you the contact information for my forger. With a good set of fake ID's and a decent actor you should be able to take control of the remaining assets without too much trouble.

I'm sorry to burden you with the knowledge contained inside of these volumes, but I find that after everything I've been through that I'm unable to just let all of this knowledge be destroyed. I give you permission to read any and all of them should you desire, but all that I ask is if we should meet again that you'll give these journals to my future self so that I can truly understand what I gave up in the pursuit of a possible future with you.

—Geoffrey

My hands started shaking as I set the note down and picked Geoffrey's final journal back up. I would need to read it to get access to the money he'd left me, but that wasn't what was driving the surge of emotion that was overwhelming my ability to hold my hands steady.

This was probably as close to the real truth behind Geoffrey's actions as I was ever going to get. He would have written these entries only for himself and therefore there would be much less in the way of deception inside of them than I'd find anywhere else.

I opened the journal and carefully thumbed through the stiff white pages, skipping past the older stuff. I got into the more recent entries and was tempted to stop and follow along through the development of his feelings for me, but ultimately I knew that I needed to read about his last moments before I'd be able to focus on anything else.

The first entry took me by surprise. I'd never imagined Geoffrey capable of feeling fear.

I've decided and it's the right decision, but I still must confess to a degree of fear. I've possessed the capability to do something like this for years now, but I never would have considered using it before now.

All of the arrangements have been made. I've moved all of my most liquid assets into an account under Lucy's name, I've provided a healthy shot of capital to Venice and discussed my wishes with her. Venice has agreed not to hurt Lucy as a result of what I'm about to do, and I believe that she actually means her promise, although I think she herself is a little surprised by her own willingness to let bygones be bygones.

All that remains is to talk to Lucy, to tell her what I have planned.

There is a part of me that wants to just disappear without saying anything to her. I keep trying to rationalize it as some innate love of big, dramatic gestures, but if my goal is to create a universe in which there is a possibility, however small, that Lucy and I might be together, then going with my first instinct would be counterproductive in every way.

In the harsh light of day I can only surmise that there is a hidden streak of cowardice that has persisted despite all of my efforts to eliminate such things.

I would say that I'm disappointed with myself but for two things. I've come to realize that so much of the cold calculation I'd prided myself on for so many years wasn't an achievement but rather a lack of something vital.

ELDON MURPHY

Once you eliminate the good emotions from your being it becomes easy to view everything as a dispassionate analysis of the odds simply because you no longer view your life as being worthwhile. I always wanted to continue living simply because the alternative would be to cease to chart my own course, but I lacked any kind of attachment to anything or anyone that would drive the kind of hopes and dreams that make life more than just a series of choices.

I said there were two reasons by which I justify my cowardice. The second is simply the fact that the sacrifice I'm about to make is on a scale that I've never experienced before and never will again. I'm about to wipe away every emotion and memory gathered over my decades of life.

I'm committed to doing this, but it still causes me to feel a unique strain of terror that I haven't felt since those first few years after Imastious killed my family and turned me. Doing this will take all of my willpower and it is going to be exquisitely hard to convince Lucy of the rightness of my path given how hard it was for me to decide on it.

It's done. Not the dissolution of my being, obviously, but rather the act of telling Lucy of my plans. She was so beautiful sitting there in a pool of sunlight from the window. I arrived only seconds after she did, and was able to observe her for quite some time before she noticed me.

The minutes passed as seconds though and all too soon I was deprived of the pleasure of tracing the lines of her face with my eyes. As she looked up and saw me, a cloud momentarily covered up the sun and some of the luster of her hair vanished.

The symbolism wasn't lost on me. Interaction with me in any form, no matter how insignificant, has always dimmed some of the light inside of her. Pursuing her as I am now would lead her to a darkness even more severe than what I saw in that moment, but the only way to stop that is for me to accept a different kind of darkness which is even more absolute and enduring.

I can't lie to myself any longer. I truly don't want to do this. I don't want to proceed, but I can't see any other way forward. I'm not strong enough to maintain my distance from her of my own free will. I might succeed for a period of time, a few days or even months, but it would only take a single moment of weakness for my defenses to crumble and for me to go running to her.

No, this is the only way to preserve the goodness I see inside of her, the goodness that drew me to her more than any other thing.

I will do this. I just wish I wasn't so scared, although I suppose that is an impossibility. Barring that, I wish that I had someone I could talk to. I wanted so badly to tell Lucy just how *terrified I am, but that would have only made it harder on both of us.*

Sitting there across the table from her and not letting on regarding the true state of my feelings is without a doubt the hardest thing I've done to date. I could see that I was hurting her with my words, but failing to hurt her now would have just led to a bigger hurt later on.

I'm finally here. I rented a small apartment last week and had two extra copies of the key made. Venice has one and my courier pickup choice has the other one. The rest of my journals have all been packed up, leaving only this one here in the bedroom with me.

I've never been as hedonistic as some of my kind become after centuries of life, but there is still a level of Spartan simplicity to my current surroundings that is completely different than my normal apartment and yet it's perfectly appropriate for this undertaking.

I have food and water sufficient for a week as well as enough blood to last for at least that period of time. I only expect my dissolution to take a day or two, but in cases like this it is better to over prepare than under-prepare.

Looking back at what I just wrote, it is apparent to me that I'm just stalling. While the urge to do so is understandable, now that I've recognized it, I must proceed. If I don't my determination will swiftly unravel.

The sense of loss is both more and less than I expected it to be. It's still early on in the process, but I have made significant progress nonetheless. Although the possibility still exists that my journal entries are a form of procrastination, I've decided that it is important nevertheless to document what I'm doing. It is possible that my notes will provide help to some future version of myself, and this is an undertaking that likely has never before been attempted.

While meditating to prepare myself for the first phase of memory destruction I realized that my memories arranged in concentric rings around my mind with the oldest memories out on the edges of everything.

I can only surmise that new memories are anchored in the center of my mindscape and that each new set of memories then tends to push the older memories further out away from the center. I've chosen to begin working from the outside of my mind inwards so as to maintain my more recent memories for as long as possible. This should help me maintain my determination to proceed until the very end as the memories that are driving to this action are all relatively recent.

ELDON MURPHY

There are two groups of memories which are located out on the end of my mind that I've chosen to delay destroying. The first is the hidden blind where I've traditionally moved memories to protect them from Imastious. The knowledge of how to destroy and move memories around is located in this blind and therefore it too logically must be one of the last few things to be destroyed.

The second is the memories from my early life. Recollections of the times back before I became a vampire are of questionable value, but I find myself oddly unwilling to lose them yet. Possibly the physical resemblance between my older sister and Lucy is what is giving me pause.

Regardless of the reason, I've decided not to proceed with wiping away those early memories quite yet. There are still plenty of other memories which need destroyed. I expect that I'll be quite occupied with those other memories for some time still before I'll need to circle back and deal with my previous life.

I said that the sense of loss was both more and less than I expected it to be. It's less because I have no recollection of what I've lost, and the oldest memories are already insubstantial and transparent. I'm generally unable to see where memories have just faded away and been forgotten and where I've artificially destroyed a group of memories.

I expect that will change as I progress on to memories that are more recent, but for now the only way for me to even know that I'm missing anything is my recent memories of destroying stretches of my mindscape.

Not knowing what I've lost, what is now gone, is really what is eating at me right now. I can foresee a problem developing as I progress where I start second-guessing the destruction of a particular group of memories and wondering if I should delay their sanitization similarly to how I've delayed the erasure of memories of my sister.

I've started to notice that my short-term memory is holding onto more and more of the content of the memories I'm destroying. It seems to be a kind of mental self-defense mechanism similar to what I encountered with Mrs. Agosti.

I'll be forced to destroy pieces of some memories two or even more times to accomplish what I've set out to do.

It is odd the things that my mind has started focusing on as this process has continued. Mrs. Agosti has taken up more and more of my thoughts over the last twenty-four hours. I paid lip service to understanding what I took from her, but I truly didn't understand until just now. It is a terrible thing to have a stretch of your life completely disconnected from what came before and after.

I've now destroyed enough memories that I'm feeling a sense of dislocation. I remember bits and pieces of my early life still, but nothing of growing up. All of the terrible things that Imastious did to me in the decade or so after he first turned me are now gone.

Yet again I must admit to a level of fear as I examine the future and contemplate being completely unanchored from the experiences that went into making me who I am today. I'm not entirely happy with what I've become, but the more that I lose the more I come to appreciate the strengths that I do have. It seems a waste to destroy the good qualities I've managed to hold onto along with the bad qualities that Lucy so rightly despises.

It's becoming harder with each passing hour to continue with the destruction of my memories. The sense of loss continues to grow and seems to be compounding as my recent memories tell me that I've lost things I value greatly.

I see only one route forward. I'm going to have to start destroying my recent memories at the same time that I destroy the older memories.

I am loath to do so, but I know that any sacrifice is worth it if it will create a chance for Lucy and me to be together.

A DARKNESS MIRRORED

My sense of dislocation is growing. It seems as though there is more of an interconnected nature to memory than I've ever before realized. From my past journal entries it is obvious that I was determined to preserve my earliest memories. I have no reason to think that I've done otherwise, but those memories hardly seem worth preserving now.

All I have left of the time before I became a vampire are hazy fragments of experiences that seem more constructed than real.

I live in an odd twilight world now. I remember nothing from the time that I entered this apartment and began the process of removing my memories. My life seems to have no beginning and the end is likewise insubstantial, meaning I remember only a disjointed period of time that is separate from anything else.

While my new situation is quite distressing, it seems as though my rate of memory destruction has increased substantially since I began removing items in my 'working' memory.

My entries have historically been made either before I started a session of memory destruction or after one had been completed. I suspect that this has been done intentionally as a way of saving myself from reading an entry done while in the midst of wiping memories from existence.

Honestly I know that I should be continuing that policy, but I can no longer force myself to be silent while experiencing the terror and regret that washes through me each time I begin destroying the bits of myself that make me more than just another eating, breathing animal.

I would give nearly anything for all of this to stop, but my memories of Lucy drive me onward even as they start to lose some of their cohesiveness as well.

Things haven't gotten any easier. I've completely lost track of time, but I've started noticing odd moments of insight. It's as though stripping away some of the distractions inside of my own head, some of the spurious layers of detail woven through my memories, has allowed me to see things that I couldn't see while living my experiences out.

Venice really has been better to me than I deserved. I've known that for quite some time on an intellectual level, but I truly felt it deep down for the first time today. She has done nothing but love me in the best way she knows how for year after year. If I were a slightly different person, this knowledge would have been enough for me to go back to Lucy and tell her that I want for the three of us to leave together, but I'm not that different person and neither is Lucy. I'm still beneath her in every way that matters. There is nothing left for me to do but continue forward with my original plan.

Lucy no longer means anything to me. I've read back through some of my entries and I can see that she was important to me, but I'm no longer able to say with any certainty that she is worth what I've done to myself.

I still have memories, but they are timeworn and moth-eaten, so riddled with holes as to be almost unintelligible.

I'm not just free of time and space, I now exist in a place where the only thing that exists is my knowledge of the methods used to destroy my memories and a question that I have to ask myself on an hourly basis. Do I trust the judgment of my past self enough to continue onward with this ritualized destruction of everything that I've ever known or been?

I only thought that my universe had shrunk down to a single point. What I had before was an infinite sea of experiences and possibilities. What I have now is nothing more than the memories from the last few hours. Lucy, I don't remember you, but if you ever read this, please be worthy of the sacrifice done in your name. I have no idea what

I've lost, but I can't escape the feeling that it is immeasurable.

I've left instructions to myself to slide this journal underneath the door, but I can't bear to make myself do it yet. Even the knowledge that reading through my journal entries is the only thing repopulating my memory isn't enough to make me sever this last tie with the outside world, with my past.

I'll leave myself a message on the next page and just hope that it's enough to convince me not to look back at the earlier entries.

In a very real sense this is goodbye.

Geoffrey, I know that you're scared and disoriented, that you don't know how you got here or why you're locked inside of this room, but it's very important that you don't read this book. People you care about will die if you ignore this warning. When you're ready, slide this book underneath the door and then dial the first number on your phone and ask them to conduct a pickup. The address to the apartment is on the wall next to the phone. They'll know what to do, but if they ask questions tell them that Jackson knows what to do and that the code word is 'new beginnings.'

Don't make any noise when you hear them arrive to pick up the journal. Once they are gone you can text the second number and ask Venice to come get you. It's going to be hard, but do the best you can to trust her.

I'm about to follow the instructions in this book. I haven't read it, other than the page telling me not to read anything else. I feel very odd. I don't remember anything about my life, but I still remember stuff like how to use a phone or read and write.

What kind of person wakes up in a strange room with no memory of who they are? My only clue is in this book, but I left myself a message telling me not to read it. The handwriting is the same as this handwriting, so I know it was me, but it's still a lot to be taking on faith.

I...I feel sad. I don't think it's an emotion that I feel very often, but I just want to sit here and cry. I feel like I lost someone special, like the world changed and it can never be what it was before.

A part of me wants to just stay here in this room. Outside represents possibilities that this version of me has never even considered, but it also represents everything that I don't know, everything that could hurt me.

That's not normal, is it? Why should I be scared of everything out there?

I'm going to slide this book underneath the door and then I'm going to call the numbers just like I told myself to.

Heaven help me.

Chapter 27

July
Lucy's Age: 19

I felt like I'd been run over by a truck. There were depths hinted at in Geoffrey's journal entries that he'd never exposed to me, but even that paled against the fundamental truth I'd learned.

Venice had been right all along. There was a core of goodness to Geoffrey that exceeded even my wildest dreams. He hadn't done what he did out of cold calculation. He'd done it because it was the right thing to do, the only way to begin atoning for his sins. He'd paid the ultimate price to redeem himself, to create the possibility of a future with me, and in doing so he'd proven to me that the darkness inside of him was weaker than the light.

He'd erased the doubts that had plagued me since finding out he was a vampire, but now that he'd proven himself to me, there was no longer any way for me to tell him that I wanted to run away with him. His act of redemption had killed the man that I'd known.

I wanted to dive into his journals, to begin scouring them for every detail of his life. Even the darkness I knew was contained inside of those leather volumes no longer scared me. My knowledge that the light had been greater than the darkness rendered the darkness somehow less.

I forced myself to put down the journal and instead picked up my phone and texted Venice.

We need to talk. Something has just come up and I think you deserve to see it.

Nearly three hours passed before I got my response.

I'll do what I can to break away tomorrow. I really need to see you right now too. Imastious is on to something. I'm not sure how much time I have left.

Chapter 28

July
Lucy's Age: 19

Everything about Venice looked different today. It was almost like she was a different person. Gone were the thin, frilly tops and the short, almost indecent, bottoms that she so often wore. Instead she had on black leather pants that looked like they'd been through a war zone, and her customary tank top was mostly hidden by a heavy leather jacket that looked like it would be sheer agony to wear in the heat of the day like this.

Her hair wasn't the platinum-blond veil that usually framed her face to perfection. Instead she'd pulled it back into a no-nonsense ponytail.

"What gives, Venice? Are you slumming?"

"No, this is combat wear. Leather holds up a lot better than my skin if I get thrown through windows or sent skidding along the blacktop. Besides, the jacket has ceramic plates in it."

Her response put a sudden stop to my euphoria in a way that even her appearance hadn't been able to.

"How much trouble are you in?"

Her shrug looked tired, and I suddenly wondered just how many hours you had to keep a vampire up to make them look that exhausted.

"I'm not sure, but the crap seems like it's somewhere between neck and eyeball deep. I can still see, so it's not past my eyes yet, but I think I'm starting to have a hard time breathing."

"What do you need? I've got money, lots of money. Anything you need that I have is yours."

"I wish it was that easy, love. Enough about me. What did you want me to see?"

I hesitantly held out Geoffrey's final journal. I felt like she needed to see it, but I also knew it would probably cause her as much pain as joy. He'd finally realized just how much she'd loved him, but even after that he'd still been mostly focused on me.

A slight intake of breath was the only clue to Venice's emotions as she accepted the journal and flipped through it.

"Presumably there is a specific part you think I need to read?"

"Yeah, right here."

I waited while Venice read through all of Geoffrey's final entries and then nodded to herself.

"It looks like I was right all along. He really did love me, he just never quite got past the fact that we were both vampires. Do you believe me now when I say that he's worth saving?"

It took me a couple of tries to find my voice. In the end I'd probably have been better off just nodding.

"I'm sorry that I've had such a hard time coming to grips with this. I've ruined everything. He's gone and now you're in trouble."

"Don't sweat it, love. I've known that my days were numbered since the first day I met you. Honestly, I've made it longer than I thought I would."

"Please tell me what's going on, Venice. I'm ready to hear whatever you think I need to hear. I've started reading some of Geoffrey's other journals. I'm a lot less naive than I was a few days ago."

"The sixty-second version? The werewolves are kicking the crap out of us. Geoffrey and I have had a better run of luck than most, but even so we can't keep dodging metaphorical bullets forever. Imastious and some of the other powers-that-be have decided that Geoffrey has got some kind of mojo though because they have put him in charge of coming up with a plan to save every vampire in the city."

"Can he do that?"

"Maybe. If anyone can do it, it's him and his damn unorthodox approach to problem-solving, but it's going to be tight. The werewolves seem to be able to sense us so they only attack when they have us outnumbered."

Venice shifted slightly and I realized that she had a bandage around her ribs and that blood was slowly soaking through her shirt.

She waved away my concern as soon as she saw what I was staring at.

"Don't worry about that, seriously, I've got much bigger concerns than something that will be healed up within the next couple of days."

"What aren't you telling me?"

"It's Geoffrey, and Imastious, but mostly Geoffrey. This deal that Geoffrey has agreed to with Imastious won't end well. No deal with Imastious ends well but Geoffrey doesn't remember that anymore. Even if Geoffrey manages to pull our collective bacon out of the fire he's still going to be as good as dead. He'll get all huffy about Imastious double-crossing him and then he'll leave, only this time Imastious won't just collect him after a few days and then torture him to drive home the lesson that Geoffrey isn't supposed to try and escape. Geoffrey is too popular now. Some of the rank and file are starting to look up to him like he's some kind of vampire elder in his own right."

The things that I'd read last night after texting Venice flashed through my mind. It made a sick kind of sense. Imastious held onto his position and power out of fear and the rest of the vampire elders were likely cut from the same kind of cloth. If the foot soldiers were ever able to unite behind a single figure then all of the power and riches wielded by the elders wouldn't be enough to save them from the more numerous younger vampires.

"So convince him not to leave, convince him to be a faithful grunt until we can figure out a better plan."

Venice's smile was tired. "I'm not going to be able to convince him of that any more than you were able to convince him to go. Some things have changed and it's taken me a while to get a good read on this new Geoffrey, but he's still just as stubborn as always. No, my only chance is to convince him to take Imastious out before Imastious can kill him. If enough of us get behind him we can do it."

I knew the words that I needed to say, but it was still almost more than I could do to make them come out.

"If you can't convince Geoffrey then you need to go to Imastious and tell him everything. If Geoffrey can't be saved then we have to focus on keeping you alive. I've already lost Geoffrey in nearly every way that counts. I'm not losing you too."

"Thanks for the concern, love, but I've been lost for more years than I care to think about."

"That's not true. You're good, Venice."

"No, I've got bits and pieces of good in me still, but I've let myself fall a lot further than I should have."

Venice stared off into space for several seconds as I tried to come up with a response that would convince her to turn away from the self-destructive course I could tell she was leaning towards.

"Look, I'm not giving up hope or anything. If Geoffrey will agree to go after Imastious then there's a chance that we can make a difference in this hell-hole of a city. If not, then I'm going to do my best to do right by you. Before he left, the old Geoffrey implanted some conditioning inside of my mind that stops me from telling anyone about you. He thought it would help shield knowledge of your existence from Imastious, but he said it wouldn't be foolproof."

She looked back at me and smiled, the first genuine smile she'd given me in a long time. "I'll go to him and I'll do whatever I have to in order to make him get deep enough into my mind for him to find out about you. If I can't have my happy ending then I at least want the two of you to have yours."

"You're not planning on surviving all of this, are you?"

"Like I said, I haven't given up hope, but if Geoffrey runs and Imastious gets his hands on me then you're as good as dead, Lucy, and I won't let that happen."

"So I'll run away. I'll go somewhere he'll never find me."

Venice shook her head. "No, that won't save me. I've underestimated Imastious too many times. Geoffrey threw him off the scent for a while, but Imastious can pull stuff out of people's minds that they didn't even know was there. Given enough time he'll track you down, just like he's slowly tracked my sins back to me. He's not there yet, but he's close. Another couple of months at the outside and he'll know that I was the one who screwed him over a few months back."

Inside I was desperately looking for something else to say, some way to convince Venice that she was making the wrong decision, but I couldn't seem to get anything out. Venice pulled me into a hug and for the first time I realized just how frail and tiny she was despite her supernatural speed and strength. It would take next to nothing for Imastious to snuff her out.

Chapter 29

July
Lucy's Age: 19

I waited on pins and needles for some kind of development, desperately hoping that Geoffrey would buy into Venice's plan, but I heard nothing other than Venice's normal check-ins for several days.

Despite, or possibly because of, my long vigil, I was actually surprised when Venice's call came in.

"Hi, Lucy."

"Hi, Venice. Any news?"

"Yeah, we killed dozens of werewolves in a stunning victory that was made entirely possible by Geoffrey."

"Imastious stabbed him in the back already?"

"No, but it's coming and Geoffrey is actually smart enough to see it. I'm headed over to

Geoffrey's now to try and head things off. This would sure be a lot easier if I could just tell him about you."

"I could come with you. Maybe between the two of us we could convince him."

Venice swore under her breath. "I can't believe I didn't think of that myself. That might have actually helped, but there just isn't time now. I don't know exactly where you live, but after all of this time I have a pretty good general idea and there's no way you could make it here before Geoffrey leaves. No, this one is all me."

"Just wishing you good luck doesn't seem like enough."

"Yeah, I know, the feeling is mutual. Look, I'm going to set my phone to automatically text you in two hours. If I make it through this I'll disable the auto text and send you one celebrating our victory. If not, well, could you see to it that someone comes and takes care of my body? I know it's kind of silly, it's not like I'll be in a position to care, but I'd just feel a lot better knowing that I'm not going to lie there for weeks. The text will have his address in it."

My throat was tight, but I managed a whisper.

"Of course. If it comes to that, but it won't."

"Thanks, Lucy. You're not a bad sort, you know? You've brought me partway back from the edge and I really appreciate it."

A DARKNESS MIRRORED

She hung up before I could respond, probably worried that I'd get teary on her and ruin her ability to function once she actually made it to Geoffrey's place.

I waited for two hours for her to text me and each minute that passed seemed to freeze a tiny piece of my stomach. When my phone finally vibrated with an incoming message my fingers were shaking so badly that I almost couldn't bring up the message.

This is the automated text. Sorry, love, it looks like I didn't make it. Even in spite of all the crappy things that have happened I'm still glad that we met, for my sake if for no other reason.

The tears in my eyes made it almost impossible to read the address she'd appended to the end of the text, but I forced my trembling fingers to dial the police as my frozen insides shattered into a million pieces.

Chapter 30

September
Lucy's Age: 19

I didn't go to Venice's funeral, but I arranged for a large cash donation to be dropped off at the morgue with instructions on how I wanted her laid out for burial.

The funeral was the only thing that almost managed to bring me out of the desolate numbness that had taken me over ever since I'd found out that Venice was dead. The nightmares took on an even more sinister cast. Sometimes it was me walking through the house with a bloodied blade instead of the shadowy figure whose face I'd never managed to see.

I stopped sleeping in stretches longer than half an hour and almost completely lost my appetite. Movies, books, financial research, it all lost its appeal. Instead, I spent every waking minute and even most of my dreaming ones analyzing my life, looking at all of the places where I should have acted in a different manner, dwelling on all of the places where I'd failed and thereby killed Geoffrey and Venice.

Hal and the others didn't know what was wrong, but they'd still clued into the fact that something was up, and it had taken several attempts to get them to just leave me alone, but I'd finally succeeded by the time that Venice's funeral rolled around.

Once the funeral was past there wasn't any reason to keep track of time, so I didn't know how long it had been since the funeral when I heard a knock on my door. I answered it and found not, Hal as I'd expected, but a pale old man who made my skin crawl.

He stepped into the room without asking for permission, which set off an additional round of alarms, but when I stuck my head into the hall to ask Hal for help, the old man grabbed the back of my shirt and threw me into my own living room. As I was sliding across the floor I realized that the motionless mounds in the hallway that my mind had been struggling to make sense of were my bodyguards.

"I'm afraid that I can't have you going out in to the hall, my dear. I have to apologize, I would have been here quite a while ago, but other matters temporarily took precedence. Please allow me to introduce myself. My name is Imastious."

Author's Note

The Greater Darkness is the third novel I ever wrote. I wrote it approximately seven years ago and asked some of my friends to read it. They all hated it, but I look back on the first installment of Geoffrey's novel with a lot of fondness because in a lot of ways it was the beginning of me being a 'real' writer. The first two books were fan fiction and I don't expect that I'll ever go back and rework them so that they can be put up for sale.

Back when I wrote The Greater Darkness I had no idea where I wanted to take the series; I just wrote and figured that subsequent books would take care of themselves at some later point. I had no idea how far away, and yet how close, that later date would end up being.

Once I finished up The Greater Darkness, I proceeded to write Frozen Prospects and Thawed Fortunes. Partway through writing Thawed Fortunes I started my third accounting job (The

Greater Darkness and *Frozen Prospects* were written in between jobs) and consequently *Thawed Fortunes* took a while to finish, which was okay. Meanwhile though my attempts to get *The Greater Darkness* and *Frozen Prospects* published weren't going anywhere, which was incredibly disheartening.

I finished up *Thawed Fortunes* and stopped writing altogether for a while. When inspiration next struck I found myself writing a new novel, one with shape shifters in it rather than werewolves and vampires. This new novel was pretty different in tone, but I knew almost from the start that it was set in the same world as *The Greater Darkness*.

Broken took me somewhere in the neighborhood of half a year to write, but about the time I finished it I once again found myself between jobs. I wrote some short stories and then wrote *Torn* as I attempted to get *Broken* traditionally published. The new few books in the *Reflection* series—*Splintered, Intrusion,* and *Trapped*—were all written while working a day job once again, and then I decided to do this writing thing full time.

I wrote two more *Guadel Chronicles* books, as well as *Forsaken* and *Riven* in the first six months that I was writing full-time, and then I realized that it was time to write this book, a book that started out as nothing more than an idea that 'I needed to write about Geoffrey's adopted daughter.'

The most amazing thing about writing A Darkness Mirrored has been how easy it was to weave a second storyline around and behind the original story line from The Greater Darkness. There were so many things that I never contemplated doing while I was writing Geoffrey's story, but which fit perfectly once I got into the meat of writing Lucy's story. I especially love the way that this second book has given both Geoffrey and Venice more depth than I was able to provide in the first book, but even more exciting still is that now that Lucy's story has been started it's time for me to weave the Eldon Murphy Reflections books in with the Dean Murray Reflections books.

If seeing the interplay between Geoffrey's story and Lucy's story was amazing for me, seeing that same interplay between the Eldon Murphy and the Dean Murray books has completely blown my mind. A minor character from The Greater Darkness has become one of the two or three most pivotal individuals in the entire world. Some oddities as far as werewolf behavior in The Greater Darkness have been completely explained by one of the villains from Alec's world, and a host of other things have just worked out much better than I ever could have hoped.

There are probably only a few of you who have stayed with me through this ridiculously long author's note, but for those who have I guess what I really want to say is please go read the Dean Murray books. Start with Torn, or maybe Broken if you want something with a little more romance and a little less action, and read all the way through Riven. You're going to want to know the background behind the characters Geoffrey and Lucy are going to meet in the next book!

Acknowedgements

My Eldon Murphy books tend to go through a slightly different vetting process than the rest of my books, but if anything the smaller number of people involved in these books means that this group needs even more thanks than normal.

As always, Katie is the glue that holds everything together. She's done great work on the cover and editing for A Darkness Mirrored as well as serving as my primary sounding board—Thanks Katie.

Claire Farleigh graciously read through my rough draft to make sure that I hadn't crossed any lines that fans of The Greater Darkness wouldn't want crossed, and then the book went off to RJ Locksley and Amy Jirsa-Smith for editing and then the final version was sent to Chris in the Netherlands and Mei to make sure that my fixing of the edits everyone else found hadn't introduced yet more problems into the manuscript.

I'm very grateful to all of those individuals for their help in making A Darkness Mirrored much better than it otherwise would have been.

About the Author

Eldon Murphy is an open pen name for Dean Murray, a prolific author with dozens of titles across multiple pen names and more than half a million copies of his work currently in circulation.

Dean started reading seriously in the second grade due to a competition and has spent most of the subsequent three decades lost in other people's worlds.

Things worsened, or improved depending on your point of view, when he first started experimenting with writing while finishing up his accounting degree. These days Dean has a wonderful wife and two lovely daughters to keep him more grounded than he used to be, but the idea of bringing others along with him as he meets interesting new people in universes nobody else has ever seen drags him back to his computer on a regular basis.

Keep up to speed on Eldon's/Dean's latest projects at deanwrites.com.

Torn

Shape shifter Alec Graves has spent nearly a decade trying to keep his family from being drawn into open warfare with a larger pack. The new girl at school shouldn't matter, but the more he gets to know her, the more mysterious she becomes. Worse, she seems to know things she shouldn't about his shadowy world.

Is she an unfortunate victim or bait designed to draw him into a fatal misstep? If she's a victim, then he's running out of time to save her. If she's bait, then his attraction to her will pull him into a fight that'll cost him everything.

Frozen Prospects

The invitation to join the secretive Guadel should have been the fulfillment of dreams Va'del didn't even realize he had. When his sponsors are killed in an ambush a short time later, he instead finds his probationary status revoked, and becomes a pawn between various factions inside the Guadel ruling body.

Jain's never known any life but that of a Guadel in training. She'd thought herself reconciled to the idea of a loveless marriage for the good of her people, but meeting Va'del changes everything. Their growing attraction flies against hundreds of years of precedent, but as wide-spread attacks threaten their world, the Guadel have no choice but to use even Jain and Va'del in their fight for survival.

The Society

People need to be monitored, or they'll repeat the mistakes of the Desolation, a centuries-old war that killed billions of people and destroyed civilization.

Skye is part of the Society, the hi-tech, nanite-endowed group responsible for making sure that the millions of surviving people—grubbers—are confined to the ancient, decaying cities where they can be watched to ensure they aren't redeveloping the weapons technology that came so close to extinguishing life on the planet.

When the Society's monitoring programs pick up troubling developments in one of the grubber cities, Skye is ordered in to deal with the man responsible, but what—and who—she finds once she arrives will change everything.

Reborn

True love never dies.

A new arrival at Selene's high school is about to turn her entire world upside down. She's never met anyone so attractive—or so mysterious—before this, but Jace's unyielding insistence that they've known each other for decades can't be denied—not given how familiar he feels to her.

In the hidden world of gods and fairies what you don't know can get you killed faster than anything else and only those you love have any chance of saving you.